JC Wardon Books

Available in Print and/or ebook!

Mystic Thunder (Book 1 - The Cavanaugh Sisters Trilogy)

Touch of Lightning (Book 2 – The Cavanaugh Sisters Trilogy)

Tempest's Embrace (Book 3 – The Cavanaugh Sisters Trilogy)

Jewel of the Nile ~ Cavanaugh Series - #4

Sapphire Blues ~ Cavanaugh Series - #5

Diamond in the Rough ~ Cavanaugh Series #6

Luna's Landing ~ Cavanaugh Series #7

Celestial Liaison ~ Cavanaugh Series #8

Zeus: Unbound! ~ Cavanaugh Series #9

Apollo: Unleashed! ~ Cavanaugh Series #10

Blood Moon Rising ~ Blood Moon Series #1

What Reviewers are saying about…

JC Wardon's Mystic Waters Books

I would say that J.C. Wardon is a shining new star in the paranormal genre. MYSTIC THUNDER is the first book in a new trilogy that features three identical sisters who are blessed, or cursed at times, with mystical abilities. It centers around the three sisters, their tumultuous journey toward love, and the danger that seems to follow them. This was a totally engrossing story, unlike anything that I've ever read. It captivated me from the beginning and kept me hooked until the end." **Debra Taylor, The Romance Reviews**

"Wardon has crafted a page-turner with the first of the Cavanaugh Sisters Trilogy." **Karen Sweeny-Justice, Romantic Times Book Reviews**

"J C Wardon weaves a great story with memorable characters and a small town life found in the breath-taking atmosphere of the Great Smoky Mountains. I look forward to reading the next sister's story and finding out more about the murderer that is still living among the good people of Mystic Waters." **Susan, Night Owl Reviews**

"Wardon continues her Cavanaugh Sisters Trilogy with a second page-turner that ratchets up the action and the heat faster than the first book did. The romance between Rayne's sister and Garrison's best friend is a literal scorcher…." **Karen Sweeny-Justice, Romantic Times Book Reviews**

"Wardon concludes the Cavanaugh Sisters Trilogy with another page-turner that successfully mixes romance, paranormal elements, and the darker aspects of life." **Romantic Times Magazine, reviewed by Karen Sweeny-Justice**

"I very seldom buy books. Yet I bought all 3 in the series within 36 hours. The characters and story line are believable and there is the addition of the spiritual and paranormal. I look forward to more in the storyline." **A "Verified" Amazon Customer.**

Sapphire Blues

Sapphire Blues

The Cavanaugh Series

JC Wardon

Mystic Waters Books
JC Wardon

Mystic Waters Books
JC Wardon

SAPPHIRE BLUES
Copyright © 2016, JC Wardon
Trade Paperback ISBN: 978-1-944454-97-5

Editor, Gilly Wright
Cover Art Design by Calliope-Designs.com

Digital Release, 2015
Trade Paperback Release, 2015 – 1st Edition
Trade Paperback 2nd Edition Release – March 2016

Media > Books > Fiction > Romance Novels
Category/Tags: Werewolves, action, police, witches, magic, romance

JC Wardon
www.jcwardon.com

SAPPHIRE BLUES

Can a werewolf be defeated when a mystic denies her magic?

Police officer Sapphire Cavanaugh-White turned her back on magic soon after her ascension eight years earlier and hasn't looked back. But now, with all the local humans and wildlife living in fear of a murderous maniac, Sapphire may have no choice but to hunt down the animal who may also be a man.

To protect their nearly extinct species, Nicolae Lupei must find and destroy one of his own, while keeping their existence a secret. But, when he runs across the policewoman his brother may have infected, he finds his loyalties torn. Save her, or those he calls family?

Chapter One

Sirens blared, lights flashed and blinded, fiery emergency flares marked off areas where hundreds of bits and pieces and a few larger chunks of human remains lay in drops or pools of blood. The air held the scent of death, of decay, of fear and vomit. Even Mystic Waters' seasoned police officers weren't accustomed to seeing this kind of carnage. Having only been on the force for a few months, Sapphire Cavanaugh-White tried to distance herself emotionally from the horror as she held a sanitizer-covered hand over her nose to mask the death smells with the scent of rubbing alcohol. There was no way to soften what she was seeing while she studied the largest piece of the deceased's carcass.

Chunks of flesh clung to what remained of the hip, but it was clear only two-thirds of intact spine was still attached to the sacrum at its base. The coccyx was missing as well as any sign of genitalia or digestive organs. Whatever kind of animal tore this person apart had been indiscriminate as to what it was eating. The lack of a crotch area as well as the fact that there was only a four-inch stub of one remaining leg could have made it difficult to identify the sex of the victim. Were it not for the completely intact tattoo of a big-breasted woman on the remaining butt cheek, it could have gone either way.

"I've found what I think is part of the liver and a kidney, and Jackson found both eyes—blue—but everything else looks like skin and muscle so far. What do you think?"

Sapphire rose slowly, only realizing she'd been stooping for too long when her legs protested the movement. She shrugged, taking in the distaste on Brad Cunningham's face. The veteran officer was her partner and was basically training her on Mystic Waters police procedure. She thought it ironic he was asking her. "I don't know. Maybe a pack of wild boars?"

Brad nodded. "Possible, but where is the rest of it?"

It was Sapphire's turn to shrug. "It's a *him*. I'm thinking maybe the rest was carried off for later, or maybe Mr. Casey scared them off when he came around the curve, but he said he didn't see anything but what we're looking at now. He thought at first it was an animal hit and broken up by a car." Sapphire sighed. "He's pretty upset now he knows it's human."

Brad nodded again as he lifted his hand to hold it over his nose. "Yeah, I think we all are. I've never smelled anything like this. It makes me want to puke."

Sapphire nodded, still keeping her hand close to her face as well. "I know. There's something strange about it. But I can't put my finger on it." She glanced back down at the chunk of meat that was once part of a man. "I wonder who he is, and what he was doing out here on a mountain road in the middle of the night."

Brad shrugged. "Guess we'll never know. Isn't much to identify him by."

Sapphire pointed to the butt cheek. "It's a tattoo. If he's a local we'll see if anyone comes forward claiming a missing person. That's a pretty clear identifying mark."

"You're right. I didn't notice it before. It's hard to look at this too closely. How do you stand it?"

Sapphire almost smiled but knew it wasn't appropriate. "I wanted to be a nurse when I was growing up and spent a lot of time watching law enforcement shows that leaned heavily toward forensics. By the time I got to college, I was captivated with the idea of studying forensic science, which led me to law enforcement. So I got a degree in criminal justice, with a specialty in forensic science, and hope one day to work in a law enforcement lab or for a coroner. Maybe even for the FBI."

Brad looked at her for a long moment then shook his head. "That would be a terrible waste. You're too attractive to be hidden away in a lab somewhere studying things that used to be human beings."

Since Brad's tone didn't carry any *flirt* in it, Sapphire let the comment pass. She wasn't one of those people who jumped on the sexual harassment bandwagon without due cause. So she took it as the compliment she was sure he'd meant it to be, but it was still an issue she wished never arose. "Thanks, but one of the perks of being hidden away is your work is what matters to people, not your looks."

"I didn't mean it that way."

She did smile now. "And I didn't take it that way. But you've heard some of the guys at the station. It gets a little old after a while. All I want is to be good at what I do."

Brad nodded. "I get it. But men are men, and you are gorgeous. You can't expect us to ignore something that is impossible to ignore. That isn't even fair." He looked down then and his brows pulled together.

Sapphire sighed heavily. "I appreciate my genes. But they don't define me." She didn't know what else to say. To continue to try to make her point would continue to force him to make his, and neither one of them were comfortable now.

"Look, don't worry about it. I appreciate it that you are always respectful and have never treated me like a piece of meat rather than a colleague. Let's get back to work."

Brad nodded. "I never will, you know. Treat you like that, I mean. I like you. You're smart. You are willing to work as hard as it takes and you never complain. If we didn't work together, I might have eventually found the courage to ask you out. But this way is better because girls who look like you don't look at guys who look like me."

Sapphire was too stunned to speak at first. "Brad—"

He shook his head and looked back up at her with a grin. "Don't say it. You're nice. I don't want you to have to lie to spare my feelings. Just friends works for me."

Sapphire smiled and held out her hand. "Friends it is then. Not just friends, but good friends." She glanced over to see the coroner was finally arriving. He pulled his black ambulance as close to the wandering police officers as possible. She hoped the new coroner was already in place and had replaced the one who was to retire.

Doc Parsons had held the position long before she was born, and though she knew there had once been a mass murderer in Mystic Waters, and because that *too* had been before her birth, she didn't really know any details and doubted it had resulted in anything like she was seeing now. She was certain Doc Parsons would have a heart attack if he had to deal with this.

To Sapphire's relief, the man who stepped from the ambulance was the new guy. From the little contact she'd had with him so far, she figured he fit the bill as a coroner. Middle-aged, thick glasses, thinning buzzed hair but not yet bald, he looked born to wear a lab coat. He walked right to her, his lips pressed together.

"Hope you didn't touch anything."

Feeling more than slightly offended, Sapphire shook

her head. "No." She didn't add that she wasn't stupid. There was little point. She grinned at the coroner, doubting he knew the falsehood of the pleasant gesture. "We've identified several body parts, have concluded it is a male by the tattoo on the remains, and will be here to help start packing it all up, whenever you're ready."

The coroner nodded though he wasn't looking at Sapphire. His attention was glued to the remains she'd been studying. "It doesn't look like this is a homicide. And if it is, there are too many people here making a mess of the scene for it to matter. Clean it up and bring the parts to me. We'll see if we have enough to make an identification."

Sapphire nodded. "Yes, sir." Again, she didn't add her thoughts that had he been on the scene when he'd been called, he could have orchestrated the process. She watched as the coroner headed in the direction of the different flares. He barely bent over as he glanced at each body part the officers had marked, before heading back to his vehicle. Sapphire waved her partner over. "Looks like we get to bag it all up."

Brad nodded, his eyes filled with distaste. "I was afraid of that. Doc Parsons would have looked harder."

Sapphire nodded. "Maybe. I don't think anyone is too anxious to look too hard," she said, looking at the group of officers standing together across the road. She had to get to the squad car to get supplies from the trunk but approached the more senior officers first.

"Doc says we are to bag it all up."

They turned to look at her, and irritation set in, as several pairs of male eyes looked her up and down with appreciation. She ignored them and turned to head to her car. Brad was already there pulling out a body bag and the black toolbox they used in such cases. The sound of a wolf's howl startled them both, and Brad looked at her warily. "Is that what I think it is?"

Sapphire shrugged. She hadn't seen any wolves in the area in all the years she'd lived in Mystic Waters. Though she knew there had been reports of them from time to time when she was growing up on Mystic Mountain, she'd never once gotten a chance to lay eyes on one. "I don't know."

"Would a wolf have done all this?"

Sapphire frowned as she pulled on a new pair of latex gloves. "I don't think so. This is too aggressive. I can't imagine wolves tearing a man apart like this. If they felt their pack was threatened, one would hold him off while the others got away. And we would see signs of them. There are no tracks. With all this blood we'd have seen bloody paw prints. We'd also see scat and hair. There's nothing here to indicate a wolf."

"Well, it's giving me the creeps."

Sapphire nodded as she followed him back to the biggest chunk. The wolf was continuing to howl, its call singular. She handed Brad a pair of gloves and knelt down to open the toolbox. "I think it's just one wolf. From my understanding, if a pack was close by, the alpha male would begin the communication and others would respond with howls as well."

"That's a relief. All we need is a pack of wolves moving onto the mountain. We'll get calls day and night."

As Sapphire began lifting and bagging the smaller pieces of flesh with the long tweezers, she agreed. "I think once word gets out something tore a man into a thousand pieces, we will get those calls anyway. I just wish we could identify him before word gets out. I'd hate for someone to have to speculate if a son, father, or husband is gone longer than someone expects."

Brad pointed at the largest chunk of flesh and bone. "If you'll hold the bag open for me, I'll put it in."

Although she normally wouldn't have blinked at handling a dead body, Sapphire didn't argue. She was thankful, in this case, to hand that particular job over to his willing hands. Unfortunately, just holding the bag didn't stop the smell from nearly knocking her over, as Brad had to hold it just below her face as he placed it in the plastic. She gagged, and chills washed over her body. Though she wanted to close the bag as soon as the body was in it, she knew there were other big chunks the coroner would want in the body bag as well.

She and Brad made the rounds gathering the larger pieces while the other officers used varying sized plastic baggies to gather the smaller pieces. By the time she was able to zip the bag closed, it only weighed about forty pounds. As well as they could tell, whatever killed the man ate him as well.

Fire trucks arrived on the scene, ready to spray off the road once the police left. Sapphire immediately looked to see if Apollo was among those on duty and smiled when she caught a glimpse of him jumping out of the extended cab. He was so cute in full fireman regalia, though she knew other women, those not related to him, would think him hot, not cute. He spotted her and smiled.

"Hey, cuz. We got the call about this. Can't believe something like this would happen on Mystic Mountain. Dad will be sick. You know how he reacts whenever anything violates Mother Mountain."

Sapphire nodded. "I imagine it will affect our mothers and Aunt Haven too. They are all so attuned to everything around here."

Apollo nodded as well, his gaze going to the officers loading the various remains into the black ambulance. He looked back at Sapphire and shook his head. "How do you stand it? The smell is enough to make me sick."

"It isn't easy, but it's my job. And I can't let the guys see me flinch. They've already made noises that my looks got me the job."

Annoyance flashed across Apollo's classic features making Sapphire smile. His Native American genes were slightly tempered by her aunt Destiny's, but he and his identical brothers Zeus and Heracles were their father made-over.

"Does it never occur to them that you being at the top of your class has something to do with it?"

Sapphire shrugged and pulled the latex gloves from her hands, making sure they ended up inside out. The last thing she wanted was to get the deceased's bodily fluids on her. "I'm glad you're here. Something is really strange about this. Not only about the way the remains were mutilated and left behind, but also the smell. There's something off about it."

Apollo glanced back to the officers and other firemen before speaking quietly. "I can smell it. I did as soon as I stepped out of the truck." He looked back again to make sure they were still far enough from the men moving in their direction. "Is there any way you can get a sample of the blood? We could have the parents look at it."

Sapphire nodded. "I'll try. Thankfully Aunt Soleli and Aunt Lune Brille decided to stick around to make sure Jewell and Amen-ra aren't in danger of being sent back to ancient Egypt. There's a good possibility they might know something, too. Or at least be able to help us find out if it's anything a *normal* police investigation couldn't make sense of."

Apollo smiled at her. "Since when do you involve yourself in the possibility of magic?"

"Never. And I hope that isn't what this is. But I feel really creepy about more than the obvious. And that makes me think it does have something to do with the mystical."

"Hey, Whitehawk! You gonna spend all evening talking to the pretty girl or you gonna help us clean this mess up?"

The flare of anger in Apollo's eyes was enough to keep

Sapphire from pulling her gun on the other fireman. She placed her hand on Apollo's arm to calm him and then turned her attention to the idiot. "Apollo is my cousin. And you are out of line. You can call me Officer White, or you can just call me officer, or even ma'am, but pretty girl is not acceptable."

The fireman bowed mockingly. "Sorry about that, *ma'am*." Then he smiled at her. "But since the chief here is your cousin, maybe you'd like to get a drink later?"

Sapphire fumed, unable to believe how completely inappropriate the jerk was. This time it was Apollo who was the one calming her. "Don't bother. He won't last long in this job with an attitude like that. It doesn't bother me. But I'll bust his mouth for talking to you like that if you want me too."

She grinned at him. He'd always known how to make her feel better. It had been that way since they were kids. Apollo was a good guy who used his human skills to help others, and in that they were alike. Of all her cousins, and for that matter the rest of the family, she felt closest to Apollo because neither of them felt the need to call to their mystical side to get things done.

"Thanks, but no. I can fight my own battles, and he isn't worth the time for either of us. I'll head on into the woods and see if I can find evidence of the body being carried into the trees. Whatever did this somehow knew to keep their feet out of the mess, but too much is missing for there not to be more somewhere. Hopefully I can get us a blood sample, without anyone knowing what I'm doing. You head on, and get everyone done and out of here as quickly as possible. I feel like someone or something is watching." She bit her bottom lip as creepy-crawlers skittered up her spine.

Sapphire sent Brad a signal that she was heading into the woods. He nodded and continued packing away their supplies. It didn't take long to find where the animal dropped what must have been a large chunk of flesh onto the ground. From there, following the blood-trail was much too easy as the beast, or whatever it was that had destroyed the human, hadn't worried about hiding anything. With the high beam of her flashlight pointed only a few feet in front of her, it was clear a pretty good-sized body part had been dragged. The flattened bloody grass was fairly wide, not just a line, and there were additional bits and pieces of flesh or muscle that left a trail behind.

The smell got worse the farther she walked, which made her concerned the animal was definitely something out of the ordinary. Sweet yet vinegary, the scent was like nothing she'd smelled before.

As thinner young trees gave way to millennia-old established forest, Sapphire unsnapped her holster and pulled her gun into her free hand. She stepped over broken branches, decomposing leaves, and the wild bushes that grew whenever the canopy overhead gave way for daylight's solar rays to allow for it.

She wished for daylight now.

A pop to her right caused her to freeze before she thought to swing the light in the direction of the noise. Sapphire searched the area but saw nothing save more trees and shadows. A chill covered her body, sending goose bumps to dance over her skin, though she assured herself it was only that the wind was picking up. With a shaky breath, she turned the beam back in front of her until she had it lighting the blood-trail again.

"Hey!"

Thinking she was about to pee on herself if she didn't get over being spooked, Sapphire swung her body around until she had Brad in the flashlight's beam. He was frowning at her, which, she realized, never happened. "You nearly gave me a heart attack!"

He shook his head, his brows pulled together. "Sorry, but we need to get out of here. Dispatch just sent out word that a storm is moving this way rapidly. We're under a tornado warning."

Sapphire nodded, almost relieved she wouldn't have to go any further into the woods. She started to walk his way hoping he would turn around and lead them back. She'd been so focused on the bloody trail she hadn't stopped yet to get her sample. When he continued to wait, she sighed. "Go ahead. I'll just be another minute."

A hard blast of wind whipped through the trees, nearly knocking her to the side. She caught herself and spread her stance in an effort to keep her feet. "Okay, run! I'm right behind you!"

Brad took off at a sprint and she followed, fighting to stay upright. The sound of what she could only imagine was hail sounded loudly overhead. The canopy didn't hold it off for long, and ice rocks pounded her head and shoulders painfully. Desperate to get out of the downpour, Sapphire sidled up against a large tree and called for Brad, but she had no idea if he responded. She could hear nothing over the deafening onslaught.

Blinding white light replaced the darkness, turning harmless trees into threatening beasts with flailing arms. The immediate crash of thunder followed so quickly Sapphire knew the storm was right above her. She debated her options as she pressed herself against the tree's trunk. If she stayed where she was, there was always the danger of the violent lightning striking either the tree or bolting through the canopy and setting a fire, even zapping her. Brad had obviously opted to get out of the forest fast, and she knew she should have too, but the violence of the wind and the harsh sting from the hail kept her glued in place.

A flash of movement caught Sapphire's attention seconds after her hair came undone and smacked her already watering eyes. Whatever was there was gone too quickly for her to be able to identify if it was an animal or a large branch flying by. Belatedly, the growing fiery heat across her wrists alerted her to the possibility of injury. She pushed her hair away from her face and studied the slash, realizing *something* had scraped her, as it passed by. She didn't have time to dwell on the pain as the hailstorm intensified, pelting her with the stinging ping pong-sized ice-balls, making her cry-out as she was slammed by it again and again. Knowing she would have bruises all over, she slid down the tree's trunk and curled into as small a target as she could.

Sapphire expelled a long breath and tried to gauge the extent of her injury only to gasp in terror when something covered her head and body, pinning her arms down in a tight grip. She struggled against the blinding material, not knowing if it was a blanket or tarp someone was using to hold her down. Fury filled her, and she screamed, desperately trying to push whomever it was away, and then sanity returned and she stopped. "Dammit, Brad! Get off me!"

There was no response in either movement or sound, and Sapphire growled. "I said get off me!"

The pressure around her eased and Sapphire fought against the covering until it finally landed at her side. There was no one around. The wind and the hail had stopped. She sat, frozen with confusion, before remembering to look at the arm that was still burning and now starting to itch. Blood seeped slowly from the three-inch-long gash. Sapphire clamped her hand on the wound to stop the flow as she struggled to her feet.

It was eerily quiet after the noise from the wind and the hail; *nothing* stirred. It seemed as if she'd stepped from one planet to another. She took a shaky breath, then more, until she was almost breathing normally. Swallowing, she looked around for her flashlight, but it was so dark it took her several minutes to find it. Once it was in-hand, she shined the beam at the ground and saw her gun was beside what turned out to be nothing more than a wool blanket lying on the ice. She frowned, wondering where its owner was, concerned he or she hadn't even stayed around for introductions, or to let her know that they were all right too.

Surely, if it *had* been Brad, he would have stayed put long enough for her to apologize for cursing at him. With that in mind, Sapphire shined the light around her, looking for any signs of...*anything*. She shivered, not just from the cold wetness against her head and skin, but from the reality that whoever, or *whatever* had come to her rescue, may have also been the person or *thing* that now had her forearm swelling.

Ignoring her purpose for entering the woods in the first place, Sapphire made a quick trip back the way she'd come. The melting ice balls and forest debris made her progress slower than she'd hoped. It was a relief to finally see the flashing blue and red lights through the trees, and it was only then she realized she had been on the edge of panicking.

At last she stepped from the woodlands and into the clearing of the roadway. The activity at the site of the massacre now was that of crews loading up to leave and of those already pulling out to head back to their stations or their homes. Relieved her shift would soon be over for the night, Sapphire took a deep cleansing breath. Which only reminded her that something smelled very wrong....

"Sapphire, over here!"

She rubbed her nose and turned at the sound of her cousin's voice. Apollo squatted next to Brad, who was sitting on the asphalt beside their cruiser, with a cloth held to his head. She hurried over and squatted down too, sending a glance to her cousin.

"Is he hurt badly?"

Apollo shook his head and rose from his crouched position and she followed suit, still looking at her partner.

"I don't think so. I think a branch hit him while he was running back."

Brad glanced up, his blood-covered face either regretful or embarrassed. "I'm sorry I left you. I didn't realize you weren't right behind me."

Sapphire shooed away his comment with a wipe of her hands. "No problem. Are you okay?"

Brad frowned, and nodded, But Sapphire wasn't sure she believed him. He looked like he'd been in a prizefight, and he'd lost.

Apollo grabbed the arm she swung and lifted it to inspect it before looking at her with a frown. "What happened?"

Though he was gentle, the pain of his grip caused Sapphire to pull her arm away. "Something flew by me and scraped it." She frowned. "*I think.*" She glanced down at Brad. Knowing he already felt bad enough about abandoning her, she kept her next thought to herself. Apparently Apollo caught her vibe, though, as his eyes grew concerned.

"Brad, I need to talk to my cousin. Are you okay enough for us to step away for a minute?"

Sapphire's slid her partner a glance, frowning when he hunched down into himself. He seemed much more injured than his small head wound indicated. When Brad nodded, again, Apollo put his arm around her shoulder and pulled her away from everyone's earshot.

"What really happened out there?" he asked, lifting her arm again, this time taking her flashlight to shine it on the wound.

Sapphire winced at his touch. "I'm not sure. The storm

came up so fast. Everything was flying all around me. Then suddenly something hit me, or something…" Sapphire bit her bottom lip, afraid the sudden onset of nausea was going to cause her stomach to revolt and embarrass her.

With his lips pressed together and his brows furrowed, Apollo slowly turned her arm to inspect it before releasing her and looking into her eyes. "I don't think that's a scrape. You need to go see Aunt Haven."

Chapter Two

Sapphire was so glad to be home. As much as she loved her job, nothing had prepared her for the night she'd had. Not only was there someone, or *something*, running around Mystic Mountain that threatened the peaceful world in which they all lived, now she had this darn injury that would require her to fill out an on the job accident report at work. For a rookie cop, that was never a good thing, which was why she hadn't reported it when she'd taken her partner to the hospital. Thankfully, she'd been able to leave him there in the capable hands of the hospital staff, and no one saw the wound she'd hidden beneath her jacket.

Apollo had overreacted. As much as she loved him and respected his opinion, there was no need to wake Aunt Haven at two in the morning to have her work her magic to heal what was probably nothing more than a nasty scratch. A good washing and an antiseptic should do the trick nicely.

She stepped from her little Jeep and couldn't wait to get inside to get Ellie. Her eleven-pound Shih Tzu was the love of her life. No matter what kind of workday or, in her case, *night*, she'd had, Ellie would welcome her home with joy and kisses. That was the best thing about adopting the sweet baby months earlier, when her previous owner had died. Once her confusion over not seeing the elderly woman anymore passed, and Ellie had accepted Sapphire as her new mommy, she'd embraced the relationship and was nothing but a little ball of love.

For Ellie, life was nothing but a joyous romp.

Sapphire smiled at the excited barks coming from behind her front door. Ellie always knew when she was home, and Sapphire was sure she'd slept soundly until she'd heard the crunch of tires on the quarter-mile-long gravel driveway, so she'd be filled with energy. As tired as Sapphire was, and as much as her arm was aching, nothing could take precedence over letting Ellie know how much she was loved.

Since she always left lights on so Ellie wouldn't have to awake to a dark empty house, and the television on the animal station, so she'd have company, Sapphire was able to step into her cabin as if she'd been there the whole time. True to form, Ellie's white tipped black tail flew back and forth in welcome, as her tiny front legs hugged Sapphire's knee with all her might. The pup stared up at her adoringly with large, dark brown eyes that always filled Sapphire's heart. Laughing, feeling the horrible night fall away, Sapphire lifted her, and they snuggled and kissed each other as if they'd been parted for months.

"Let's go potty!"

Immediately Ellie was struggling to get down. Sapphire opened the door to let her out then followed, stopping on the front porch to watch the show. Since she'd been gifted the cabin from her builder father, nestled within the deeply wooded ancestral land from her uncle Tom, there was no need to worry about Ellie running off or going out into a street.

Though she'd just stepped into the house for a moment, stepping back out was like doing it for the first time. Now she could take a moment to breath in the mountain's pine trees, smell the sweetness of the dense vegetation that outlined her land, and embrace the slight breeze winding through the trees. Amazingly, the storm hadn't hit her house, so Ellie could take care of her business without having to traverse ice and mud, just the normal tiny broken pine branches and needles that always covered the yard. Sapphire knew it wouldn't be too long before the air started cooling and the vegetation beyond the small yard would start dying down. Fall was approaching, and within the Appalachian Mountains it would either be breathtaking and lengthy, or kick-start winter weather with a vengeance.

She was hoping for the first, but today's sudden unusual storm had her concerned it could be the second.

Sapphire watched as Ellie squatted in the clearing that made up her yard and then grinned as the pup sniffed around even more furiously so she could finish her quest. As Ellie always had to find just the right spot to poop, the quest often took longer than Sapphire expected it should, but she knew the routine and waited patiently as she allowed the night's horrors to wash away.

Lulled by the peace of the night sounds, Sapphire settled into one of the two large wooden-slat chairs her father had fashioned and enjoyed the moment. She loved her home. Not only because it was built with love, but because Garrison White was such a masterful builder that it was flawless. Even though the loft bedroom structure was new, it was designed and built in a way that blended in with its ancient surroundings, as if it too had sprung from the earth. That was true of all the cabins built on Mystic Mountain regardless of their age. Not only was it required to honor those who first settled the area before white men's feet ever touched the land, it was her father's way of doing things. Though his blood was diluted by generations of Anglo-Saxon marriages, Garrison White, too, was related to those who first settled the mountain.

His very distant cousin, her uncle Tom, shared a tribal ancestral homeland, which was unique to the mountainous region and was guarded by those whose stewardship meant more to them than their own lives. Unlike other West

Virginian mountains mined for coal, Mystic Mountain was still pristine, untouched by modern mankind as much as possible. The mountain, from which a spring fed from top and flowed to bottom, lorded over Mystic Lake below. And like the mountain itself, the waters were filled with mystical elements that enhanced the magic of those mystical beings who called it home.

Both sides of her family had been a part of the mountain's history and were, once again, a part of its present. Although Sapphire had no desire to have any link to those mystical hereditary traits, she was more than happy to embrace the beautiful land her immediate and extended family called home.

Her father had lived in Mystic Waters all his life, though he'd only lived on Mystic Mountain following his service in the military over twenty-five years before. Her uncle Tom was native not only to the mountain, his Native American ancestors had staked their claim to the entire region so many millennia ago that no one knew just exactly when the tribe had migrated south from the mid eastern part of what is now Canada. Her mother, Aunt Destiny, as well as Aunt Haven, had only moved from California to Mystic Waters, a year and a half before Sapphire and her identical sisters' births. But, according to her mother, the Cavanaugh women had found their way here time and again, though Sapphire didn't want to know why. Her desire to leave magic behind years before had resulted in her tuning out any talk of their ancestry whenever possible. And though they hadn't seemed to care, she wondered now if her rejection had stung.

Ellie's sudden hoarse bark startled Sapphire from her musings and she stood to see what had captured her baby's attention. A chill rolled over her, from head to toes, but she could see nothing as Ellie continued to bark in the most aggressive way she ever had.

"Ellie! Stop that, and come here! You've scared me to death!"

Ellie glanced back at her and then turned back toward the stand of trees she'd been facing. She threw back her head and let out a long howl, followed by several shorter ones. Even though she loved the silly little howl, Sapphire felt unnerved by the continued vocalizations, as well as by the fact that Ellie was disobeying her. "Ellie! Come here!"

Resigned that her pet wasn't going to budge, Sapphire took the three porch steps quickly and walked into the small clearing with purpose, not catching Ellie's attention until she was right over the little dog. Ellie immediately turned and pawed at her leg and Sapphire lifted her into her arms.

Soft whimpers and frantic snuggling was so out of character for the dog that Sapphire's gaze went immediately to the forest-line. More chills covered her arms in goose bumps, making her injury ache more. After the massacre she'd witnessed earlier, her heart raced in fear. She clamped Ellie to her with one arm, freeing her to unlock her holster and hold her gun in her free hand. Cautiously she backed toward the cabin, while surveying the tree line with each step. She glanced back once, relieved to see she'd made it to the porch. Without hesitation, she turned and made it up and into the house. She lowered Ellie to the floor before slamming and locking the door.

A great sigh escaped as she placed her gun on the key table she kept just inside the door. She lifted and hugged Ellie to her, before she kissed all over the shaggy little head. "What was it, girl?"

Shivering with energy, Ellie licked her face as if it were a salt-block, while sharp little toenails dug into Sapphire's shoulders; her long tail didn't move. The tail not swinging like windshield wipers was what worried Sapphire the most. Ellie was always happy to be held and kissed on. "What is it, baby?"

As she came from a boisterous, large family, one of the best things about dogs, as far as Sapphire was concerned, was they didn't talk. At the moment, though, she'd have given anything to know what had her little dog so agitated. She walked to the large front-facing window and glanced out, but even with her floodlights lighting the area immediately around the house she could see nothing amiss. Still, knowing it was just as easy for something to see in, she did something she'd yet to do since moving into the cabin. She closed the large curtains her mother had bought and hung, when Sapphire first moved in.

"Don't you worry about it, baby. We're safe."

But assuring her pet did nothing to quell her own shivers.

****

Nicolae Lupei breathed a sigh of relief once the beautiful police officer and her little dog were inside. It was stupid of him to have alerted her to his presence by covering her with his blanket to start with, but he'd followed that up by shadowing her first to the hospital and then home. He'd justified his detour from hunting his brother by telling himself he'd had to know how she would handle all that had happened. Which was true. But his real reasons were less honorable.

Admitting she pulled at the male in him in some way meant he was putting his own needs and desires ahead of his pack. Nicolae sighed, ashamed at the truth of it, even though he was certain it had nothing to do with her beauty. There was a strength about her that appealed to him, but even that didn't explain what had him dropping the most important mission of his life.

He settled himself on the side of the tree facing away

from her cabin, uncertain how to proceed. In a way, he was glad she hadn't sought medical attention for her wound, but he knew she would have to since she'd become very sick, and eventually die a painful death, if she didn't. The questions were, just how that would play out, and how soon would he be forced to step in?

He glanced back around the tree, knowing no matter how exhausted he was, he'd have to find his way back to his clothing soon. Wandering around the mountain as a wolf was all good and well, but falling asleep outside of a woman's cabin as a naked human male would get him in all kinds of hot water once the sun came up, and she and her pup were out and about.

He was just glad the little dog hadn't come to him and exposed him. Staying in the form of the wolf until they were inside had served him well, but that little dog would know he was still close, and wouldn't settle down until he made himself scarce.

Embracing his wolf, Nicolae transformed and stood. With one last look back, he put his nose to the ground and sniffed around, but his brother was long gone. Picking up his trail would have to wait for another night. He just hoped Ion wouldn't kill and dismember anyone else before he could be found and put down.

Sorrow was becoming a common feeling not only for Nicolae, but for his pack as well. Ion, translated from their Romanian language to John in English, was once their Alpha. His bold heart and astute ability to protect and lead the pack was legendary, but his stubborn refusal to allow others to help him when confronting adversaries had come at a hard price. Not only had he taken on and been horribly injured, while fighting and killing the rabid wolves that had recently threatened his pack, he'd ended up bitten himself and was now as dangerous as they had been. The difference being they were pure wolves, and he was Lycanthrope, so much more dangerous to human and animal alike, as his diseased mind no longer allowed him to think clearly.

As the next oldest male and current Alpha, Nicolae was now charged with hunting Ion down and taking his life, preferably while he was in human form and less likely to bite. It was a hard pill to swallow, not something he could allow his pack to participate in. If Ion changed in the midst of the battle and bit more of the pack, there would be more than one rabid werewolf running around. At that point it would be nearly impossible to keep the dominoes from falling, and there would be many more twisted-minded, diseased creatures, terrorizing the planet.

That, Nicolae could not allow.

Spreading the disease wasn't the only threat to their kind. Knowledge of their existence, in a world of those who thought them only mythical beings, would cause all kinds of havoc and likely take them to the edge, or possibly over the edge, of extinction. Even now, his pack was all that was left on this continent. He knew of several more packs in existence, but most, unlike their king's in Bucharest, Romania, were small like his own. With less than twenty pack-members left in the United States, every one of them counted, and Nicolae could only pray that no more, himself included, became infected with the terrible disease.

Which brought him back to the cop.

Ion scratched her. Whether it was with a claw or with his teeth, it was too soon to tell. Either way he could have infected her with rabies if his saliva had transferred to a foot while licking himself, or even while he'd been holding down meat if still able to eat. Nicolae just hoped he could find a way to figure that out before it was too late. If it was nothing more than a scratch from a toenail that didn't contain the infection, then she would only require the painful shots to keep her from dying, but if Ion had actually broken the skin with his teeth or a tainted nail, more than rabies would affect whatever life she had remaining.

Nicolae took off at a run and headed to the area where he'd first transformed to track Ion's movements. He was completely exhausted by the time he made it and had to take a moment to just lie at the base of the tree where he'd hidden his clothes. He changed back into the man everyone believed him to be, gave himself a few more minutes, and then dressed as quickly as possible. Fortunately, his campsite was less than a mile away.

Tonight's hunt was done. Tomorrow, he had to try tracking his brother again, but now that wasn't his only charge. He'd also have to check on the policewoman and figure out a way to get close enough to her to see just what he could do for her…if anything.

Chapter Three

Sapphire knew she was in trouble.

Not only had her forearm swollen to nearly twice its normal size, it was streaked with red and black lines, and she could tell the injury at her wrist was filled with pus. And as much as she hated to alert her family, Sapphire knew she had no choice. Not only hadn't she slept, she was feeling sick to her stomach. If she went to the hospital now, there would be questions about her not doing so the night before. But before she went anywhere, she'd have to take Ellie out. It infuriated her that she felt hesitant at doing so, as she loved her secluded home, and had never know a fearful moment, until the night before.

Fortunately, her anxiety was unfounded, as the bright morning sky peeking through the forest's canopy showed she had nothing to fear. Whatever animal had spooked Ellie the night before was apparently gone. The little dog wandered around the yard, squatted a couple of times, and then made her way back in a playful spirit.

Sapphire laughed at her, but the pain in her arm didn't allow for either cheer or play, so she took her pet inside and reluctantly lifted her cell phone. Before she could hit the screen to call first her mother—otherwise she would be mad—and then her aunt Haven, the healer of the family, her aunt Destiny's ringtone startled her into nearly dropping the phone. She bit her bottom lip and answered.

"Sapphire! What's wrong?"

As an Intuit, who, like her identical sisters had so many mystical abilities it was mindboggling, Sapphire didn't even have to ask how her aunt knew... although, there was always the possibility Destiny's middle triplet, Apollo, had said something after expressing his concern the night before.

"I was just about to call Mom. I got scratched last night while on duty."

"Why are you *just now* calling someone for help?"

The sternness of voice wasn't unusual coming from her mother's older sister, and it made Sapphire feel like she was a little girl again, caught doing something she shouldn't. She sighed. "I thought I could take care of it by myself."

"Obviously that isn't the case. Call your mother and tell her you're coming over. Haven and I will be there shortly."

Sapphire couldn't bite down the smile that instantly came to her lips. As early in the morning as it was, she could just imagine what Aunt Haven's reaction would be to being awakened. "I don't think that's necessary, yet. We can wait a few hours."

"Your aunt can get her butt up out of bed just like the rest of us. Now call your mother. I'm calling your uncle Logan, and he can deal with his lazy wife. See you shortly."

The connection was lost and Sapphire exhaled, actually relieved everything would get taken care of quickly. Although she avoided even a hint of magic whenever she could, and she'd done a stellar job of it since moving out of the house she and her sisters shared following college, Sapphire had to admit having a healer in the family was a blessing, given the circumstances.

"Ellie-girl, we're going to see Grandma."

Ellie's tail wagged furiously, and Sapphire laughed again. "Yes, baby. And she'll be just as happy to see her little grand-pup." Sapphire didn't want to think about how furious she'd be for finding her daughter had ignored help when it was so readily available.

After making a quick call and getting lectured as she'd expected, Sapphire loaded Ellie and took off. As much as she'd appreciated her long driveway in the past, the jarring of her injured arm had her cursing it today. Relief washed over her when she reached the end. She settled in for the five-minute drive up the mountainous road leading to her parents' cabin, and although she was looking forward to a quick fix to her problem, the drive was over way too soon. Her mother and her mother's identical sisters were standing on the porch, and they all looked like they wanted to kill her.

Thankfully Ellie got to them first, and all were oohing and awing when Sapphire reached the porch. Laughing, Rayne lifted a wiggling Ellie before looking at her daughter. "Let's see it."

Knowing what was coming, Sapphire lifted her arm and turned it so her wound was completely visible. The happy puppy smiles fell from three identical faces, and each set of emerald eyes changed; her mothers were aghast, Aunt Destiny's were furious, and Aunt Haven's sparked with fire.

Storm clouds gathered in an instant. Lightning streaked the sky in angry bursts. Thunder rumbled and boomed, shaking the earth beneath their feet. Sapphire, as well as her mother and Aunt Destiny, looked at Haven, all three realizing the atmospheric conditions were a direct result of her distress.

"Haven, calm down," Destiny said softly, placing her hand on her sister's shoulder.

Haven blinked and the sky cleared, but the frown on her face had Sapphire worried. Haven was the most lighthearted of the three Cavanaugh sisters, and she never looked worried, unless one of her children was unhappy.

Haven walked forward and grasped Sapphire's wrist. The warmth in her hand was startling but not painful. When she lifted her other hand to place it on the wound, the pain eased, but not by much. She looked up into Sapphire's eyes, her own still a kaleidoscope of fiery emerald with sparks of yellow and red.

"What bit you?"

Sapphire shook her head. "It isn't a bite. Something scraped me when the storm hit last night. I thought it was a flying branch, but the hail was pounding me and my hair flew in my face. So I can't be sure."

Haven stared at her silently and then shook her head. "You were scraped by the teeth of a rabid animal. We have to get you medicated immediately." She bit her bottom lip, and turned her attention back to the wound. "But there is something more here." She looked up at Sapphire, her eyes filled with fear. "And I don't know what it is."

Rayne was at her sister's side immediately, her concern causing deep lines around her eyes. She looked at the wound as well, then at her daughter. "You will come inside now."

Though her mother wasn't one to panic, the softly spoken command held a world of alarm. Sapphire nodded, and then glanced up to Destiny. She held Ellie in her arms; her lips were pushed firmly together. That Aunt Destiny wasn't saying anything at all worried her almost as much as had the words of the other two.

They made their way into the house and Haven lifted and punched at the screen of her cell phone. "Hi, babe. I need you to get a vial of rabies immune globulin over to Rayne's right away. Sapphire has been bitten, and we need to act fast."

She hesitated and Sapphire felt her stomach lurch, causing her to seek the couch. Rayne joined her and took her hand as they waited.

"Yes, go on and get the series. We'll give her those shots when they're required. But there is something else, and I don't know what it is. We'll need to take blood and test it."

Sapphire listened as the conversation continued, feeling more sick by the minute. She had no idea if it was because of the rabies, or if her fear was increasing to the point her mind was sending vomit signals to her stomach. Either way, she had to hit the floor running, glad the bathroom was close enough to prevent her from soiling her mother's pretty hardwood floors.

Rayne was at her side immediately, holding her hair back. Sapphire continued to wretch until dry heaves burned her throat. By the time she felt she could lean back and sit on the bathroom floor, Destiny had joined them and was wetting a cloth. She handed it to Sapphire as Ellie came in and lay at her side. Even her baby knew she wasn't well.

Tears spilled from her eyes, which made her mad. She never cried. Ever. Not since the one and only time she'd used her magic. With everything else she had to worry about, Sapphire turned her thoughts away from that horrible day and focused on her mother's words.

"You will have to stay here. At least tonight, so we can make sure you're doing okay. I'll take care of Ellie and you, and we'll let your sisters know you're here, and a dangerous animal is running around the mountain." She glanced up at her sisters when Haven made an appearance. "Fix my baby."

Haven nodded, though Sapphire could see the doubt in her aunt's eyes. She moved forward to place her hand on Sapphire's brow and then stepped back.

"You're running a fever. We need to get you into a bed. Why don't you take a tepid shower, if you feel up to it? It will help you feel a little better." She turned her attention on Rayne, who had settled at Sapphire's side as well. "She'll need to be watched for several days. She'll feel like she has a bad case of the flu. Possibly even hallucinations, and likely anxiety and agitation." She turned her attention to Sapphire again. "You will get through this. I promise."

Sapphire nodded and allowed her aunts to help her and her mother to their feet. That her mother needed help worried her. Rayne Cavanaugh-White was as healthy as they came.

The aunts left the room and Rayne assisted her in undressing, though she didn't need assistance. She allowed it because she saw that her mother needed to be there, needed to be doing whatever she could for her sick child. It made her smile, remembering how often her mother had prepared her and her sisters for their baths when they were little.

"I'm going to be okay, Momma. Aunt Haven will make sure of it."

Tears filled Rayne's eyes as she nodded. "I know. It's just that I never expected you and Jewell to be the ones that had to deal with anything frightening. First Jewell being transported to a past life, and now you, with this. Dia was always the one who concerned me. To this day I'm afraid when she blows something up in her quest for magic, she'll end up getting blown up too, but there is no stopping that girl."

Sapphire rarely found Diamond Cavanaugh-White's *experiments* amusing, one reason they'd all been so relieved Uncle Tom provided her with his secluded cabin way up the mountain, but she knew where her mother was coming from and couldn't help but smile. "I know. She's a mess." Rayne laughed, which was exactly the reaction Sapphire had hoped for.

"You shouldn't talk about your sister that way. Dia is just... *Dia.* I celebrate each one of you children, no matter what you pursue." She looked at Sapphire pointedly. "Or don't."

Sapphire stepped into the large, elaborate shower Uncle Tom had fashioned back when her father built the cabin he and her mother loved. She had always loved it too, even though the only other bedroom besides their master, which was a loft like her own, had been rather crowded for their triplet daughters to grow up in. But they'd made do and had been happier for the closeness. *If you discounted Dia's aggravating exploits.*

Water flowed over her like a soft rain. Sapphire ignored the guilt she felt at being so mean where Dia was concerned. It had always been that way between them, even though there was no doubt about the love they had for each other. She adjusted the spray, making it a little harder, but was careful to keep the injured part of her arm from being hit. The pain was only getting worse.

Once she'd bathed and shut down the spray, Rayne was there, holding out a towel. Sapphire took it and quickly patted herself dry, before winding it around her hair like a turban. She held out her arms and truly felt like a little girl again when her mother helped her into a soft cotton nightgown. Since she hated to sleep with panties on, she was relieved it reached the floor.

"Let's get you into bed. Logan is here, and they want to get your treatment started."

Sapphire nodded, though she thought she might be sick again. This time she was certain it had more to do with the thought of the needles going into her. But she smiled when she stepped across the hall to find both Haven and Logan standing side by side, their arms locked around each other's waist.

Logan released his wife and stepped forward, looking into her eyes. "What have you gotten yourself into, baby girl?"

Sapphire smiled at him. "A mess, apparently. How are you?"

Logan grinned. "A lot better than you, *apparently.*"

"Tom's on his way."

All eyes turned to Destiny, where she stood in the doorway. "I think we need to find out what else is going on as well, if he can."

Haven nodded. "Thanks. I don't like not knowing what this other threat is."

"Me either," Rayne said. "Garrison is on his way, too. He may not usually pay any attention to our world of magic, but this is his baby."

The others nodded, and Sapphire wondered if the entire clan would descend on her before the day ended. She was seriously afraid they would. But for the moment... "Can I lie down now?"

As if they'd forgotten she was the reason they were crowding the room, everyone moved to allow her to crawl into the single bed that was once flanked by a set of bunks. It was the room she and her sisters had shared. Now the remaining bed was moved away from the wall, allowing someone the ability to stand on that side. Since the twin bed had always been hers, she really did feel like she was little again. Unfortunately, she was a lot longer now than she had been then, and everyone chuckled a little when she had to move her pillow higher so her feet wouldn't stick out at the foot of the bed.

"I guess we need to at least get a full-sized bed in here."

Sapphire looked at her mother. "You think?"

Even she had to laugh at herself, until Logan opened his black bag and pulled out a number of syringes. Hers weren't the only eyes that got serious of a sudden. She watched as he and Aunt Haven filled the first and then placed empty tubes in three more. She held out her hand, and her mother immediately took it. Logan's eyes were serious when he looked over at her, though she could tell he wasn't trying to let his concern show.

"I'm going to take blood first. I want to take it from

the arm that isn't infected. Then we'll give you the rabies shot in the arm that is. I have to tell you, it's going to hurt."

Sapphire swallowed and then nodded. It wasn't like she had any choice. He nodded, too, and approached her with the first empty vial syringe and the rubber tube he'd use to tie off her circulation. Aunt Haven followed, holding the small tray that held the remaining syringes.

"What the hell happened?"

Everyone turned as Garrison entered the room. He went straight to Sapphire and leaned down to kiss her forehead before looking down at her infected arm. His gaze immediately sought Haven. "Can't you fix this?"

Haven shrugged. "I could pull the rabies from her body, and burn it, but something else is at play here, and I don't know what it is, or what my magic will do to it. I was hoping we'd be able to kill the rabies virus with modern medicine, then let me have another look at what's left."

"Tom's coming too," Destiny interjected, pulling Garrison's gaze to her. "He may be able to look into her... maybe. We don't know yet. There is little Haven can't do for an injury or illness, but she's blind here. Maybe Tom won't be...."

Garrison glanced at his wife then looked back down at his daughter. "We'll do whatever it takes, baby. Magic or regular medicine. We'll get you well."

Sapphire nodded and smiled for her father's sake. But the number of people in the room was starting to make her feel claustrophobic, and she really didn't want everyone to see her if she cried. "I don't mean to sound... ungrateful, but there are so many people in here, it's making it hard to breathe."

Garrison leaned down and kissed her again before leaving the room. The fact that he didn't speak told her he couldn't, not without crying himself. Destiny smiled at her and turned to follow, leaving only her mother and the healers in the room.

When her mother looked down beside the bed and then lifted Ellie up to place her at Sapphire's side, she smiled at her gratefully. "Thank you."

"I'm not leaving."

Tears flooded Sapphire's eyes. "I didn't expect you would."

Rayne looked up at her brother-in-law. "Get this over with."

Logan nodded and walked around the bed. He tied off the circulation just above the elbow and Sapphire was thankful for his expertise when she barely even felt the needle go in. He gently replaced the first vial with two more once they were filled to his satisfaction. She kept her gaze on her mother's face and breathed again when Logan released the band, allowing her blood to flow. Haven handed him a cotton ball and then a Band-Aid, and the needle slid out with as much finesse.

"Now comes the hard part," he said, pulling her gaze to him. "I'm going to have to inject the serum as close to your wound as possible."

Sapphire nodded. "I know."

He shook his head and rounded the bed. Rayne lifted Ellie and walked around him and stood on the other side before placing the little dog back on the bed. Sapphire looked up at her mother again. "I'm scared."

Rayne nodded, but didn't speak as her throat muscles worked furiously. She took Sapphire's hand again, and held it tight.

"I'm going to stick you now, and it will likely hurt like hell since this arm is so swollen. But I need you to be completely still."

Sapphire nodded but didn't look at him, determined to keep her gaze on her mother. When nothing happened, Sapphire looked over at her uncle. "Just do it!"

Logan shook his head. "I can't." He handed the syringe to Haven and walked out of the room.

"Men are such pussies," Haven said. Though her tone was teasing, the strain in her eyes said she wasn't any more anxious to do the deed than her husband had been. She shook her head and took a deep breath. "Like your uncle said, I'll have to get this as close to the wound as possible. This is going to *really* hurt. Do you need me to call your dad and Logan back in to hold you still?"

Filled with fear, Sapphire shook her head then turned to her mother. "Will you do it?"

Rayne nodded and climbed onto the bed quickly, as if hesitating would stop her all together. She draped her body over her daughter's, careful not to squash Ellie as she settled. Lying flush against Sapphire, she slid one arm around her daughter's neck to hold her in a secure hug. With her free hand, she held the injured arm just above the elbow.

Sapphire felt another pair of hands take her wrist and hold it to the bed, and she knew Aunt Destiny had returned. She tried to fight the fear and struggled to take a breath, but before she could, her arm exploded in pain.

Sapphire's scream ripped the fabric of the air and continued until the burning liquid filled her forearm. By the time the needle was pulled from her flesh, and those holding her down loosened their hold, all four of them were crying, *hysterically*.

Chapter Four

Nicolae awoke with a start and threw himself into a sitting position. He looked around his tent, relieved to see a bottled water within reach, and startled to see Sabia Ilie's naked behind facing him. He looked away from her, downed the remaining water in one long drink, before crushing the bottle and pitching it in the container he used for trash.

"Awww," Sabia said, rolling over as she stretched. "My man is alive. You were in such a deep sleep I would have thought you dead, if you hadn't grumbled in your slumber."

Annoyance had Nicolae pressing his lips together. "Put your clothes on."

Sabia pouted. "But why? You know we will be good together." She switched to a seductive smile when the pouting didn't work. "I will pleasure you and bear the next Alpha for you."

Nicolae pushed away from her reaching hand and crawled from the tent. He looked around, relieved to see the rest of the pack hadn't followed her and equally aggravated he'd have to take the time to take her back to them. He had more important things to do.

Sabia joined him, a light summer dress now covering her human form, though Nicolae had no illusions about underclothing being beneath her dress. She walked up to him and placed her hand on his bare chest. "You fight me, yet you know your duty. I am the strongest female. And the most attractive. Not to mention, you know of my lineage. I was meant to be an Alpha, even more so than you." She reached down and grabbed his penis, the devilment in her eyes saying she could caress or injure.

Nicolae slowly removed her hand and stepped back, not giving her the satisfaction of seeing his fear should she decide to hurt him in his most vulnerable spot. "You are making assumptions. I am not ready to pick my mate."

Sabia shrugged. "You will ultimately choose me. Everyone knows it."

Nicolae didn't respond. He walked a short distance then turned back. "Are you going to watch as I relieve myself?"

Sabia said nothing but finally turned to face the tent. "It would not matter to me one way or the other." She frowned as she glanced back at him for only a second, before turning away again. "And there was a time it would not have mattered to you. You know, from the day we found you, when you were but a pup, my father was going to have us mated. Why do you hesitate now that we are both of age, and you are in charge?"

Nicolae ignored her question and took care of his needs, before turning to face her. Her back was still to him, and he knew he couldn't afford to make an enemy of even one of his pack. His place as their Alpha was new, and though none had been willing to fight him for the position since Ion had decreed it would one day come to pass, and had trained him accordingly, he knew one misstep would have the others questioning their easy acceptance of him as their new leader.

He placed his hand on Sabia's shoulder and she turned his way. The hope in her eyes had him taking a step back. He would not give her false hope, only honesty. "I am not sure who I will chose. But more importantly right now, I don't even know if I will survive finding Ion. If he should bite me, I will kill him, then I will take my own life to end this threat."

Sabia shook her head. "You should not do this alone. You shouldn't be doing this at all. There are other males who are not as important to us."

Nicolae stared at her, bewildered she expressed no concern for her brother or for those who provided her with esteemed care. All that mattered to her was her place should he chose to make her what equated to the queen of their pack. "We are all equally important, Sabia. Your fear is not for me, but for yourself. You know if I should fall before siring a son, the next in line is Heburue. You have feared him since we were children. And we both know he would chose to take you whether you were willing, or not."

Sabia swallowed. "You cannot allow that to happen."

Compassion filled him, but he wouldn't allow her to hold him emotionally hostage. The woman he chose to mate with would have to be more interested in his welfare than her own, just as he would have to put her needs over his. But more importantly, she'd have to be willing to die to protect their family. "I will have you mate with Jaspon. He worships the ground you walk on."

Anger flashed in Sabia's eyes. "You would force me to marry that wimp? I would rather rut with pigs. Have I no chance with you then?"

Knowing the truth would be more than she could bear at the moment, Nicolae shook his head. "I told you. It isn't something I can give thought to right now. I was only trying to ensure you would not be taken by Heburue should I fall."

Mollified, Sabia nodded, and then slowly smiled. "I knew you had feelings for me. And I will give you space if that is what you desire of me. But I will not agree to mate with Jaspon. He is not worthy of me. I *am* of the royal line."

And you've made sure we all knew it since the day you started talking.

Nicolae didn't have time to argue with her, but he also knew she would have no choice but to go along with him if he decided she was to marry Jaspon, unless she was willing to be shunned from the pack. That wouldn't be good for any of them. Sabia would be alone, with no protection in her wolf form, and the pack would suffer another loss, or revolt if they strongly disagreed and try to kill him.

"Why did you come alone? You could have been captured or worse. You are placing us all in danger with your selfishness."

Sabia's annoyance was clear in the set of her lips. "I came to see you, to make you understand your duty. I am a true Alpha by birthright and deserve to carry the next Alpha male."

"Had Ion had a son, he would have carried the title, and you would never have had that chance, anyway. Why is it you now believe you do?" Nicolae asked, exasperated he had to deal with this now.

She shook her head. "You are talking foolishness. You know I have this right. I will not refuse you mating with the others, to increase our numbers, but you will allow me my due as Alpha Female."

Nicolae knew she was right. His duty to the pack dictated he follow protocol, but as beautiful in both wolf and human form as she was, Sabia's spirit of selfishness, and her superior, rather mean attitude with the rest of the pack, made him hesitant to mate with her.

And then there was the policewoman.

Nicolae sighed, knowing he had no right to even think of her when his pack was in such danger, but she was *all* he could think of. Even the mumbling in his sleep Sabia spoke of was likely a result of the dream he'd been having about the beautiful black-haired woman, with her amazing sapphire eyes.

He'd watched her, with vision that was never blinded

even by the darkest of nights. He'd listened to her from afar, with hearing that could reach miles and penetrate walls if he so chose. He'd seen her bravery in the face of carnage and her care for others, allowing their needs to take precedence over her own. He'd felt her heart when she talked and played with her little dog, treating it like her baby, unlike so many pet owners he'd seen in the past. And he'd felt the little dog's love for her. Its joy at her homecoming. Its desire to protect her with its cute little barks and howls when it realized he was near.

"You are angry at me, I know. But there is no need to ignore me. I will go back when the moon rises."

Having forgotten Sabia was even still there, Nicolae smiled and then nodded at her. "I will call to Jaspon and have him meet you halfway. I would take you back myself, but your brother tore a man apart last night and left the mess for others to see. I must find him as quickly as possible and put a stop to this. We will talk about other things then."

Sadness entered Sabia's eyes, and Nicolae was relieved to see she actually had a heart.

"My brother was a great Alpha. But his time is done. Kill him quickly so he may not suffer any longer."

With that Sabia transformed into a delicate female wolf and turned her back to him. She lifted her tail and he could smell that she was fully in estrus. Startled, Nicolae felt his form shifting without it being of his will and had to fight to keep it from happening. "You shame yourself, and now you must stay. Unless you want Jaspon to mate with you this night, you will stay here until this time has passed. He will not be able to resist your condition. He has only just reached his sexual maturity."

Sabia changed back into her human form and grinned at him. "I guess then we will see just how strong an Alpha *you* are."

Nicolae turned away and headed for the cold stream that ran down the mountain, angry the wolf in him wanted to give in to her, just to relieve the ache that now filled him. But the man in him wouldn't be so easily manipulated by wolf or woman.

Three mountains to the north, where his pack had established a territory long before he'd joined them, Nicolae knew the rest of his pack would be going about their daily lives. In human form they would be bakers and bankers, mechanics and lawyers, brick layers and office clerks, and as much as he knew he should miss his normal life, he didn't. This quest had been a blessing in disguise, though he would never have wished Ion's fate on the man or on his wolf. Mostly, he was straining with the burden that he now held all their futures in his hands. He hadn't expected it to weigh so much.

It was a welcome change to be free of their squabbles, to be free to hunt, to travel, and to find himself in the presence of those who would never know he lived two lives, by day as a home construction worker and by night as a wolf, who never had a moment's peace among a pack who were increasingly becoming dissatisfied with their lives.

His leave of absence from the job was something he missed, though. He loved to build things. To feel the strength of the wood, to wield the hammer, to hit the nails. But even building houses forced him to follow the dictates of others. Making cookie-cutter houses wasn't what he'd had in mind when he'd chosen his career. All he'd thought about was being able to work outside because he could never stand the thought of sitting in an office all day.

His dream was to design and build something like the policewoman had as her own home. A structure that was unique and looked as if it belonged to the landscape. Something that he could put his special stamp on, something that said *Nicholas Wolfe built this.*

Nicolae smiled, realizing he was thinking of himself as others did. His Romanian name was who he was in his natural form. Nicholas Wolfe was the man he chose to be, to live among all those who could not fathom his real identity.

The stream he'd chosen to build his camp near was wide and nearly two-feet deep. It didn't allow for a full immersion unless he stretched out to lie down, but he had no problem with that. The natural heat in his body allowed him to ignore the icy coldness, so he stepped into the stream, and enjoyed the chill, before seconds later it felt nothing more than tepid.

It was amazing to feel the water rushing over his body when he lay prone and was lifted to float on the surface. There was something about it that instantly invigorated him, and though he couldn't figure out what made this water different than all the other lakes and streams he'd visited, he knew there was a definite difference.

Like silk fluttering over his skin, the water caressed him, and elevated the level of his sexual appetite, rather than cooling it down. The music of the passing water sang to him, whispering words of enchantment and desire. The fish that occasionally passed by stopped, either out of curiosity or by design, to nibble at his flesh, tickling and teasing, and made him laugh.

Nicolae lay staring up at the sky through the thin line breaking the canopy of the large trees that outlined the stream. He closed his eyes and allowed his mind to go back to the woman who should have been an unwelcome distraction, but was in fact a distraction he couldn't wait to explore again. Her injury would need immediate treatment, and that scared him because he had no idea how to approach her to make it happen. She'd think he was a nutcase if he told her she might have been infected by a rabid werewolf.

Fortunately, her arm wound was such that she'd have to seek treatment of one kind or another. Though he feared the rabies wouldn't be caught in time, he was more concerned about the possibility she could have contracted the element that would turn her into one of his kind...if she survived the transformation.

Those, like himself, who were born Lycanthrope pups, transformed at will. But one who was infected, and not killed, would die on the night of the first transformation, by going through such a horrendously painful physical change that crushed and broke bones and stretched and ripped muscle. To his knowledge no one had ever survived, except in movies or books.

It pained him to know such a beautiful and brave creature would die because of one of his own. And it scared him that he wanted her to live, not because he should want any innocent to survive, but because he wanted to get to know *her*. He wanted to smell her magnificent aroma, and he wanted to know if her skin felt as soft as it looked.

"You are no better off now than before. You should give us both that which we desire."

Nicolae opened his eyes, knowing his interlude of peace was over, relieved Sabia couldn't read his mind unless he opened it to her. If she had been able to, she'd know his cock was heavy because of someone other than herself. He sat up and felt his butt hit the mossy bottom of the stream. "I am more than my desires."

At her lifted brow then swift exit, Nicolae hoped his words were true. If they weren't, he might just find himself in the struggle of his life. And this time, it would have nothing to do with his rabid brother.

As he prepared to once again track Ion, he knew how futile as it was to think of her, but Nicolae couldn't help but wonder how his beautiful cop was doing and how long it would be before he could find that out for himself. For the first time since they'd adopted him into the pack, he wanted to put his duty to his fellows aside.

But that wasn't an option.

****

The room had expanded then retreated repeatedly, increasing the nausea that perfumed the air. People came and went, wetting her brow, bathing her body, and whispering in low tones with words she could not follow. Windows were opened, and the air would sweeten, and then were closed when shivers overtook her. Hot soups were put to her painfully cracked lips, but she couldn't force the liquid down her raw throat, knowing it would soon reappear, and her sheets and gown would once again need replacing.

The excruciating pain of being moved as they rolled her one way and then the other as they changed her sheets was not nearly as horrible as having to raise her diseased arm to change her gown. Thankfully, her mother had given up on clothing her the last time she'd soiled everything around her.

Sapphire wanted to die.

Once she could see that night was once again approaching, and her delirium gave way along with the chilling fever that alternately froze her to the bone and felt like a furnace had settled in her form, Sapphire's mind cleared enough for her to realize the house was quiet.

She glanced to the side of the bed where her mother's head rested and felt shame she'd allowed her pride to keep her from seeking help as soon as the incident happened. Her family had to be sick and tired of her by now. "Momma?"

Rayne lifted her head and immediately reached for Sapphire's hand, before she straightened and stood. The way in which she rotated her head bespoke the discomfort of falling asleep in the chair sitting beside the bed. She reached forward and gently placed the back of her hand against Sapphire's forehead, then smiled.

"The fever broke."

Sapphire nodded and licked her flaky lips, wanting to ask for water, but afraid to. "How long?" was the most she could get out, as her throat burned with each breath she took, and talking was so much worse.

"Three full days, two nights. It looks like this one will be easier on you."

Sapphire nodded, hoping it would be easier on her mother, as well. "You should go to bed. You look horrible."

Rayne laughed. "Thanks. You don't look all that great yourself. But don't try to talk. You sound even worse."

Sapphire nodded again, even though she had so many questions to ask. She pointed to her lips and mouthed the words, *Dry, hurt.*

"I know. We've tried to keep them moisturized, but you would lick it right off. Maybe now will work better." Rayne lifted a small tube and removed the lid before rolling the ball within it on Sapphire's lips.

There was an instant difference, and Sapphire was certain the mixture in the tube was something her Aunt Haven had concocted. She smiled at her mother then raised her brows when there was a knock at the door.

"I'll be right back," Rayne said, before leaving the room.

Sapphire listened and was surprised she was able to hear every word spoken between her mother and Uncle Tom.

"We need to have a family meeting, but I need to talk to you and Garrison first. I'm afraid we have a problem."

Sapphire swallowed and then winced at the pain of

doing so. She waited, as she listened to her mother, not knowing how, but knowing she could hear each step as Rayne climbed the loft stairs and then awakened her father. When they spoke in low tones, Sapphire closed her eyes and could still hear, which both amazed and frightened her.

"Tom is here. He needs to talk to us about Sapphire. I think it is really bad."

Sapphire wanted to close off the sounds of her father's feet hitting the floor, then of both parents descending the stairs. She wanted to ignore the solemn greeting that passed between her father and uncle but couldn't help waiting to hear just what Tom Whitehawk had to say.

"I've talked to Logan and Haven, and I sought the council of Mother Mountain, and my own father, and I think something is going on that will change all our lives. Sapphire's in particular."

When he hesitated, Sapphire was certain her parents were straining to hear what he would say next, just as she was.

"A creature, possibly more than one actually, has desecrated the earth with a sickness that has the potential to poison those who abide on it. And we all believe this creature has placed its poison inside of Sapphire."

Silence followed, and Sapphire waited, wondering if her uncle didn't know she was infected by a rabid animal. She couldn't imagine he didn't, but this was not news.

"We know she was bitten by a rabid animal, Tom. As do you. What are you not saying?"

After a slight pause, Sapphire thought her neck would break if Tom didn't just say what he'd come to say. But her uncle was like that, speaking in a way that always had his listeners straining on the edge of their seats.

"The creature that did this is not native to this land, though its origins are as old as man. If what we believe is true, then the wolf people, known only to us as fictitious legend, are real, and have come to Mystic Mountain."

"Are you saying my daughter was infected by a werewolf? That's ridiculous, Tom!"

Sapphire's head reeled at her mother's question. It couldn't be true. It was impossible! But as she finally took the breath she hadn't known she was holding, she knew it could, in fact, be true after all. As crazy as it sounded, there were more unique creatures on God's green earth than mankind knew about. Like her aunt, who could turn into mist and send her spirit to other places. Like her other aunt, who could instantly change the molecular structure of the sky and bring on a tornado. Like her own mother, who could cast and conjure and form that which was not previously there. And like her sisters and cousins and more than three millennia of ancestors, who had documented their own unique abilities. As a Cavanaugh, she knew nearly anything was possible.

Sapphire lifted her injured arm, relieved to see the streaks were nearly gone, and the swelling was down, making the appendage look almost normal. Even that didn't make her feel much better. What if Uncle Tom was right? And if he was, just was did that mean for her?

Chapter Five

Nicolae chewed on his bottom lip as he stood in the small clearing before the log cabin. He'd been by the past two nights after exhaustive hours searching for Ion, but his efforts on both had been futile. His brother was close but still clever enough to hide his trail, and his policewoman hadn't returned home at all, he was almost certain, since he'd last seen her there. He'd even made his way to town yesterday morning, putting on his construction clothes, including his tool belt, before going into the Mystic Waters Hospital in the valley below. He'd passed every room he could make his way in front of, to listen in, but she hadn't been there either. He'd walked the old-fashioned Main Street, had ducked into one store after another, hoping for any word of her. But it seemed she'd disappeared from the planet.

The sound of tires on her long driveway alerted him early enough to hide his naked form within the coat of his wolf, before he made his way to the line of trees that would protect him from view. His hope that she was returning home was soon dashed. A redheaded beauty and a blonde, who both shared her face, emerged from the little red sports car that would have cost more than he'd made over the past year.

It took only a moment for his eyes to feed his mind with the startling realization that these two women shared his policewoman's face, even though their hair and eye colors were vastly different. He inhaled their scents, and his tail wagged of its own accord. Their aromas held genetic similarities that classified them as his woman's family, yet each also had an individual identifier that made her unique.

Like his own ancient pack of old, they were from a long line, though that was a startling realization. In a world where races mixed and meshed, to find such was nearly unheard of in the world of humans.

"Mom said to get Sapphire a couple of gowns, some panties, and her slippers for now. She won't need anything else for a few more days."

"I hope she appreciates what we pick. If I know Sapphire, she'll bemoan what we didn't."

"Dia, that isn't nice. We almost lost her. You two need to quit fighting."

"We don't fight, *exactly*, Jewell. She just doesn't understand my needs, and I don't understand hers."

Sapphire!

Nicolae allowed the name to roll through him. It fit his policewoman to perfection. He watched as they unlocked her door, threw on the lights inside, and then listened as they continued to chat about the woman who had captivated his mind while both awake and asleep.

Even the power of Sabia's hormonal scent and seductive actions hadn't worked the magic she'd hoped for or detracted from his need for a woman he didn't even know. Nicolae sighed. Sabia was already a problem, but she was going to be a much bigger one if she ever found out about Sapphire. Which meant she'd have to be sent back home as soon as possible.

Opening the telepathic lines exclusive to his pack, he focused on Jaspon only, sending him instructions regarding Sabia's protection and directions to Nicolae's camp. There was no way he'd allow another male access to his present location, not even one who cowered in servitude, and he had no desire for the rest of the pack to involve themselves in what were his problems.

That done, Nicolae refocused his attention on the two women, who were no longer talking as they opened the door and turned off the interior lights. He hoped he hadn't missed anything important but knew it didn't matter now. He would follow them back to wherever Sapphire was being kept, and he would see what was what, for himself.

While Nicolae kept to the trees, he followed the car down the long driveway, remembering the conversation between the sisters. The one called Jewell said Sapphire had almost been lost to them, and a shiver went through him. He hoped he was interpreting that incorrectly, and whatever Jewell meant didn't confirm his worst fears.

The desire to stop and throw his head back to howl was almost more than he could resist, but he had no desire to alert anyone to his presence, whether human, Lycan, or local wolf. And he knew, once they hit the road, the little car would be able to outrun him if the blonde driving it was as feisty as he sensed.

Not willing to take the chance he'd be left behind, Nicolae waited until they turned to the right and headed up the mountain, before making his own plans. He knew the road was curvy and would wind back once or twice before settling into a continuous left-hand curve. Given the amount of time he'd invested, and the number of miles he'd traveled over this area in his search for Ion, he was pretty certain he could beat them to the second curve. The problem was just where things would go from there.

His heart pumped and his paws traveled at breakneck speed. He was so familiar with the landscape now he didn't hesitate to leap and jump his way over fallen trees and sudden dips. He knew the placement of every tree, of every vein of the stream, and of every rock or cave opening.

Nicolae breathed heavily as he jumped from the small cliff and landed in the center of the road. He realized his mistake immediately when headlights blinded him and the squeal of brakes collided with the smell of burning rubber. He skittered to the side of the road where he was safer, before he was nearly hit by on oncoming truck coming the opposite way.

The car he recognized, as it came to a dead stop, while the truck kept going. Nicolae debated his options, knowing he couldn't afford to get caught by the sisters of his Sapphire. But he also couldn't leave when both were getting out of the car, endangering themselves, he assumed, to make sure he was okay.

He wanted to tell them another car could come around the curve and hit them. He wanted to lecture them it was never a good idea to approach a wild animal. But mostly he wanted to tell them to take him to the woman who owned his mind. He couldn't, of course. So he turned and ran until he jumped over the guardrail that edged the road and climbed awkwardly back up the cliff.

He heard their voices, their expressions of concern, but all he could concentrate on was keeping his footing. When he finally made it to the top he looked back, and the women were pulling off. Relieved, Nicolae dropped to the mossy earth and tried to catch his breath.

It served him right, he figured, knowing his priorities had gotten completely skewed. He had to make himself stop thinking about her. And he had to do it before he ended up doing exactly what he was trying to avoid. He had no right to expose his pack to humans and humans to his pack.

Still... he wondered if the sound of tires on not too distant gravel meant his Sapphire was near.

****

Sapphire felt so much better.

After three days of sponge baths, most of which she

didn't even remember, a real shower was pure heaven. Her arm felt much better, and she was pretty sure she'd be able to eat her mother's soup without fear it would come right back up. Her throat still hurt like the dickens, but overall, she felt pretty great... as long as she didn't let herself think.

"Mom said to bring you a fresh gown and help you back to bed. Do you need anything else?"

Sapphire pushed back the shower curtain and reached for her towel, before shaking her head at Jewell. "No. I'm going to lay back down, in a bit, but I need to be up for a while."

Jewell nodded. "I understand. I hate being in bed, sick. It always gives me a headache."

Since she didn't remember Jewell every being sick, Sapphire frowned. "You've been sick?"

A slow smile lifted Jewell's lips. "I haven't told anyone yet, but I think I'm pregnant."

Sapphire smiled and grabbed the towel to wrap around her body before throwing her arms around Jewell. "That's fantastic!" She stepped back. "But why haven't you told anyone yet?"

Jewell shrugged, and wiped at the water that had transferred to her during the hug. "I've only missed one period, so it isn't for sure. But I was still going to, then we got the call from Mom about your...*situation*. It didn't seem like the right time."

Sapphire didn't want to think about her *situation*, so she focused on her sister's good news. "How can you keep this to yourself? You have to tell them..." She grinned. "You are having a *baby*!"

Jewell bit her bottom lip, and then they both squealed and hugged, again.

The bathroom door flew open and Rayne appeared. Her eyes were large and desperate as she looked from one daughter to the other and then huffed out a loud breath.

"What are you two smiling about? You nearly scared me to death!"

"Me too," Garrison said, as he appeared behind her.

"And me, three!" Dia added, wiggling her way under their father's arm to stand in front of him.

Sapphire ignored the fact everyone had invaded her private bath and smiled at Jewell. "Looks like as good a time as any."

Jewell looked from Sapphire to their family, as tears filled her eyes. "I think I'm pregnant."

Rayne immediately pulled her into a tight hug, Garrison looked a little stricken, but Sapphire figured that was because he purposely forgot his daughters were grown-up women and sexual creatures. Dia just grinned stupidly and grabbed Jewell for a hug once their mother stepped back.

As happy as Sapphire was for her sister, the fact was, she was naked beneath the towel, dripping all over the floor. "Um…*guys?* Can I have a minute here?"

Everyone turned to her, their brows raised inquisitively. Then understanding dawned one after the other. Garrison cleared his throat, winked at her, leaned in to kiss Jewell on the cheek, and then turned to leave. Rayne and Dia nodded and followed him, and Jewell turned back to her and grinned. "Sorry!"

Sapphire laughed and hugged her sister again. "No problem, Sis. I'm so happy for you and Amen'ra. You'll make a wonderful mother. And I'm sure, because he's your choice, he'll make a wonderful father, as well."

Jewell nodded, and wiped at her eyes. "He will. I haven't told him yet, because I haven't taken a pregnancy test, but my breasts ache horribly, and I'm as sick as a dog every morning. The only reason he hasn't noticed is because Daddy has him at work so early, and I'm right as rain by the time I see him in the evening." She turned to the door and then looked back. "He'll be over the moon."

Sapphire smiled and nodded before Jewell shut the door behind her, though she didn't know her brother-in-law all that well yet. He was new to all of them, really, since he'd somehow made it back with Jewell after she'd been pulled into the ancient past. Although not sure about all the details of her sister's time travel, or reincarnation visits, or whatever had happened, she knew Jewell was completely in love with the man who was once charged with guarding her ancient twin, and then when the princess had fallen from grace, marrying her. By the time they were both firmly back in the present, Jewell was deeply in love and knew his betrothed, Princess Anippe, was long dead and likely mummified. She hadn't felt the first qualm in making him hers.

Unlike her mother, who, once Jewell was safely anchored in the present, accepted all that had happened with Cavanaugh aplomb, her father had been a lot more hesitant to accept the ancient Egyptian into the family. But he loved Jewell, as he did all his children, and was doing everything in his power to teach the former palace guard to build the unique furniture that was Garrison White's passion and trade. Now that a grandchild was likely on the way, Sapphire had no doubt he'd be as great a grandfather as he was a father. But more importantly, according to her mother, Amen'ra was an eager and quick learner, gaining their father's respect by the day.

Finally dried off, dressed in a fresh gown of her own, Sapphire left the bathroom and headed to the living room, combing her long black hair as she walked. The sounds of her family chatting made her smile. It had been too long since the five of them were together in their parents' home, without more of their extended family around for one celebration or another.

All eyes turned her way, and the light in them sobered

and smiles melted. Sapphire sighed, knowing they needed to talk and face whatever was coming. "Hi."

As was her mother's way, Rayne stood and walked to her, pulling her into a secure hug. She released Sapphire and stepped back, then took her hand to lead her to the couch.

"We've been talking baby showers. But that's still a ways off."

Sapphire nodded and took the seat beside her mother after Rayne settled next to her husband. She loved that her father immediately took Rayne's other hand, but all eyes were still on her, making her uncomfortable. "Stop looking at me like I'm about to die."

The room seemed to expand at her words, and Sapphire was afraid her hallucinations were returning, before she realized it was simply the tension. She expelled a breath, knowing her life was never going to be the same. Eyes that had always looked at her with love and respect, or in Dia's case, *reserved resignation*, now looked at her with caution and pity.

She inhaled with as much force as she'd exhaled and dove right in. "Mom, what am I facing?"

Rayne's grip on her hand tightened. "We aren't sure, but Tom thinks it a possibility that you've been infected by a rabid...*werewolf*."

Stunned silence filled the room, even her mother looked like she couldn't believe the words had left her lips. Sapphire wasn't as shocked as her sisters, but hearing their mother say the word still took her breath. She allowed the nausea that was resurfacing to settle, while the others processed Rayne's damning words. When she could finally speak, her voice shook. "Is that really a possibility?"

Rayne shook her head. "I don't know. I'll call a family meeting, and then we will begin to search in the family diaries to see if anything like this has happened before."

"So many were read when Jewell was being taken back in time to deal with that. Wouldn't someone have come across this?"

Rayne shook her head. "We were just skimming them for anything that referred to dreams or out of body travel. Once we focused on ancient Egypt, things happened so quickly. Then Jewell and Amen'ra were here, so we put them away. But I think we need to pull them all back out."

Sapphire knew what a major undertaking that would be. The family diaries spanned more than three thousand years; the oldest being written on sheets of papyrus, then animal skins, then the progression of parchments that made up paper. The languages were numerous, many of which were no longer used either in speech or writing, as the Cavanaugh women had been forced to move often throughout time to protect themselves and their offspring. Were it not for her mother's lifetime of studying ancient and foreign languages, the oldest of them would have never been translated or read.

"Sapphire, honey, we'll find a way to fix this."

Sapphire looked into her mother's emerald eyes, and though she found fear, she also saw resolve. She knew she couldn't allow her own fears to immobilize her in terror. "Can't Aunt Haven cure me?"

Rayne shrugged. "We don't know. This isn't a broken bone or a failing heart. Those things are of the natural realm. She's studying and trying to alter the blood Logan drew the first morning after you were scratched, but so far she hasn't been able to break down the virus. When she's tried, the blood cells multiply instead of die."

Nausea hit Sapphire again, and this time she was certain it was a combination of fear and whatever that *thing* had put inside her body.

"We saw a wolf tonight," Jewell said quietly.

Sapphire turned from her mother, only then

remembering Jewell and Dia were present. "What?"

Dia spoke up, her eyes haunted, "When we went to your place to get your clothes…we almost hit a wolf. He leaped out onto the road, nearly making me wreck."

Garrison leaned forward, reached across Rayne, and took Sapphire's hand, though he was looking at her sisters. "There are a lot of wild animals all around us, but we rarely see a wolf. Did this one look unusual in some way? Did it act threatening?"

Both Dia and Jewell shook their heads before Jewell spoke. "No. He was beautiful, healthy, and seemed curious, as he watched us until we got out of the car to shoo him off the road. We were afraid a car would come around the curve and hit him."

"You got out of the car and approached a wild animal?" Rayne asked, an edge to her tone.

"We're not children anymore, Momma. We wouldn't have gotten too close, and it was obvious he was more afraid of us than we were of him. He practically climbed straight up the cliff to get away from us."

"And we didn't know werewolves actually existed, or that Sapphire had been infected by one," Dia added.

Sapphire turned back to her mother. "Are you sure that is what this is?"

Rayne shook her head. "No. But Tom thinks it's a possibility, and he knows things we don't."

"What if it's something else?"

Rayne shrugged, and sighed heavily. "We're trying to figure that out. But no one in the family who is currently alive has ever encountered whatever put that virus in your bloodstream. Logan is studying the blood too, and he says it isn't human. They are going to have Celestia look at the blood in the morning to see if she can identify what we're dealing with. She's been at a veterinarian conference, but she's taking the red-eye tonight and will get in before daylight." Rayne's eyes filled with tears. "I can't believe this is happening."

"Don't cry, Momma. *I'm* trying not to."

Rayne bit her bottom lip, but a tear fell anyway. "I'm sorry, baby. I just feel this is somehow my fault. If my sisters and I hadn't broken the family curse...."

"Then we wouldn't have each other, or our children, or even our nieces and nephews," Garrison finished, pulling her closer. "You are not at fault for any of this. We just have to figure out what, or *who*, is, and fix it."

Rayne snuggled into him, and Sapphire knew no matter what she was facing, she had all anyone could ever ask for just by being a member of this unique family. She closed her eyes for a moment, wondering if her desire to be *normal* rather than mystical was childish, as her aspiration had originated soon after she'd first *ascended*. Yet memories of that horrible day, *that precise moment* when she'd realized the cataclysmic consequences of her powers, brought back the same feelings of horror and overwhelming sorrow. Even now she couldn't fathom using the gift that was her birthright. It seemed the universe was paying her back for the deed, or the subsequent denial of her mystical power. Either seemed like a cosmic joke that wasn't funny at all.

"Sapphire? Are you feeling ill again, honey?"

Sapphire opened her eyes, only realizing tears fell when she sought her mother's face and it was blurry. She nodded, unable to continue with the visit, desperately needing to seek the bed. Fortunately, the others stood when she did, and her sisters allowed her and her mother to pass as they headed back to the bedroom. She *was* feeling ill again; her head hurt, her stomach as well, but mostly—remembering the night a child had died because of her—her heart hurt worst of all.

Sapphire allowed her mother to settle her into the bed and asked her to open the window because she needed the fresh air. She denied wanting food, or drink, or even another blanket. She just wanted to be left alone to lick the newly reopened wounds from the long ago memories. But she knew it wouldn't be that simple. She'd buried the incident, and the reasons for denying her hereditary gifts, from both her family and herself for eight long years. She buried the guilt as well. Unfortunately, suppressed memories had a way of breaking free, and Sapphire knew she'd have to allow herself to remember everything, before she could try to bury the past again.

His name was Steven Hart and he'd been a nasty little bully since they'd all started kindergarten together. He'd made fun of her, her sisters, and her cousins, from the start, though the others had somehow been able to ignore him for the brat he was. She hadn't. She'd fought back, had given as good as she'd gotten, and had even ended up being sent to detention after school a time or two for punching him in the face or stomach. Once, both. That hadn't stopped his behaviors at all. If anything, it made him meaner. By the time she'd come into her own, and was filled with the gift of magic, the then fifteen-year-old Steven was several inches taller than her, nearly outweighing her twice over. He'd thought that an advantage and had badmouthed Dia for the hundredth time. He'd called her a freak, a nutcase, a witch, and finally said he'd make her into his whore.

Then it happened: energy filled her, thunder clapped in a clear blue sky, and anger like she'd never known had her lifting her hand to point at him. Her mouth opened and words spilled out of their own accord, and she told him to *drop dead*.

She hadn't meant it to happen, and she'd have taken that moment back in a heartbeat because only three hours later he was rushed to the hospital, already dead. They said his heart just stopped. They said it must have been something doctors had missed all along even though he'd had yearly physicals. But she knew, and she never told, that it was she, and she alone.

Chapter Six

Nicolae wished himself mentally deaf at times, and especially now, since Sabia's telepathic tirade was louder than any words she could have spoken in his presence. He tried interrupting her, to tell her to stop yelling at him and at Japson, but there was no stopping the angry she-wolf when she was furious.

He knew he should go to Japson's rescue, but then he'd have to deal with her face-to-face. It wasn't that he couldn't, it was that he'd have to put up with a tantrum that could last days. He didn't have days. Or even another minute to listen to her complaints. If she wanted to hold out for him, he couldn't stop her, but it didn't mean he had to live with it up close and personal.

No way will I mate with her!

The tirade stopped immediately, and Nicolae realized he'd had the thought while their communication channel was still open. He thought to apologize, to tell her he was only thinking that because she was being obstinate and disobedient, but that would only serve to delay the inevitable.

I'm sorry, Sabia. I did not mean to relay that thought, but you are driving me crazy with your pushy ways. I am looking for your brother, to eliminate the threat he brings to us all. You should have no purpose right now but to support me and my mission. I do not know what the future will bring, but it would be best for you to accept Jaspon as your mate and have done with it, before you return to the pack. We have spoken of these things already, but I will say again, should I fail, and ultimately fall, he would protect you from my successor. You will always hold a place of honor among our kind, no matter if you hold a title or not.

Nicolae's hope that his words would soothe her was short-lived.

Do not trouble yourself with thoughts of me, Alpha! I am well able to decide my own fate. But it would do you well to remember who I am, what power I hold in my own right. This slight will not be forgotten. Find my brother and kill him as you must, but know this, I will be the Alpha Female, with or without you.

She abruptly closed off the communication, and Nicolae shook his head in resignation, which also shook the thick fur of his neck and shoulders. He knew she was fully capable of turning others against him if she went on an all-out assault of his character, but he hoped the pack would see her ploy for what it was, and would know she only sought to elevate herself, and that her words and actions had nothing to do with his ability to lead. Though he had been accepted into their family as a pup and had been made a full member of the pack by Ion and Sabia's father, when his own large family—save him—were completely annihilated, he was not a blood relative to his current pack. That in itself gave Sabia an advantage. Whether he lived through his mission and was still Alpha, once it was done, would have to wait to be seen. Right now he had other things to worry about. One was an elusive rabid werewolf, the other a beautiful woman who could die because of that werewolf.

As he'd suspected, the sisters he'd seen earlier had turned into a driveway not far from where he'd seen them on the winding road. He stepped even closer to another well-built log cabin, much older than the one Sapphire lived in. Delicately, so as not to alert man or beast, he lifted one paw and placed it on the ground slowly, before easing forward and moving another. He knew Sapphire was in the home. He would have even if the little red car were not sitting out in plain sight.

He lifted his nose and allowed the breeze to carry scents his way. Immediately a growl stirred in his throat, and the hair along his spine stood on end. There was a male in the house with the women whose scents he now knew, as well as a new one that was a mixture of the three. He choked down the growl and remained still, until he was once again in control.

It took little time to deduce the forth woman was their mother, and once he'd completely calmed down, the male was their father. Relief washed over him, and Nicolae could once again breathe easier. Though he had no right to claim Sapphire in any way, the presence of another unattached male would be dangerous for them all, if he didn't find a way to release the hold she had on him.

He crept closer to the house and then froze again before slowly lowering himself to the ground when the front door opened, and several family members stepped out. He flattened himself as much as possible, hoping the shadows kept him hidden, though he knew he was depending on fate as much as luck to keep one of them from turning his way.

"You girls be careful. No more stopping for wild animals. At this point, I want you all to start carrying a gun. Daddy will teach you how to shoot it."

"Mom, I am *not* carrying a gun. Amen'ra will be waiting on the porch when I get home, and I'll be super careful and not be out at night unless I'm with someone else."

"Me either. I'll just try to turn it into gold."

As the family laughed, Nicolae would have frowned had he been in human form, but all he could do was pull his brows together at the odd comment from the feisty blond. From the response she'd gotten, he figured it must be a family joke and let it go. He was glad neither the redhead nor the blonde planned on packing guns, since their mother indicated they didn't know how to use them. In his case, as well as Ion's, it would do nothing but slow them down, even if they used the *much-overused-in-movies* silver bullets. The truth was nothing—short of old age, incineration, decapitation, or drowning in an act of suicide—would kill him and his kind, and the last two were not easy tasks to accomplish.

"Bye!"

"Bye, baby, tell Amen-ra hi, for us!"

"Okay, Mom. Bye, Daddy."

"Bye, babies. You girls be *very* careful."

Nicolae listened to their parting, relieved when the two drove off, and their parents reentered the house. He waited a bit to make sure no one else was coming out and then stood on all fours and proceeded forward again. He listened to the sounds from within. The parents were heading to the back, chatting quietly as they went about the possibility of a new baby, and the dangers Sapphire faced. They stopped talking abruptly, and he waited and then heard the click of a door. Once the mother indicated Sapphire was sleeping, he knew he'd found his target. Now all he had to do was figure out a way to get to her without alerting the others to his presence.

Nicolae transformed and approached the house, trying one window after another, and was relieved someone had thoughtlessly left one open. He pulled himself up and looked in and then felt his heart jolt. A nightlight, which cast her mostly in shadow, illuminated his beautiful Sapphire, but his eyes needed no light at all to see her clearly.

He almost lifted the window higher but spotted the little dog sleeping next to her just in time. He couldn't wake the pup without alerting the household. Nicolae glanced back at the woman and debated his next move. More than anything he needed to get close to her, to see what she was suffering from, to find out if her illness was in fact due to the virus that could change her physical makeup. He inhaled deeply, but all he could smell was the flowery scent of her shampoo.

****

Sapphire relished the wind on her face, heard the magnified sounds of the night as she ran at breathtaking speed, and knew her paws barely hit the ground as she jumped over a fallen log and then continued. Small animals skittered away, but they were not her intent, so she ignored them completely and just embraced the freedom of the night.

The howl of a lone wolf caused her to stumble, and she slowed to a stop next to a wide branch of the stream that ran from the top of the mountain all the way to the large lake below. She looked around, trying to gauge the direction from which the sounds continually came, but the mountainous terrain caused sounds to echo and bounce, and she ended up turning her head sharply time and again without success. She shivered with pleasure, causing her black coat to capture the moon's light in a cascading shimmering mass that was only visible to her because the water reflected her movements. She smiled her wolf smile and then glanced up through the naked branches above, allowing the full moon to caress her senses and soothe her spirit.

A sharp bark broke into her peace and this time she shivered in fear, as the male had moved closer, and his tone held menace. Now knowing the direction from which the threat came, she rose and quickly headed the opposite way. As she ran faster, so did he, and she was afraid she was being hunted. She increased her speed even more, but she could hear that he continually gained ground, making her frantic that he would soon catch her. Another howl sounded before her and Sapphire skidded to a stop. With her heart beating painfully against her chest, she looked one way, then the other, and took off at an angle away from them both. She hoped the two males were after each other and not her, but she wasn't going to stay around to find out.

When a loud scream rent the air seconds later, she was relieved to be out of the line of fire.

Sapphire awoke abruptly and sat up, panting as if she'd actually been running in the woods, as if she'd actually been a female wolf, being chased by a male. Ellie was immediately upon her, her tail wagging furiously, her little tongue licking all over Sapphire's face. She hugged the little dog to her, kissing her back, relieved to find she'd only been dreaming. She was sure it was because of the yet unconfirmed fear she'd been infected by a werewolf, but knowing it was a dream didn't make it feel any less real.

The howl of a wolf broke the silence of her room, startling her, and making her heart pound painfully. Not because of the suddenness of the sound, not even because of the threat that a rabid werewolf might be out there, but because it sounded exactly like the howl of the first wolf in her dream. Something inside of her wanted to howl back.

That scared her more than anything.

What if Uncle Tom was right? What if she was in danger, not from rabies, which was still an ongoing threat but being treated daily with the shots, but from the saliva of a werewolf? If so, what did it mean? Would she turn into one? Would she die anyway? Was the moon an important factor? Silver? Was she to be a mindless monster, who could bring harm to her own family? To others?

Shaking hard, she tried to remember every possible tale she'd ever heard about the creatures they'd all believed were only fictitious characters in movies and books. But she couldn't think, couldn't move past the terror that kept her immobile, frozen in place on her bed. Tears threatened but she choked them down. She'd never been a coward, and she wasn't going to allow this *thing*, whatever it was, to make her one now.

She lifted Ellie and crawled off the bed and then set her pet on the floor. She slid on her slippers, once again thankful her sisters had been kind enough to go and get some of her personal things so she didn't feel completely out of place. She padded across the room and approached the window and then lifted it higher so the cooling evening air could caress her body and hopefully clear her mind.

The scents that assailed her went deep and were richer than she'd ever noticed before. The night-songs of insects and frogs seemed magnified, almost overpowering. The wind rose and slid from the opposite side of the house, through branches and leaves that had transformed during her violent illness. Though the moon was but a sliver of light in the night sky, she could see vivid oranges and reds, yellows and burgundy. Sapphire frowned as she realized she shouldn't have been able to see things so clearly, and another shiver went through her.

Sapphire smiled and looked down when Ellie placed her little paws on her leg. With all the misery that was now her life, the cute little smashed-in face with the adoring large button eyes was guaranteed to lift her spirits. She reached down and lifted her, rewarded as she always was with snuggles and kisses.

As quietly as she could, she moved through the house. She clipped on a retractable leash on her excited pet, and they both slipped out onto the large porch. Sapphire allowed the pup to head off down the steps her father had long ago made from split logs, now dented and dinged from age. She loved the workmanship of her parents' log cabin, just as she loved the one she now called home, but she didn't have time to dwell on either as Ellie's nose was already to the ground in her frantic search to find just the right spot. When she lifted her head abruptly and growled, Sapphire froze and cautiously looked in the same direction. Without meaning to, she inhaled deeply, but the wind was blowing from the opposite direction. There was no way to determine what had captured her pet's attention. That she'd thought she could, by breathing in, added to her concerns that something within her brain had accepted Tom Whitehawk was right, and her life would never be the same.

****

Nicolae was once again flat against the ground, unmoving, and focused on the woman and her little dog. Gone was the playful and laughing beauty he'd first seen only days before. She was certainly still beautiful, but the ravages of illness were clear, in the dark circles under her eyes and in the hard jut of cheekbones, sunken as a result of sudden weight-loss. He knew what the first signs of rabies looked like, as he'd witnessed it with Ion. But unlike her, Ion hadn't been treated for rabies. They couldn't take the chance that hospital staff would draw blood and realize there was something more there than the virus.

Ion's entire human form, if he were even able to transform now, would be nothing more than sore skin over skin-covered bones. The two weeks they'd tried to keep him contained after the bite had ravaged a once healthy body and mind, made both diseased and twisted beyond recognition. His natural form had suffered equally, as chunks of hair fell off in patches, the exposed skin on his body and face split open with sores that soon festered, and his intelligent eyes, once clear brown, had changed to red, watery, and filled with rage. Ion had escaped from the cage they'd been forced to build for him. Now Nicolae had no idea what shape his brother was in, but he knew it could only be worse than before, and everyone, including Ion, would be better off if he were dead.

He hated that Sapphire was sick, too, but relieved she wouldn't have to suffer from the rabies beyond the two weeks of shots required. Still, other issues faced them all. He was certain, now that the wind blew his way, she was going to transform or would die trying. The taint of his kind was even now manifesting, as he'd witnessed her attempt to sniff him out when her little dog either sensed his presence or caught a whiff of his scent. Fighting sorrow for Ion, and the woman who had captivated him, he silently continued his vigil until she finally scooped up the little dog and hurried back into the house. He turned away then and started moving back the way he'd come, not willing to take a chance the wind would shift and set her little dog off. Or, perhaps, even her.

Chapter Seven

"It's good to have you back. I was afraid we'd lost you."

Sapphire smiled at her partner, more than happy to be back herself. In the three weeks during her leave of absence, she'd been through hell and back, but between the shots, the fluids Haven and Logan insisted be pumped into her, and more tender loving care than anyone should have to endure, she'd finally gotten to go back to her own home. Against everyone's wishes, including her captain's, she was starting back to work as well. "Thanks. I'm doing okay. What about you?"

Brad shrugged. "I don't know. Something has felt off since that night. And I'm having weird dreams all the time." He frowned. "I've been to the doctor twice since spending the first night in the hospital, but they can't find anything wrong with me."

Sapphire stared at him, wondering if the wound she'd seen on his head had anything to do with the werewolf her family was convinced hurt her. "Are you ever sick to your stomach? Does your head hurt? Anything like that?"

He shook his head. "No, I feel fine. Just different. I can't explain it without sounding crazy."

Sapphire didn't want to think he could have somehow been bitten or scratched, too, and he hadn't gotten sick like she had. Maybe it was nothing more than a bump on the head. At least she hoped so. She opened her mouth to ask him what his dreams were about, but his phone rang and he lifted it to his ear.

"Cunningham, here."

Sapphire listened to Brad's side of the conversation for only a moment and then turned when a beautiful young woman ran in, her eyes spilling tears. She stopped short and looked from one officer to another, and Sapphire rose, intending to see what she could do. Brad hung up and pointed her back into her seat. "That was the captain. He says I'm with Dunlop this week, and you're on desk duty." He grinned. "That means I don't have to write my own reports."

Sapphire felt an inner growl and closed her eyes. She loved being a cop, loved getting her hands dirty, and hated with a passion writing her own reports. But at least she could read her own handwriting. Transposing anything Brad brought in would be nothing short of a nightmare, and she was going to be stuck doing it for an entire week. When she opened her eyes, Brad was staring at her strangely, making her wonder if she'd done more than think the inner grumbling. Before she could ask, he turned and walked away, apparently to follow the woman back to whichever room they'd taken her to.

"Hey, White, Captain says you're on the desk. How about getting the rest of us some breakfast food?"

Sapphire almost told him where to put his order but stopped herself just in time. It wasn't unusual for one of the guys to take an order for everyone, regardless which meal was involved. Then they'd head out to get it filled at one of the local restaurants. With the option being to sit at a computer, catching up on Brad's paperwork, or getting a chance to take a walk in the cool morning air, it was a no-brainer. She smiled. "Be glad to." She stood and addressed the squad room. "Put your orders on paper, guys, I'm out of here in two."

Satisfied, she pulled her small purse from her file drawer, headed to the ladies room to take care of necessities, then headed back and gathered each officer's slip of paper. They all grinned at her, and she grinned back, knowing once she was off the desk, and back on the streets, they'd have to find someone else to fetch their food. In the meantime, she'd do it every chance she got.

The air was amazing. Crisp, not cold. Just breezy enough to keep the sun from making her uniform jacket too hot, and it smelled of the evergreens blanketing Mystic Mountain on the other side of the large lake to the west. She could have taken a squad car, or even her own, but after three weeks of so little activity, mostly because the medics in the family insisted she be tied to an IV once she started looking like the walking dead, she was thrilled for the chance to stretch her legs.

Mystic Waters was home, but even if she'd just been passing through or visiting, she would notice what a quaint little town it was. The buildings along Main Street faced each other, the continuous long line of one shop after another one would expect within any small southern town. But unlike so many other small towns whose original structures had fallen into disrepair or had been replaced with something newer over the years, those responsible for the care and upkeep of Mystic Waters had made sure anything that needed replacing with something new, or even just in need of repair, was done in a way that looked as it always had.

Though three times larger than most of the shops along the street, Mystic Waters Police Station was part of that strip of buildings and was located at the western corner of the U-shaped section, which rounded the courthouse square. The front entrance faced Main, but there was an emergency exit that faced the courthouse where prisoners were often made to walk around the police cruisers parked along that area. Sapphire was taking the opposite direction, choosing to head to a diner nearly at the end of the strip.

She knew everyone would be waiting for her quick return and would likely complain their Styrofoam-encased breakfast had gotten cold, but she didn't care. She'd bat her eyes, smile apologetically, and laugh on the inside when the men fell over themselves to forgive her.

Not allowing herself to feel any guilt at all, even though she'd spent her short career trying to prove herself as a cop and not a wily woman, Sapphire embraced her looks for what she figured was the first time in her life. She understood the captain's concerns that she'd been deathly ill and probably needed some additional time to recuperate, but the truth was she felt not only well, she felt great. Her speedy recovery would have been marvelous if not for the fact that she was probably turning into a monster.

Fortunately, a full moon had come and gone, and nothing happened, if she discounted the nightly dreams. In them she was always a wolf, of the regular variety, not the big scary kind that walked on two legs as seen in movies. Neither did using her mother's sterling silver utensils faze her in any way. If not for her ability to hear others' conversations through walls, see in pitch-darkness as if she was standing in full light, and her nearly instantaneous recovery only a week into the rabies shots series, she'd almost have believed her family's concerns were unfounded. The most telling thing was the gash on her arm had not only healed, it hadn't left a scar or any sign at all that it had once been there.

Sapphire approached Tinker's Café with her head down as she mulled over her situation and accidently ran into someone. Instantly contrite, she looked up with an apology on her lips, but found, instead, that her tongue was tied. The man was as tall as Uncle Tom, but instead of being built like the muscular, yet slender, aging Native American, this man had the build of a long-legged prizefighter, whose broad shoulders tapered down to slim jean-encased hips. But the most arresting part of him was his chiseled face and the penetrating blue eyes that held flakes of gold. She felt herself respond to his smile but could do nothing more than stand there like an idiot.

"I'm sorry. I wasn't looking where I was going."

Something inside of her slipped and slid at the sound of his deep voice. She shook her head slowly, thinking she had to somehow acknowledge his kindness for her own mistake, but she couldn't form the words. He continued to look into her eyes before he reached out to her. Though Sapphire normally would never allow a stranger to touch her, she found herself not only awaiting his touch but craving it as well. The honk of a car's horn broke the spell he had on her. Sapphire turned to see who it was, but by the time she could make her gaze break from his, the car had already passed by. She turned back to the gorgeous stranger, suddenly embarrassed by her behavior.

"I'm the one who should apologize. I was lost in thought and not paying attention. I'm Sapphire, by the way, and you are new." Instantly embarrassed again, she continued hurriedly, "I mean, *new in town.*"

His smile widened, and Sapphire was glad for the swift gust of wind that hit her in the back and not only knocked her forward a step, but knocked some sense in her as well. She was seriously concerned she was about to make a complete fool of herself and melt at his feet.

"I am, new in town, that is. I'm Nicholas Wolfe."

She grinned and was afraid it probably looked stupid, so she immediately pulled herself together and held out her hand. Without hesitation he took it, and shook it gently, but he didn't let go as was expected. She studied their joined hands, hers delicate and smooth, his large and rough, yet he gripped hers with gentleness. Sapphire glanced up again and delved into those amazing eyes. She knew she was completely befuddled, how else could she explain the flare of passion she was seriously afraid must be reflected in her own eyes?

"Have breakfast with me," he said, and opened his hand, allowing her to pull hers away.

As much as she wanted to say yes, Sapphire knew she couldn't. Not only were there people awaiting their own breakfast, she was in no position to consider a breakfast, or anything else, with a man. Especially one that completely captivated her. "I can't."

"Then have lunch with me."

Sapphire shook her head. "I can't."

"Then have dinner with me."

She laughed then, and her tilted world straightened to almost normal. Her smile melted with all the regret she felt. "I'm sorry. I can't.

He nodded. "You're married."

"No."

"Engaged."

"No."

"In a relationship."

Again she shook her head. "I'm sick."

He frowned then. "Mono?"

This time her laughter made him smile. "No."

"You just aren't interested."

The disappointment in his tone caused her to waver, but only for a second. "I might die."

He stared at her, but surprisingly, he didn't back away, or offer platitudes.

"I won't allow that to happen."

Her breath caught, and held, and everything inside of her melted. Tears filled her eyes, but she refused to look away. "I have to get breakfast back to the station. I'm a cop."

He smiled gently. "The uniform kind of gave that away." Then his gaze sobered. "If you're so sick, why are you waiting on others? They should be waiting on you."

"I've been ill recently, so I'm temporarily on desk duty. They don't know the rest. And I offered to do it. I needed the walk."

He nodded. "Can I help you take back the breakfast? Then take you for a ride?"

Sapphire shook her head. "I just got back today. I need to work."

"No you don't. You need to play."

It was so tempting. And that was a reason not to. "I can't."

He reached for her hand, before staring deeply into her eyes. "I can't take no for an answer. I think I've been looking for you all my life."

Sapphire knew the feeling, knew he wasn't feeding her a line. The honesty of his words enveloped her like a caress. "Why?"

"Why what?"

"Why have you waited until now to come into my life? Why would you want anything to do with a woman who just told you she might die? Why do you make me feel as if we should have known each other all our lives?" Nicholas allowed her questions to hang in the air for a moment, and then he simply smiled.

"Because sometimes fate knows more than we do."

The tension within her eased and Sapphire relaxed as much as her excitement at being in his presence allowed. She didn't want him to take no for an answer any more than she wanted to keep saying it. She knew this was probably a terrible mistake, and that one or both of them could end up getting hurt, but she desperately needed to embrace whatever *good* life was willing to throw at her, while she still could. Even if it was only this once. "Let me get the squad's breakfast to them, and then I'm going to decide I'm not quite well enough to start back today."

"Why don't you make it the week?"

****

Nicolae couldn't believe he'd convinced her to push back her return to work for a full week, but he understood why she had. The connection he'd felt, he was certain she felt as well, but he didn't believe that was her reason at all. If anything, he'd sensed her fear of getting close to him, *or anyone*, at this point in her life. He was convinced her decision was based on the need to experience something fun, something daring, even, while she still could.

That she knew her life was still in danger was something of a problem, because that meant she had some awareness the rabies virus wasn't all she'd faced during the illness. He just had no idea if she knew what was happening to her. If she had any knowledge werewolves existed, that was a real dilemma he'd have to work through. It endangered his pack and his kind in general.

Surely not.

Convincing himself it wasn't a possibility, he crossed the busy Main Street to where he'd parked his Harley on the facing side. The beautiful black machine was his mode of transportation while in human form, and it nearly equaled the thrill of running in his natural form, whenever he got the chance to open the throttle fully and burn up a road. He hadn't been able to do that lately since the winding roads up the mountain made it too dangerous, even for him. But he would fix that today, once he had her sitting behind him.

Nicolae smiled at the thought as he placed the shiny black helmet on his head and strapped it beneath his chin. He hated wearing the thing, but it was the law in the area, so there wasn't a choice. He straddled the motorcycle, started it, and kicked back his booted foot, lifting the stand.

The vibration throughout his body nearly equaled that of a she-wolf's growl while in the throes of passion, and he couldn't understand why any man would choose any other form of transportation. He backed away from the diagonally painted parking space and waited for a few morning commuters to pass before heading in the direction she'd taken. She hadn't allowed him to help her. She had instructed him to pull into the courthouse square to wait while she delivered her bagged packages and then to follow her to her cabin once she was free to go.

He'd almost made the mistake of telling her he already knew where she lived but caught himself just in time. That she hadn't hesitated to allow him access to her home concerned him, though. He sensed she was a loner, and a woman who didn't allow strange men easy access to her in any way. Their attraction to each other aside, it made him fearful she was truly convinced her life would be cut short, and she was throwing caution to the wind.

It took only a moment to make it to the location she'd indicated, so Nicolae parked in one of the many still vacant spaces facing the courthouse and turned off the motor. He reset the kickstand and stood, taking a moment to enjoy the relative peace of the town awakening to start a new day. It was still too early for the shops to open, the courthouse as well, so no one was milling about. He glanced over to the corner of the building when he heard a woman's voice. His heart stuttered when he realized the voice belonged to none other than Sabia Ilie. Trepidation skittered down his spine when he heard the click of a door closing behind her. Why was she still here? And what was she doing, exiting the front of the police station? As tempted as he was to round the building and demand answers, he settled back onto his seat, hoping she'd head the other way. The last thing residents of Mystic Waters needed were two werewolves fighting in their streets.

Sapphire chose that moment to exit the side door, and Nicolae knew his problematic she-wolf would have to wait. His senses stayed on full alert, however. The only thing he could think of, that would be worse than Sabia and him having a throw down in public, was her getting a look at the woman he desired above all others.

Sapphire walked toward him, a big smile on her lush lips. "Nice bike!"

Nicolae smiled back, relieved Sabia's scent was lightening, indicating she had, indeed, headed off in the other direction. "Thanks. Which way do we go?"

Sapphire pointed in the direction he'd feared, so he knew he had to stall to give Sabia time to get far away. "Come here."

Fire flashed in her sapphire eyes, and everything inside of him flared to life. He tamped down his libido as well as the hungry growl struggling to leave his throat. When she came the remaining steps to stop only inches in front of him, Nicolae realized he was in serious trouble.

His wolf was struggling to come out.

And for the first time in his adult life, he wasn't certain he could stop it.

Chapter Eight

Sapphire normally enjoyed the peace of the long drive home from work. She'd always embraced the serenity of the view while circling around the large glistening lake, as she approached the base of the majestic mountain. More often than not, she'd glance over again and again as she drove, sometimes to find kids or their families swimming or fishing from the lake's banks, or sailing on the calm waters. She often spotted some of the multitude of wildlife and birds that made their homes close by and had always envied the simplicity of their lives.

It was too cold now for swimmers and all but diehard boaters or fishermen, as the Autumnal Equinox had passed. October forecasts promised the first signs of an early snow and, up the mountain, possibly even freezing weather. As much as she had always loved the vivid colors brought on by the season, she also mourned the loss for those who would be forced to spend the coming months bundled against the cold or stuck inside, when they were not at work or school.

But today her mind was on the remaining length of the road home, and the man following closely, but safely, behind her.

She'd though he was going to kiss her, and she'd been more than disappointed when he hadn't, but he'd really no choice. Brad had chosen that moment to lead their one and only prisoner out the side door, to take him to the holding room in the courthouse, to await the opening of court. Neither of them had moved until she'd turned to nod at her partner, then she'd headed straight to her Jeep. Nicholas hadn't questioned her retreat but had simply started the loud engine of his motorcycle. Once she was strapped into her seatbelt, they both waited to pull out until Brad and his charge were permitted inside the courthouse's back door.

It was a relief to reach the base of the mountain and begin the ascent. The circular climb would take another thirty or so minutes before they'd arrive at the long driveway that led to the cabin. She was so thankful she didn't live as far up it as Dia did, or the drive would have been nearly twice as long. As antsy as she was to see what would happen once they arrived, *that* would have had her in worse shape.

That she was feeling reckless, even more so than she ever had felt before, didn't escape her notice. She'd never allowed anyone, except family, to know where she lived. Even her address on her personnel file at work was the same one she'd used when she, Jewell, and Dia had all shared the house her father built for them following college. She hadn't deliberately meant to deceive anyone, but she hadn't cared enough to change it either. Her paychecks were directly deposited into her checking account every other week, and her mail was delivered to a box at the post office in town. Other than her monthly bills, she never got anything but junk mail anyway.

When at last she spotted her turn, Sapphire slowed, braked to a near stop, and took the hard turn onto the gravel. She glanced up and smiled to herself when the Harley followed, and her excitement increased. She kept glancing back the closer she got to the house, and each time she saw his helmet covered head, her heart rate jumped another notch. Something flashed across the front of her car just as she returned her gaze to the end of the driveway. Memories of the night of the storm swamped her, and her thrill turned into trembling terror as she stomped on the brake and skidded to a halt right in front of the cabin.

Nicholas was at her door and pulling it open immediately, though she had no idea how he'd gotten there so quickly. Shaken, she frantically searched the tree line on each side of her home and then felt herself pulled into his arms. Since his massive chest blocked her view, and his tight hold held her immobile, she gave into the panic, and let herself go. Great choking tears clogged her throat and spilled from her eyes, and there was nothing she could do to stop either.

"You're okay. You're okay. I've got you. You're okay."

Sapphire nodded and tried to calm herself. She was nearly there moments later when he loosened his hold. He allowed her to step back, only a bit, but didn't release her completely. "I'm okay. I'm sorry. Something ran across the front of my Jeep and it startled me."

She didn't add that she shouldn't have been looking at him in her rear view mirror, or that the something she was talking about could only be the creature that now placed her life in peril. Fortunately, he seemed to accept her words and wasn't going to do anything but continue to try to calm her.

"Let's get you in the house. You're as pale as a ghost."

Sapphire almost smiled at that. Her mother was the only person she knew of who'd actually seen and talked to ghosts, except for the one time Rayne had allowed her own sisters to see what she saw on a regular basis, until she shut them out. Sapphire moved forward and placed her head against his chest, securely held once more. It was disconcerting to realize she didn't want him to ever let her go. "Thank you. I'm not a ninny, normally, I promise."

"I never thought you were." He allowed her to pull back, his eyes filled with questions. "Was it an animal?"

Sapphire shrugged. "I'm not sure. It was there, and gone, in a flash."

He nodded; his brows drew together. "Large, like a… man, or small like a dog?"

Sapphire didn't know how to answer. She was afraid it was something of a combination of both. But she couldn't tell him that. "I don't know. It happened too fast, and I wasn't paying attention."

His gaze remained serious, but his lips slid into a grin. "What were you paying attention to?"

If she hadn't known she never blushed, Sapphire would believe the heat in her cheeks was just that. "You. I was paying attention to you."

His nostrils flared, and the flecks within his irises seemed to expand, changing so much that the blue was completely replaced by purest gold. Something inside of her stirred, even as she was stunned. She reached up and touched the sides of his face just below the temple, but when she blinked, his eyes seemed normal again, and she was sure the trauma, of only moments before, was playing tricks with her mind. She shook her head slightly and turned to make sure whatever had caused her fright was no longer in sight and a threat. The last thing she ever wanted to happen was for him to face the same frightful future as she.

"Let's go inside," she said, turning to face him. "I think I may need to lie down."

He searched her eyes and, apparently, saw what she wanted him to see because he smiled. "I think that would be a great idea."

They were no sooner in the door before Nicholas reached back to lock it. He kept what she could only think of as *hungry eyes* on her, as he slowly moved closer with a stealth that set her heart racing. Anticipating the taste of his lips, she took a step closer and was surprised when he didn't immediately pounce. Instead he lifted his large hands and cradled her face with a tenderness that stole her heart.

Oxygen was hard to find, and she struggled with each breath. Bones loosened, and she found it nearly impossible to stay upright. To her relief he dropped his hands and swung her into strong arms, to cradle her against his body. He continued to stare into her eyes; everything inside of her demanded he proceed, but he smiled instead.

"I want this to take a *very* long time."

Her lungs wouldn't function at all now, as her body trembled with need. She nodded though, as words were impossible to form. He glanced back at the door once, and she understood he was making sure she was protected from that which had frightened her, but she couldn't allow her mind to be anywhere but on him. She inhaled deeply, once she could. "I do, too."

****

Nicolae knew he should be outside the little cabin, taking advantage of his first sighting of Ion in weeks, but he couldn't make himself leave, just yet. Not only was he completely and helplessly captivated by Sapphire, he knew she needed him as strongly as was his need for her. But mostly, the speed with which Ion had moved proved he was as aware of Nicolae's presence as Nicolae was of his. He had little doubt the sick werewolf was miles away by now, for which he was very grateful. He'd never allow the crazed man-animal near his woman again.

He swung Sapphire around and checked the deadbolt one last time before turning again, searching the room. Only a second passed before he knew he'd need to carry her up ladder-like stairs to get them to her bedroom. The flash of thought that it would be much easier to just jump the distance was discarded immediately, so he stopped at the base of the stairs and searched her eyes. "Are you sure?"

Sapphire's smile was that of a woman drunk with passion, and he couldn't help but smile back at her. "I'm taking that as a yes."

She closed her eyes, but the smile remained on her lips, so he made short work of the climb and then gently placed her on a bed that took up nearly the entire loft. "This is a very big bed for one little woman."

She rolled to the opposite side and grinned up at him. "No one but me has ever been in it."

She studied him silently as she undid the belt that held her holster, before she shoved both in a little nook against the low wall, as he struggled to contain himself.

"No one has ever shared my bed before—or my body."

His control snapped and Nicolae was immediately at her side. Part of him demanded he tear the clothing from her body; thankfully, he still held a degree of control. He pulled her into a sitting position and then across his engorged lap, making them both tremble. He sucked in a breath and focused on her eyes, determined to behave as she deserved. "You know you're killing me, right?"

She giggled, and he thought he was surely going to die. She didn't seem like a woman who giggled, and that she had was almost more of a turn-on than he could bear.

Her eyes sobered. "This can only be what it is."

Denial was on the tip of his tongue, but he understood she was attempting to protect them both from her uncertain future. He didn't want protecting, but he wasn't the only one involved. "Let's just take it one moment at a time."

She nodded and then leaned into him, pressing her breasts against his chest, keeping her tempting mouth only a hairsbreadth away. He breached the difference with a soft slide of his lips upon hers, then repeated the process before engaging her mouth fully to tease and sample with a gentleness he'd never before employed with either woman or she-wolf. But then, his previous sexual encounters had never meant as much, so he continued to tantalize, equally tormented in return.

He lay back, taking her with him, keeping the kisses gentle yet increasing them in depth with each required breath. She lifted her hands from his shoulders and slid her fingers through his hair, and all that was wolf within him silently howled in glorious delight.

It took everything he had to remain a man.

He rolled so she was beneath him and eased back to work on his control, but he did so under the guise of unbuttoning her dark blue shirt, only then remembering she was in her uniform. If he thought the separation would do anything to assist him, he soon realized his mistake. He parted the opening and found, beneath her no-nonsense work clothes, she wore a lacy little bra that would have taken him to his knees if he weren't already on them.

He looked up from the glossy globes the material barely covered to her face. "Seriously, you're killing me."

Her laughter was that of a woman pleased, and he shook his head before pulling her up to slide the shirt from her shoulders. As much as he admired her choice of underclothing, he unhooked the bra as well, and heard her moan of pleasure. Knowing his promise to take things slow was getting terribly close to impossible, he gave himself a moment before looking down.

Sapphire took that as an invitation to pull the tail of his shirt from his jeans before she started unbuttoning it from top to bottom. He found her fumbling fingers endearing, and her hesitancy to touch the remaining two, which covered his zipper, adorable.

He undid those himself and shrugged out of the shirt, before capturing her jaw with his hands and ravaging her mouth, as he'd been dying to do for too long. Her response was as immediate and crazed, and Nicolae knew he was seriously close to changing. He was glad his eyes were closed, so she wouldn't see their reaction while he struggled with his inner-self. When a growl worked its way up from his core, he trapped it in his throat and broke the hold of her lips. He moved back, not looking up until he was standing and facing the other way. "I have to go." His heart sank at her silence. "No. Not go. Just give me a minute."

He struggled in silence, taking several deep breaths, and then felt his wolf retreat. He turned to her once he felt he was back in complete control. "I'm sorry. *Damn!* I'm sorry."

Sapphire stared at him, her eyes filled with confusion. She bit her bottom lip before crawling to the foot of the bed. "I don't understand."

Nicolae nodded. "I know."

"Is it because I'm sick?"

He pulled her to him and held her there. He had nothing to offer, but as much of the truth as he could give her. "No! It's because you bring out the animal in me, and I was losing control. I don't want to hurt you."

She studied his eyes, her own still filled with adoration. "Nicholas, I won't break. I want this as much as you do." She grinned. "And it was starting to get really good. I can do wild. In fact, I was into it as much as, or maybe even more than, you were."

He knew there was nothing else he could say that would make any sense to her, unless he told her who and what he was. He'd give anything to be able to tell her, to tell her he knew what she was going to go through. But there was no way he could. Not unless she was willing to give up the life she knew and make one with him, for however long she had. They'd have to go where neither her people nor his pack could find them. Her family would never understand, and his would kill her, *and her family*, just to safeguard their existence. As illogical as it was to expect anything from her, he couldn't help but want everything. An urgency to make her understand his desire overrode every argument he thought of to just go along with her need for the here and now. "I want more than just sex."

Her eyes went flat and she moved away. "I told you. That isn't possible."

"Sapphire..." Nicolae shook his head. "I...can't let you go. We need each other."

She looked back at him as if he were crazy. "I know why I need you, but, if not for sex, why do you need me? We literally just met!"

What could he say? Anything but the truth would be the end for them, he knew. He couldn't let that happen. Not and retain an ounce of sanity. "I know what is happening to you."

She barked out a laugh. "You don't know anything."

"I know you were...*infected* by a rabid werewolf."

She visible jumped and backed away. "*How do you know that? How* could *you know that!*"

Her scream of fear held a hint of accusation and hit him square in the face. He took several breaths, knowing he was breaking the most important rule his kind had. "Because I'm hunting it. I have to kill it."

She didn't react and he was certain she was trying to process his words. When her eyes welled up in tears, his heart nearly stopped.

"So you will have to kill me, too."

"No!" Nicolae crossed to her, hating that she backed away in fear. She only moved a couple of feet though, before her terrified features revealed she'd realized she'd trapped herself between the wall, the railing, and a small dresser. She glanced down at the floor below and then at him. He stood between her and the stairs. He knew he had to calm her down before she considered jumping. "I would never hurt you. But I will do my best to help you, if you'll just give me a chance."

Sapphire reached back and grabbed a brush from the top of the dresser. She threw it at him. He didn't move, but let it hit and bounce off his chest. "Don't you come any closer to me!" She glanced over to the nook that held her gun, and Nicolae sighed.

"I wouldn't think about it, if I were you."

She turned angry eyes his way. "Who are you? *Really*?"

He was all in now, so he'd tell her as much truth as he believed she could handle. "I'm known as Nicholas Wolfe to those I work with, and in everyday life, but I'm also known as Nicolae Lupei by the family who adopted me when I was very young. Nicolae is who I really am."

"How do you know about the rabid werewolf?"

"He was once a member of my adopted family, and a good man, before he was infected." Nicolae didn't define *infected*, so he hoped she'd take it as both the rabies and the genetics that made them all what they were. She seemed to relax a little, and so did he.

"How did you figure out he was a werewolf?"

Nicolae shrugged, again telling only as much truth as he could. "I saw him change, but he was deranged with the rabies, so the family felt it necessary to cage him until we could decide what must be done."

"Why didn't you seek medical help for the rabies?"

Nicolae's brows lifted. "And tell them what? To be careful, that he might bite them, and then they might get infected too?"

Sapphire huffed out a breath and approached the bed. When Nicolae intercepted her, she shook her head and looked him in the eyes. "Don't worry. I'm not going for my gun. I just need to sit down for a minute."

He felt the truth of her words, so he allowed her to pass and then settled himself at her side. "I'm telling you the truth. I would sooner die than allow harm to come to you. And I will do everything in my power to help you, Sapphire, I swear it on my life."

"How can you? If I become a monster, you will be forced to take my life." She stared at the floor and then turned to him, her eyes resigned. "In fact, I insist you do."

Fury filled him at her words, but he had to keep from letting it show. In time he would have to tell her the complete truth. That they weren't monsters, but a species as old as man, and not nearly as harmful to either the earth or others who were not of their kind. Sadly, there was millennia of folklore that said just the opposite, and until he proved otherwise, she'd have to go on believing the lies.

"I need your word, Nicolae."

The sound of his real name coming from her lips rolled through him pleasurably. He turned to her and opened his hand. She immediately placed hers in it. He chose his words as carefully as he held her delicate hand. "I swear to you, if you become a monster, I will take your life."

She nodded and looked down. A sad little chuckle escaped her lips. "It seems I should put my bra and a shirt back on."

Nicolae didn't look over at her, just as he hadn't looked at anything but her face since she'd left the bed. It seemed wrong to do so, though he still wanted her with a passion like none he'd ever known. A thought occurred to him, and he took the time to mull it over, before turning to her fully.

"I need you to keep the information about my adopted brother, and my mission to capture and kill him, to yourself."

"Because once you kill him, he will change back into a man, and you will be considered a murderer?"

That was as good a reason as any, though she had that

wrong too. They were Lycanthrope first, born as pups, and only transformed into adult men and women once they were around five Lycan-years old. "If I kill him, it will be best to do so while he is in the form of a man, otherwise, I face almost impossible odds."

Sadness for him filled her eyes. "Oh, Nicolae, that is horrible. You will have to look him in the eyes, and he is your family."

He appreciated her sympathy more than she would ever know. "Yes. Everything about this is horrible. He was very important to us."

Staring at the floor, they sat in silence for a while before Sapphire turned to him again. "So I would have to be me, in order for you to take my life. I guess that is too much to ask of you. I will find another way before it comes to that."

Fearful she might try to harm herself, and to put her mind at ease, he shook his head. "I know you don't believe me, but you aren't going to become a monster. It doesn't have to happen that way." *Since you are no longer in danger from the rabies.* Of course there was still the almost certain possibility she would die during the first transformation, but he was determined to keep that from happening…*somehow.* He just had to figure out how, and soon. The Hunter Moon was only weeks away, and, this time, there would also be a second moon in the month of October, known to humans as a Blue Moon.

Though he had no idea when the last time both occurred in the Harvest month, he knew it was rare enough that he didn't remember it happening. His own folklore said werewolf power, when their two special moons occurred, was at its peak. Pregnant females would hold off until that night to have their pups if they could, knowing their offspring had a greater chance of achieving greatness within their own pack or in the start-up of a new one.

Unlike wolves, who only birthed their pups in the spring of the year, werewolves were more like humans, and could procreate at any time, though unlike humans, the females only came into estrus four times a year, depending on their own births and sexual maturity.

Hope lit her eyes. "How do you know this?"

Nicolae could have bitten his tongue off. That was the one question he was hoping to avoid, because he would be forced to cross the line into the realm of the white lie. But he had no choice.

"I'm a werewolf *hunter*, from a long line of hunters, and my family knows the truth about it all." Technically that was all true, and technically it wasn't. He did come from a long line of werewolves, and they were hunters, but he couldn't make the distinction for her. At least not yet.

"Tell me what is happening to me then."

He glanced at her and then down at her glorious chest. He couldn't help it. "Maybe you *should* put a shirt on first."

One brow lifted and she reached back, snatching his shirt off the bed. He watched, and his hunger reignited as she slipped her arms in the overly long sleeves. One after the other she rolled them up and then buttoned three of the centrally set ones. She looked so delicately delicious; he almost believed he'd been better off if she'd just stayed topless. All he could think to do was rip the shirt right back off her. She lifted the collar and inhaled deeply before turning to him. Her nostrils were flared, her sapphire eyes alive with hunger, and he wondered if his scent was calling to her, just as hers had to him since the first time he saw her.

"Nicolae…"

The way her voice caressed his name moved him, and he was torn between desire and honor. "Sapphire, I hunger for you, still, but I need to tell you what I believe is a solution to our problems." She blinked, as if trying to break a spell, and he understood her dilemma.

"What do you wish to tell me that is more important than what I desire from you right now?" She reached out and touched his jaw and then slid her hand back until her fingers were once again in his hair.

He closed his eyes, knowing the she-wolf was already growing strong within her. Otherwise, he was certain her sexual desires would make no sense to her at such a frightening time in her life. But unlike Sabia, Sapphire asked, not demanded. The wolf within him responded to the scent she unknowingly put off, and he couldn't help but wonder just how far into the transition she was. It explained why he'd nearly lost control earlier, and he now knew for certain he'd have to tell her the whole truth soon, but until he did, he didn't dare take her. If he transitioned against his will, she'd never trust him again.

He took her hand, kissed the back of it, and then placed it firmly on her thigh, hoping to ease the need they were both feeling. She grinned at him as her scent flooded his senses, making the effort a waste of time. He cleared his throat and blew out a breath, determined to stay in control. He had no doubt she was completely unaware of the erotic smells radiating from her body in its attempt to claim his.

He was all too aware.

"You are a hard man to figure. But I will listen."

Though he was struggling to stay on task, Nicolae knew he had Sapphire's full attention. He struggled with more than the overwhelming hunger she built within him, finding it hard to know where to begin. He wanted to stick as close to all truths as he could without frightening her into flight mode again.

"From what I have been told by those who witnessed it, the transition you will experience is very dangerous, and could lead to death."

Her eyes widened, but she said nothing, only nodded

in acknowledgement of his words. He admired her bravery in what could only be terrifying circumstances. "I know that you think all werewolves are monsters."

She held up her hand, stopping him. "Until very recently, I didn't even believe they existed. Now, I have no doubt. The things that have been happening to me...."

He nodded, knowing that this was going to stretch her ability to believe even further. "The truth is they have been around as long as there has been life on this planet. And though they were once completely wild, as early man was believed to be, they too have evolved into creatures who live their lives as men and women in the open, and as their natural selves when they so wish. But they do not kill humans and have not done so for thousands of years."

Sapphire stared at him, and shook her head. "But I saw what that one did to that man the night I was attacked. I would have been his next victim if..." Her eyes widened even more. "It was you! You are the one who covered my head and body, protecting me from the storm."

Nicolae nodded again, not at all surprised by her intelligence. "I couldn't stay once I knew you were safe. I was trying to get to Ion to make sure he didn't attack the emergency services people, too, but he got away while I was with you, and, until today, I haven't seen or heard of any deaths since. He wouldn't have done that except the rabies has ravaged his mind and body to the point he probably no longer knows who he once was. Otherwise, he would still be living his life, and none of this would have happened."

Sapphire lowered her eyes and then bit her bottom lip. "You know so much about this." She glanced back up. "And you say he is your family?"

Though she didn't say it, her question hung in the air between them. He'd wanted more time, but it looked like his time had run out. She was just too intelligent for her own good. "I am, and I am not, *family* to him and his pack…but I am of the same species."

Her swift intake of breath nearly destroyed him, but he knew he had to continue. "I was born to another pack, all killed when I was too young to remember. Ion's father found me wandering, lost and alone. His mother cared for me and raised me as her own, along with him and his sister. It wasn't until I was older that I even knew I wasn't a blood relative."

Sapphire visibly swallowed. "When they found you, you were still human?"

Nicolae smiled while blowing out a breath, knowing this was probably going to be more than she could handle, and would likely make her feel differently about him. "No. I was born a whelp. We all are."

Sapphire rose and crossed the room. This time he didn't follow and wouldn't even if she attempted to leave the loft. But she only paced the small space a couple of times before she settled back at his side. She reached over and slid her fingers through his. He glanced up at her, startled, by her reaction. She only smiled.

"You have no idea how relieved I am right now."

Surprise and excitement filled his chest so much, he could barely contain the oxygen, causing him to expel a shaky breath "Really?"

She grinned, and nodded. "I was so afraid I'd become this terrible monster that would hurt the ones I love. This is so much better than I could have hoped for." She rose again, but didn't release his hand. Instead she turned to straddle him, and Nicolae trembled with desire for her. She loosely clasped him at the base of his skull, over his long hair.

"So tell me this. I've been having dreams for weeks, and in each one of them, I am a small black wolf. Am I? Or is it only a dream?"

Nicolae lifted her legs onto the bed, grasped her hips,

and pulled her closer. She wrapped her legs around his bottom, and they stared into each other's eyes. His relief nearly matched his ardor, but he tried to ignore both. He wanted to tell her as much as he could. "You are, but you aren't. What you are experiencing is the same thing I experience when I sleep in human form. Among our kind, we call that experiencing MT or mental transformation. When we actually change, *physically*, it's called PT. Obviously, because we physically change."

Sapphire leaned forward and gently kissed his lips. When she pulled back, it took everything he had not to reignite the fires that had burned so brightly before. He swallowed, unable to grasp she not only accepted him for who he was, but was embracing it for herself as well. He had to get busy and find a way to save her.

"I need to find a way to keep the PT from killing you. I can't go to my pack. They are more afraid of humans finding out they actually exist than humans have ever been of them."

"We can go to my family."

Nicolae shook his head. "I am breaking every rule by telling you what I have. If your family knows, we place them in danger from the pack. Exposure to humans is the only justification for werewolves to kill them. Besides, what could they possibly do?"

Sapphire's gaze was filled with concern until his last question, and then she smiled. "Funny you should ask."

Chapter Nine

Sapphire looked deeply into his eyes, as her excitement grew. Yes, she knew he believed she was in danger of dying, but she didn't believe for a minute that one of her many talented relatives couldn't pull some kind of trick out of their collective hats to keep her alive during the transformation. As long as staying alive didn't mean she'd try to eat them, she was up for whatever it took.

"I have something to tell you, too, that is just as amazing as what you've told me. But before I do, will you change for me?" He smiled, and Sapphire knew he'd just been waiting for her to ask.

"Yes. Now?"

She nodded, and meant to slide back, but he rose and stepped forward so she released her locked ankles and placed her feet on the floor. "Definitely now. Where do you want to do it? Do we have to go outside?"

Nicolae's laughter was joyous. "No. I can do it here. Where do you want me? On the floor or the bed?"

Sapphire pointed to the bed. "Up there."

Nicolae started unzipping his jeans and then stopped to look at her. "It's easier if I'm naked."

Tiny little zings of thrill had her moving forward to grasp the zipper to finish taking it down. "This isn't exactly what I'd expected when I asked you to come home with me, but I had planned on you being naked all along." They laughed together, and she stepped back to watch. "Proceed, werewolf. I have never seen a grown man naked, unless you count corpses, so this is a first on two counts for me."

Nicolae grinned and chucked his jeans to his ankles, taking his boxers down with them. He stood back up, and raised a brow. "Looks like I should have taken my boots off first. You make me forget what I'm doing."

Sapphire slowly moved toward him again, taking her time, and taking in everything he had on display. He was fully engorged, and she quaked within. But she was determined to hold that off until she got to see the other, even though her mind shouted, *move, pounce, devour!* She exhaled, shaking with the need to give in, but she swallowed the saliva flooding her mouth, and forced herself to remain still until she thought she was back in control.

"Flop back on the bed. I'll take care of your boots!" she demanded and then realized she was still teetering on the edge.

His grin was knowing. "At your service."

Not only did he fall back, trusting the bed would catch him, he added a little hop to it, so all that was left hanging over the edge of her bed was his scrunched-up jeans partially covering his boots. She wasted no time moving forward to pull off first one boot, and then the other, then pulled both pant legs at the same time. When his underwear came off with them, she dropped everything to the floor and looked up to see a satisfied smile on his yummy lips. Her hunger increased as she took in bulging biceps, which teased her with their generous proportions, and the amazing pectoral muscles made her lick her lips and want to bite at the small discs surrounding the tiny nipples. He'd locked his fingers behind his head confidently, giving her a full, unobstructed view, and she appreciated it to her core. Sapphire took her time, allowing her gaze to follow the distinct line down the center of his body, and couldn't help but admire the incredibly defined abdominals, and even more amazing, the surprisingly clean-shaven area around his magnificently proud penis.

"You can touch anything you want."

Realizing she'd stared at his sex for too long, Sapphire shook her head and grinned. "Tempting, *very* tempting, but not yet. I want to see your wolf, first."

Just like that she was looking at a large black and brown wolf lounging on his back atop her bed. He slowly rolled so that he was on his side, then looked around at her, and everything within her trembled with excitement. "You're...amazing."

She would swear under oath she could see his wolf-grin as he slowly rose and padded to the end of the bed. He sat down and waited, and Sapphire didn't hesitate to move forward to slowly lift her hand to place it along his long jaw. He leaned into her hand and something inside of her melted as she caressed him. She placed her other hand on him as well and leaned forward to kiss the top of his head. Nicolae's head jerked up, and instantly he was a man again, pulling her to him, as he devoured her lips with an all-out assault that stole her breath and spun her world at least twice over.

She reveled in the hunger swamping her as she pushed him backward, off his knees. He spread his legs to accommodate the length of her body as she landed upon him, still locked within his embrace, her lips still clinging with desperation to his. He rolled them over, and slid his knees up to release her only long enough so his hands could tear the shirt from her body, and strip her of her slacks. She clawed at him with a scatter-brained impatience that went so against her methodical personality—but that was then, and *he* was now.

Everything about him threw her off balance, spun her in circles, and made parts of her ache with rabid desire. She sat up and met his lips again, unable to tolerate those seconds of separation, unwilling to let even the air hold them apart. Nicolae released the pins from her hair, allowing the long lengths to cascade down and over her back and shoulders. He tore his mouth from hers and pulled her head close so he could bury his nose in the nape of her neck. She felt as well as heard the swift intakes of breath, and she knew his wolf was as much in control as was the man. He held her tightly to him, so she was rendered immobile. She understood his need for restraint but wanted nothing to do with it. She wanted all of him. Every part. Man and wolf. But he continued to hold her as his chaotic breaths repeatedly blew against the skin of her neck and upon her shoulders, and his chest rose and retreated with the speed of a piston.

He slowly pulled back, desperation and regret in his eyes. "I'm going to hurt you if we continue. I don't want to do that."

Sapphire pushed her disappointment away and slid her arms from his neck. She shook her head and ran a finger across his lips. "What can I do, to make this easier for you?"

His laugh was one of self-derision and blew breath across her finger. "I should be walking you through this, not the other way around."

"I'm pretty good at walking myself through things." When he didn't grin, she sighed. "Okay, how would it be possible for us to proceed without you going all hairy on us?"

He did laugh at that, to her relief.

A cold rush of air accompanied the sound of her front door banging against the bookcase she'd sat behind it, but before she could react, Dia's voice came in a frantic shout, "Sapphire! Are you here?"

Sapphire was too stunned to move, but Nicolae reacted with a swiftness that took her breath and left her dangling in his arms as Dia ran up the stairs. Everyone froze: Nicolae with feet planted firmly apart and fire flashing from his eyes, Sapphire with her heart lodged in her throat as she clung tightly to his body, and Dia standing a few stairs down, her mouth hanging open and her pale blue eyes as big as poker chips.

Sapphire pushed at Nicolae, and then turned to stand in front of him once he'd released her. "What the hell are you doing here?"

Dia shook her head as her mouth fell into a smile. "I guess I could ask you the same question, but, then, it's pretty obvious." She laughed. "Oh my, wait until the family hears about this!"

Sapphire would have moved forward to throttle her sister, but she wasn't about to let Dia get another look at Nicolae's body. "How did you get in? The door was locked." She turned her head and looked back and up, and Nicolae nodded. She turned back to Dia. "*How* did you get here?"

Dia held up the single key dangling from the dragonfly key ring Sapphire had given her mother years before on Mother's Day. Sapphire closed her eyes, trying to choke down the growl she felt forming in her belly. "Why are you here?"

"Maybe you could take this downstairs?"

Sapphire glanced back again and nodded. "You're right. Sorry." When she turned back Dia was already descending the steps, so she turned again and slid her arms around Nicolae's waist. "This will only take a minute. That's my sister, by the way."

He grinned. "Never questioned that, except for the hair and eyes, you guys are identical. Take your time."

She grinned at him. "Stay put. We aren't done with this. I haven't even begun...."

"I can hear you up there."

Sapphire turned to the railing. "Then stop listening!"

"Small cabin. No walls. A little hard."

Sapphire rolled her eyes. As reluctant as she was to leave him, she had no choice if she wanted to get Dia on her way back out the door *immediately*.

"Nice to meet you! I'm Dia by the way."

Sapphire groaned and Nicolae laughed before he responded. "Nicholas. Nice to meet you too."

"Nice voice! Deep. *Manly*. Nice body too."

Horrified, Sapphire approached her dresser to grab a T-shirt and sweatpants. "Shut up, Dia!"

"Just *saying*. Isn't every day a girl gets to see a view like *that*."

Sapphire pulled the shirt over her head and leaned over the railing. "Shut up!"

Her sister's giggles carried up to the loft, as she pulled on the sweats. She sent an apologetic look to Nicolae, but he was grinning and shrugged it off. She grinned back and then schooled her face in preparation to deal with her sister as she headed for the stairs. By the time she got to the bottom, Dia was in the refrigerator, pulling out a bottle of water.

"Take that with you when the door hits you in the behind."

"No can do. Mom sent me here to make sure you hadn't died on us. So I'm here on official business." She laughed at her own joke and twisted off the top.

Seeing she'd have to physically throw Dia out, before she'd finished making life miserable, Sapphire sighed and went to the refrigerator. She grabbed two more bottles. She walked back to look up at the loft. "Nicholas?"

"Yes?"

She could hear the laughter in his voice and couldn't help but see the humor of the situation herself. "Water?"

"Definitely." He walked to the railing and she threw it up at him. As she expected, he caught it with a quick swipe of his hand.

"Nice boxers too."

Sapphire looked over at her sister, only to see Dia smiling up at him like a fool. "Eyes down. And shut the hell up!"

Dia glanced over at Sapphire, her eyes bubbling with laughter. Sapphire shook her head and grasped her sister's arm to pull her to the door. "Tell Mom and anyone who wants to know, I am perfectly fine."

Dia dug her heels in, stopping them both. "Then why didn't you answer your cell phone?"

It took Sapphire a minute to remember she'd been so traumatized by the second rabid werewolf sighting, she'd left her purse and cell phone in the Jeep. "I forgot to bring it in the house when I got home. Mystery solved. Now go."

Dia shook her head, her eyes taking on a wicked gleam. "No can do. Family meeting's been called. When they called the station to tell you Uncle Tom has some news that needed to be shared immediately and were told you'd gone home for the day, it set everyone in a panic. So I was sent here, and Jewell was sent to the hospital. When I left, Mom and the aunts were digging out the family diaries, while they ordered Daddy and Uncle Logan to fetch this and that, then to go with Uncle Tom to the place where our ascension ceremony was held, to set up for whatever spell it is they have in mind."

Sapphire looked from Dia to the loft, wondering if her sister remembered Nicolae could hear every word. When she turned back, the caution on her sister's face said she hadn't but now did. "Go. I'll be there shortly."

Dia nodded, and Sapphire could tell she wanted to apologize, but neither said anything more as she pushed Dia out the door and then stepped out herself to look around. Satisfied Ion was nowhere to be seen, she turned to her sister. "Be careful. I encountered the rabid werewolf again earlier." At the fear in Dia's eyes, she hurried on. "I was driving, and he was running across my driveway. I nearly hit him, but he's very fast. Don't go anywhere alone until we get this all figured out."

Dia nodded. "I'm sorry. I...."

Taking pity on her, Sapphire pulled her into a hug. "I know. Just go. And don't stop until you're back at Mom and Dad's."

"I'm sorry you have to leave that gorgeous man. And I promise, I won't say anything about him, just that you were home in bed, but are okay."

Sapphire smiled at how easily that could go either way. "Thanks. Now go. I need to take care of a couple of things, then I'm on my way, too."

****

Sapphire took the stairs two at a time and stopped short when she saw Nicolae had pulled on his jeans and boots. She knew his shirt was destroyed, but she had nothing nearly large enough to offer him. "I'm sorry. I have to go."

He nodded and rose from the end of the bed. "I didn't mean to listen in but couldn't help it. Tell me about your family."

She bit her bottom lip and then nodded. "I was going to later, when we had more time, but now I guess I'll have to go on and share our family secret, which, in its own way, is as sacred as yours." She hesitated, not knowing where to start, but figured the beginning, as her family knew it, was best.

"Sit back down, please. This will take a few minutes, even the abbreviated version." When he did as she requested, she walked over to sit at his side, realizing they'd been in the same position when he'd told her he was a werewolf. The irony wasn't lost on her; she hoped it wasn't

111

lost on him either.

"More than three thousand years ago, we had an ancestor who was also an Egyptian Queen. She gave birth to three identical baby girls but was told by her husband, the Pharaoh, they would have to be killed because he believed they would cause the end of Egyptian dynasties." She paused, waiting to see if he questioned why she was going so far back in time. When Nicolae said nothing, she continued. "She became very angry at him and, from my family's understanding, cursed love. Until my parent's generation, no Cavanaugh woman could keep a loving relationship. Either she would die, or the man who she fell in love with would."

Nicolae hadn't looked over at her, just stared at the floor, as if piecing her story together. He finally looked up. "So you are saying she actually created a curse, as in magic."

Jewell nodded. "Exactly. According to Mom, from that moment on, each subsequent generation of Cavanaugh women all came in triplets, but only one of the three gave birth to the next generation of three, who each carried a distinct type of magic. There's the Enchantress, who is capable of casting spells or conjuring things that were previously not there, or who can alter something's chemistry, making it something else. Then there's what is known as the Regulator, who is capable of controlling all natural elements on the earth and in the sky. And finally there is the Divine, whose spirit is free to discover truth, whether it's in the form of reading people's auras or feeling the intent of their mind and heart, and even being able to leave their own physical body, to exist as mist, or enter into another's body, if granted permission."

She exhaled shakily as she awaited his reaction, but he said nothing, and she couldn't read his expression. He sat up a little straighter, turning to her with a smile. "This is why you so easily accepted my world. You understand that there are more things on this earth than any one species is privy to, or able to comprehend."

Sapphire nodded. "Yes. That's one reason."

Nicolae's brows rose. "And the others?"

"I know now my changing into a werewolf won't threaten the lives of others, and I won't be eating people for dinner."

He smiled at that.

"And I can't wait to feel the breeze on my face and the power in my legs, when I run like the wolf in my dreams." He nodded in understanding. "And then, of course, there's you."

He took her hand and raised it to his lips. "I was kind of hoping to be at the top of that list."

She smiled. "Goes without saying."

"Say it anyway."

"You've been in those dreams I spoke about." She shook her head and frowned. "I don't know how I know it was you, but you were, and you were protecting me, even then." She smiled at him. "You are at the top of all my lists."

"Good enough," Nicolae said, before pulling her around, as they stood.

He enveloped her within his massive arms and took her lips with slow...but deadly maneuvers that threatened sanity and pride, as she was sure those sounds she heard were her own whimpers of want. She poured herself into the kiss, drowning in pleasure, grasping for more, dying with a need so powerful she could hardly stand. When he slowed the kiss and then pulled back to look into her eyes, she knew nothing would be stronger than what was between them. Neither life, nor death, nor principalities—be they celestial or human, would ever stop her from making a long life with her wolf.

"I will never let you go."

It was as if he'd read her mind. Sapphire nodded and snuggled into him. "Then we need to find you a shirt, because my father is going to have enough trouble with all this, without you showing up half naked."

Chapter Ten

The trip from Sapphire's cabin to her parents' home would have taken a lot less time if she hadn't needed to stop at her sister Jewell's house first. Fortunately, because she'd once lived there, and Jewell hadn't changed the locks, Sapphire was able to get inside and find one of her brother-in-law's T-shirts, which fit Nicolae quite well.

They resaddled and took the Harley on up the mountain's twisting and turning roads. Because she'd asked it of him, they were pushing the limits where safety was concerned, and she was having a ball embracing the speed that had only previously been part of her dreams.

"I think you are enjoying the ride a little too much!" Nicolae shouted.

Sapphire laughed. She certainly was. She'd leaned against his back and played with his front throughout the short ride, reveling in the power of being a woman.

"I'm enjoying it too, but I have no idea how I'm going to explain my hard-on to your family. I don't want them to all think I'm only after your body."

Grimacing, Sapphire realized he had a good point, and she raised her hands to a less intimate hold. This was going to be awkward enough without *that* being her family's first impression of him, and the poor man had little time to fix the not so little problem she'd caused. Much too soon, she tapped his stomach and lifted a hand to point at the upcoming driveway. Whether he was ready or not, they had arrived.

Nicolae turned into the short driveway and pulled

between Dia's little red car and her dad's old pick-up truck to park in front of the large metal building where Garrison White made, what his daughter considered, the most beautiful furniture in the world. Nicolae cut off the bike's engine and waited for her to dismount before doing so himself.

Sapphire gave him a *here goes* look and then turned her attention in the direction of her childhood home. Taking a deep breath, as she'd suddenly lost her nerve, she moved forward, only to have him take her arm to stop her.

"Give me a minute here. I'm trying to talk myself down." He grinned at her. "I have better control over my wolf, than *this*, apparently." He winked at her. "And it's all your fault."

Sapphire laughed and relaxed slightly, happy for the distraction of what was to come. Once he'd adjusted himself, took several studious breaths, and nodded, she turned and moved forward again. Nicolae followed close behind, and she wasn't completely surprised to see the three identical middle-aged women step out onto the porch. Dia followed them as did Jewell.

Dia grinned at them. "Well, it doesn't do much good for me to keep a secret when you bring it to the house. Hi, Nicholas!"

Sapphire shook her head. There was no point being annoyed. She'd brought this on herself. She looked from her sisters to her mother and aunts, and all of them had identical expressions of interest. She grinned nervously, as she stopped at the bottom of the porch steps and felt him stop behind her.

"Hi, Mom, Aunt Destiny, Aunt Haven, Jewell." She reached back and took his hand, pulling him to her side. "This is Nicolae Lupei." She glanced over at Dia, expecting the surprised expression. "Also known as Nicholas Wolfe." She looked back at her mother. "I've got a lot to tell you all." She turned to him and smiled. "Nicolae, my mom Rayne, my aunts Destiny and Haven, my sister Jewell, and you know Diamond, also known as Dia to the family."

Jewell slowly stepped forward as each of the others smiled at him. "I know you."

Sapphire glanced between Nicolae and Jewell and then settled her gaze on her sister. "You must be mistaken. He's fairly new in town."

Nicolae placed his hand on her shoulder. "No, she's right. We met once a while back, when I was looking for my sick dog."

The look in his eyes had her heart beating strongly with understanding, but when she turned back to her family, all eyes were filled with suspicion. She knew she was going to need to alleviate some fears quickly. Her family was already on edge.

"Can we go in and talk? I have to tell you what's really going on."

Rayne slid a glance to Nicolae and then back to her daughter. "I think that's a good idea."

Sapphire nodded and took Nicolae's hand before they advanced, climbed the steps, and stopped at the door. She waited until the storm door closed behind the last of her family and turned to him. "I'll have to tell them everything."

"I know."

"I'll need you to explain what I don't know.

"I know that, too."

"I'm sorry."

He smiled at her then. "Don't be. We're in this together."

She relaxed. "I'm happy. I know that makes no sense. But I am."

He pulled her to him. "It makes sense to me."

Sapphire giggled. "If we don't go in soon, they'll come

looking for us."

Nicolae shrugged. "They can wait a second…or three." He took her lips, and though the kiss was chaste, she felt it all the way to her toes. He pulled back, nodded, and opened the door.

Sapphire preceded him into her parents' living room and glanced from one questioning face to another. She smiled at them and pulled Nicolae to her side, determined to show them all she was claiming him. "I'm going to change into a Lycanthrope. Actually, I'm already changing."

Rayne glared at Nicolae then shook her head when her gaze landed on Sapphire. "It isn't going to happen. Tom's father says there is a way to stop it. That's why we've called a family meeting. Everyone is waiting for us at the ceremonial site." She turned her attention to Nicolae. "What kind of nonsense are you filling my daughter's head with, and what do you know of any of this? My daughters don't bring strangers into our business."

Sapphire would have loved to have heard of a cure only that morning, but not now. More shocking was the barely hidden rage in her mother's voice when she spoke to Nicolae. To her knowledge, Rayne Cavanaugh-White had never spoken so rudely to anyone before. "I understand your concerns, Momma, and your confusion, but I only need one thing from you all, and that is to live through the first physical transition. If I do, then I'll be okay."

Rayne sprang from her seat. "You'll be a monster!"

Knowing her mother's shout was only because she was terrified, Sapphire moved forward to take her into a hug. "I won't be. It isn't like that. That's what I need to explain."

Rayne pulled back and her sisters immediately flanked her. Sapphire felt her eyes fill. Her mother had never been the first one to break a hug, and she'd never before acted as if she needed protection from any of her girls. Sapphire swallowed and returned to Nicolae's side to take his hand, trying to ignore the hurt in her heart.

"May I speak?"

All eyes turned to Nicolae, then to Rayne, to see what she would say. Finally Rayne nodded. He exhaled heavily, and Sapphire waited with the rest of them, her heart shattered but hopeful he could make them understand.

"I know you believe what you believe, but what you are basing your information on is fantasy. Because *you* are all different from others who don't hold special powers and abilities, you should know that which others do not understand, causes them to fear, and to create stories that grow and change through time. I know many Lycanthrope, and they are not monsters. They are a species that is half wolf, half human, and usually the best of both.

"They do not kill people. They exist with them, work with them, raise families, and are of strong faith.

"Over time, because they must hide who they really are and cannot stay in their natural state except when there are special gatherings, their females rarely have an opportunity to procreate, and their numbers have dwindled to near extinction."

Nicolae allowed his words to hang in the air, and Sapphire knew her family was giving his words the consideration they deserved. Her mother and aunts, and sisters as well, were quietly staring at him, without expressions of fear or disdain, but with curiosity. She relaxed a little, until her mother's expression changed to one of denial.

"But there was a man slaughtered, and my daughter was infected, and she nearly died."

Nicolae nodded at her softly spoken statement. "Yes. His name is Ion, and he was once a proud prince from a very long line. He was bitten while trying to capture and put down a rabid wolf, in a pack of rabid wolves." He smiled. "What you think of as *natural* wolves."

His smile slid into sadness. "Because he worked with Animal Control, where the pack lived among humans, he was with a coworker and couldn't change into his natural form. Although he still had incredible strength, he lost the advantage he would have otherwise had in handling the animals. Once he was bitten, he had to hide it, and because there would be too many questions if he was hospitalized and blood was drawn, he couldn't seek medical help to treat the rabies virus. If he had been able to, like your daughter, he would be healthy, and would never have done what was done."

They all continued to stare at him until Destiny rose and walked toward him. She looked from Sapphire to him and then held out her hand to Nicolae. He stared at her for a few seconds and placed his hand into hers. Destiny immediately shuddered and then pulled her hand away.

She looked into his eyes, but addressed the room at large. "He speaks the truth. But he hasn't yet told us the whole truth."

Sapphire placed her hand on her aunt's arm, pulling Destiny's gaze to her. "I will not let you harm him."

Destiny smiled at her fondly. "We will not. He is no threat to us. But what you seek to allow, for yourself, isn't necessary. My Tom knows a way for us to flush the werewolf strain from your blood. Then your life can return to normal."

Sapphire shook her head, needing them to understand. "You are wrong. I love you all. But my life is only now becoming what it was meant to be. My heart is his. If you take that from me, I will never forgive any of you."

Rayne's gasp was loud and drew all their attention as she rose to stand by her sister. Haven joined them to take Rayne's hand, and Destiny took the other. The force that was *The Three* radiated a power that shook the pictures on the walls.

Sapphire knew only bits and pieces of the story, that her mother and sisters were the three mystics whose joint powers were destined to break a three thousand-year-old curse. The curse she'd told Nicolae about had prevented their ancestors from sustaining the love they always sought and eventually found, only to lose it again in the saddest of ways. But she couldn't believe they intended to use their massive power against her. And she would die before allowing them to use it against Nicolae.

Refusing to cower, she stepped between them and Nicolae. She looked each in the eyes and then sought her mother's understanding. "Over the years, you have told us children you and our aunts each only found happiness in your lives once you found the place you were meant to be and embraced your powers, rather than running from them. But more importantly, you were meant to be with my father. Just as Aunt Destiny was meant to be with Uncle Tom. And Aunt Haven to be with Uncle Logan. You six have been a shining example of what life between couples was meant to be. I have found my place. I am embracing my power. *This* is my happiness. Please do not force me to fight the family I love with all my heart."

Rayne released her sister's hands and held hers out to Sapphire. Hesitantly she took it, and warmth radiated from her mother to her. Rayne sighed and glanced past her to look up at Nicolae.

"I am not saying that I will allow this. But if I do, what will happen to my daughter?"

Nicolae didn't hesitate to respond. "That may depend on the strength of your powers."

The three matriarchs of the family stepped back when Rayne released Sapphire's hand, and they returned to their seats. "Please sit with us. We need to know what we are facing. We need to know *everything*."

"Give me a minute, I need to go to Tom and tell him

they need to return so we can work this out as a family, and so Nicolae will only have to say all this once."

Sapphire turned from her aunt Destiny to Nicolae and smiled. "You're going to enjoy this. Sit with me." She pulled him to the chair her father had deemed his own back when she was a child. The rather worn recliner was still plush, and she waited for Nicolae to sit before settling upon his knees and accepting the strength of his hand when it took hers. She knew the other women in the room watched with a multitude of emotions, but none protested her actions.

****

Once they all stilled, Destiny leaned back into the couch and closed her eyes. Immediately her body went limp and a mist arose from her form. Nicolae watched with fascination as the mist circled the room and then rose to slip through the planks that made up the high ceiling. When Sapphire turned back to him and smiled, he smiled back, thinking he couldn't wait to see what the others could do.

Not sure if it was okay to talk or not, he glanced around Sapphire. Her mother was staring back at them, and he wasn't sure, but he thought she was suppressing a smile.

"When did you two meet?"

Nicolae knew this wasn't a question he wanted to answer, since it required him to tell things he hadn't yet had a chance to tell Sapphire, but honesty was required if he was to build trust. "I didn't officially meet your daughter until this morning."

At the four sets of raised eyebrows, he couldn't help but smile.

"And unofficially?"

Nicolae was certain he was going to like Sapphire's mother. She didn't shy away from the truth and hadn't immediately thrown a fit that the connection between Sapphire and him was already much stronger than the length of their association allowed for. "The first time I encountered her was the night she was infected with the rabies, immediately after Ion scratched her.

"I was tracking him when the storm blew in and lost him because I was afraid he'd come back for her. I threw the blanket I carried to throw on him, over her, to keep her from seeing me, and left before allowing her to remove it. At the time I didn't know for sure he'd infected her, but I knew Ion wouldn't come back while I was with her. He knows my strength, and that I have to kill him."

His words hung in the air, and he appreciated the sympathy he saw in their eyes.

"So you just showed up on her doorstep today?"

Nicolae shook his head, knowing Sapphire was as interested in the information he needed to impart, as was her mother and the others present. "Once the storm stopped, and I was certain Ion was already gone from the area, I circled back and watched until she left the sight of the... carnage. I stayed out of sight, then followed her home to see how she was doing." He smiled. "When she got home and took her little dog out, I was lost." He looked up at Sapphire. "You treated her like she was your baby, not just a pet."

Sapphire nodded. "She is." She turned to her mother. "Where *is* Ellie, by the way?"

Rayne tore her gaze from Nicolae and smiled. "She's with your father. He's fallen in love with her and barely lets her go long enough to stand on her own four paws. I'm afraid you're going to have a fight on your hands when you try to take her back home." She laughed. "He says, besides Logan, she's the only *normal* member of the family."

Nicolae glanced from mother to daughter, grinning. "So your father has no special powers?"

Rayne answered for her. "Not mystical, but he has his own. His heart is pure and his hands are masterful, both in his craft of building things and on me."

Sapphire cringed, as did her sisters. Together they all said, "Mom! Ewwww!"

The two matriarchs laughed, as did Nicolae. No matter the species, kids never wanted to hear about, or *think* about, their parents' sex life.

"Keep it clean, Mom. *Seriously*," Sapphire said, throwing Nicolae a look. "Sorry."

He laughed again, thinking he was going to like this family very much.

Destiny's chest suddenly expanded, and she moaned quietly. She opened her eyes and looked around the room as her brows drew together. "What did I miss?"

"Nothing!" the three daughters said together, and Nicolae laughed with Rayne and Haven, again.

Destiny frowned, her expression stating she *had* missed something, but she left it there. "Well, I've talked to Tom, and he relayed the news to Garrison and Logan, so they're pretty much up to speed." She turned her eyes on Sapphire and Nicolae. "And speeding this way now, I imagine."

Sapphire's hand squeezed his, and he knew she was concerned about him facing the men of the family. He squeezed back, hoping she knew he wasn't concerned for his safety as much as for what his being in her life would do to the relationships she had with each member of her family. She smiled at him and he felt her relax.

"Your connection is strong."

Nicolae glanced over to Destiny. As cool as her magic was, he wasn't sure he liked that she could read him so easily. It wasn't that he had anything to hide, just that he had a right to private thought and feeling. "Do you read people all the time?"

Surprise lit her eyes, and she shook her head. "Only

when I want to. And usually only when asked or when my family's safety is at stake."

He nodded. "Fair enough."

"But, just so you know," she continued, "I wasn't in your mind. I was only watching the body language between you two. I understand it. My Tom and I are like that. Not even death will conquer the connection of our spirits. Where one goes, the other follows."

Nicolae relaxed completely. "Thank you. I will tell you true anything you need or wish to know, but I would be uncomfortable knowing my thoughts and feelings are open for display and dissection."

Destiny stood and stretched. "I will never enter your mind without permission. This I swear...*unless* there is need and no other option. But now, I need water. Becoming the mist dehydrates me." She crossed to the open kitchen area behind the couch and opened the refrigerator, then turned back. "Anyone else?"

When everyone shook their heads, she pulled a bottled water from the refrigerator and downed the entire thing before glancing back at them. Her smile was one of slight embarrassment. "The thirst is great."

Nicolae smiled at her. "I can only imagine. How do you do that?"

Destiny sat the bottle on the counter and returned to the living room area, but before she could answer her brows lifted. "It would seem the men have arrived."

****

Sapphire sat up straighter on Nicolae's lap and then stood. As hard as it was to tell her mother about what was happening, she knew it would be even harder where her father was concerned. Garrison White had accepted the mystical, because to do otherwise would have cost him a life with Rayne and, ultimately, his children, but he was her dad, and as such, was suspicious of any male who came into his girls' lives. He'd already been forced to accept Jewell's ancient Egyptian, but at least *he* was human. Her nerves lessened only slightly when Nicolae stood as well and sent her an encouraging wink.

Ellie was the first in the door, and she immediately flew across the floor to Sapphire. Her white-tipped tail was in hyper-speed like always, as she did her little Ellie jumps to be picked up. She stopped abruptly, sniffed, turned to Nicolae, and emitted a deep growl. He smiled down at her, she studied him, and then she sat down as if she'd been commanded to. Sapphire was so surprised by the behavior, she turned to Nicolae, but he just shrugged and reached down to lift the dog. Ellie sniffed at him when he pulled her against his chest, and then the tail was back in full swing as she licked his face repeatedly.

Sapphire laughed at them until her father, followed by Logan and Tom, stepped inside the door. Her father's eyes held suspicion, Uncle Logan's caution, and Uncle Tom's curiosity. She smiled at them all and walked straight to her father. "Hi, Daddy."

He pulled her to him, but she knew he kept his eyes on Nicolae. "It's okay, Daddy. I promise."

Garrison loosened his hold, but when he looked at her, his expression was guarded. "I'll decide *that* for myself." He released her and turned back to nail Nicolae with a glare.

Sapphire nodded, knowing there was nothing else she could do. She turned from him and held her hand out toward Nicolae. His lack of hesitancy to join them filled her with pride. He slid his hand over hers in a brief caress and then held it out toward her father. To her embarrassment, she watched as her father responded, but instead of simply shaking hands, his grip tightened and held. She glanced from him to Nicolae, and her angst eased when she saw the smile in his eyes and the teasing tilt of his lips. He kept his gaze on her father and allowed several seconds to pass.

"Mr. White. I'm Nicolae Lupei. I haven't come here to hurt your family. This isn't a contest of wills."

Garrison eventually relaxed and pumped his hand a couple of times before letting go. Silence hung in the air like a living entity until Rayne stepped to her husband and took his hand. "This is not a bad thing."

He turned to her, waited a heartbeat, shook his head in defeat, and sighed. "You girls are going to be the death of me."

Rayne giggled, and the tension filling the room evaporated, allowing everyone to once again breathe. Garrison held out his hand, and Nicolae took it; this time there was nothing but friendship in the gesture. "Garrison White. Don't you *ever* hurt my daughter."

Though the words were spoken with a hint of tease, there wasn't a person in the room who doubted her father meant every word. She put her own hand over top of theirs and squeezed. "He isn't going to hurt me or any of us, Daddy. He's going to help us make this all okay."

Their hands fell, and she slid her arm around Nicolae's waist, almost laughing when heat reentered her father's eyes. "Get used to it, Daddy. I need to be able to touch him."

"Well, that's not fair. I'm married *and* pregnant. Amen'ra still won't come near me in Dad's presence." Jewell grinned at the many surprised faces turning her way. "I figured since I was already at the hospital looking for Sapphire, I'd take a quick test. And yep, it's official."

Tom, Logan, and the females in the room all exclaimed with excitement and moved in with hugs for the new mother-to-be. Garrison simply stood there until they all noticed and turned back his way. He shook his head again as a slow smile crawled up his lips. *"Kill me, I say!* Every last one of you is going to *kill* me!" He laughed then and advanced on Jewell to pull her into a tight hug. "Congratulations, baby. Tell that husband of yours we need to have a long talk about fatherhood." He released her, grinning at them all. "He thought being transported through time was hard? He has no idea what hard is."

As the atmosphere in the room had lightened substantially, Sapphire hated to remind them of the reason for their gathering, but it had to be done. Before she could open her mouth to speak, Jewell rubbed her stomach and looked pointedly at their mother.

"I'm hungry." She grinned with delight. "And I'm eating for two... or three, or four now." Her eyes widened. "How will this work this time? Do I automatically get triplets or did that end with the last generation?"

Everyone looked at each other, but no one spoke, until Destiny moved to stand in front of Jewell. "May I?"

"Of course. *Please* do."

Destiny nodded and placed her hand on Jewell's stomach. She looked up, and smiled. "There are three! But it's too soon to tell the sex."

Everyone clapped but Jewell. She shook her head. "I don't want to know what the sexes are until they are born. There are never surprises with this family."

"Says you," Garrison inserted, fighting a grin.

As expected he got a laugh, and Sapphire knew the talk would likely have to wait until food was prepared and consumed. She headed to the kitchen with her mother, allowing the others to resettle since the kitchen area was too small for them all. She placed her hand on her mother's arm to get her attention.

Rayne smiled at her. "I know. We'll talk when we're done with this. We'd initially planned it, to just be us, but I think we should get your cousins over here too. What happens to one, happens to all."

Sapphire nodded. She'd been thinking the same thing. "Is Heracles back from Greece yet?"

Destiny answered from the living room. "He got in late last night. Knowing him, he's still getting his beauty rest, but I'll have one of his brothers go wake him and tell him food is involved. That way they won't have to knock him in the head to get him out of the bed."

"I'm texting the girls, now," Haven added, laughing at her sister. "I told them to contact the boys so they only bring two vehicles between them. Seriously, Garrison, you've got to have more parking."

"We could move this to our place," Destiny offered. "More room, and we still have the better part of the cake Logan made for Tom's birthday."

Sapphire knew that would settle that. Parking could be worked out, even the lack of space for their large and growing family. But, not one member would pass up eating a slice of Uncle Logan's sinfully decadent chocolate cakes if given the option, not even for the threat of a rabid werewolf.

It took everyone just short of a half-hour to move themselves, and the frozen deer burgers and whole-pork wieners Rayne insisted on contributing, to Destiny and Tom's cabin.

Family gatherings and meetings were nearly always held there since, of the three matriarch's homes, theirs was the biggest by far. Since they'd had rambunctious boys, Tom had built a large addition to the back to make it a play room when the boys were little, a weight and entertainment room when they got older, and had turned it into a family room once they'd moved out. Then there was the additional advantage of their cabin sitting within a large clearing of the wooded land surrounding it. Her parents' and the Hansens' cabins had very little to offer in the way of outside space unless one wanted to traipse through the woods. With the growing number of drivers in the family, Tom and Destiny's property became the only logical choice for gatherings, ever since the kids were in their mid-teens and started driving.

Nearly an hour passed before the three Hansen girls showed up one after the other. Though none of them had started relationships of their own, as far as Sapphire knew, their varying personalities dictated they each needed their own space following college, though all lived in town. Soleli, Luna, and Celestia's parents had bought each their own house. Sapphire felt bad she'd yet to find the opportunity see any of their new homes. Between returning from her trip abroad following college, starting a new and surprisingly demanding job, living through the terror of Jewell's experience, acquiring a pet, and now this, there simply hadn't been a moment for a visit, much less three.

She greeted her female cousins and introduced Nicolae to each and knew she'd have to repeat the process moments later when the Whitehawk brothers pulled up together. Since Zeus stepped from the truck first with a swollen and blackening eye, she figured he must have drawn the short straw and been left with the task of awakening the prima donna of the family. The smug satisfaction on Heracles' face when he emerged seconds later proved her right and Sapphire couldn't help but roll her eyes. Apollo finally climbed from the driver's seat and slammed his door. When he looked up with a scowl, he too had a black eye, and Sapphire couldn't help but be happy to have been born to the Cavanaugh-White branch of the family.

The three approached the porch and were nearly there when a look passed between the two oldest. With a nod from Zeus, both slapped Heracles in the closest ear at the same time. He howled, turned to face Apollo, and had his knees buckled with Zeus's boot. When he hit the ground, his brothers were instantly on him and fists flew. Destiny stepped up to the railing of the porch with a five-gallon bucket of water in her hand and threw *bucket and all* on them.

The boys froze, looked up, and all three smiled, Sapphire was sure, in a way that had gotten them out of trouble with their mother many times over the years. Apollo and Zeus jumped to their feet and each offered a hand to Heracles.

Destiny looked her sons over and smiled. "Dinner is about ready, boys. Get washed up."

Chapter Eleven

The fact that this rowdy family was nearly as large as his entire pack didn't escape Nicolae's notice, nor that they were as close-knit as any family he'd ever seen. He spent the afternoon listening to as many conversations as he could follow, certain he now knew each by name, though if not for the differences in the Whitehawk men's bruised eyes, and the fact that one didn't have a mark on his face at all, he had to concede he wasn't sure he'd be able to tell them apart.

"Did you get enough to eat?" Sapphire asked as she slid onto his lap.

"Are you kidding?" he laughed, encircling her waist loosely.

Nicolae didn't have to look up to know several, if not all, eyes were upon them, and not just because all the chatter had stopped. He smiled at her, then looked around, and knew the women were more relaxed about their position than the men. Which was understandable, given not a one of them knew him or trusted him.

"I guess we need to get to the business of the day."

Nicolae shifted his attention to Garrison White and nodded. "Yes. We should."

He patted Sapphire's rump then lifted her off his lap so he could stand. As comfortable as the large wooden deck chair was, it also made him feel at a disadvantage should any of the men take exception to what he had to impart.

Which would likely be the case.

"Though I'm sure the word has already spread among you, I guess I first need to state that I am Lycanthrope." Since he got no reaction but a couple of nods, he continued. "I was born to a pack that lived north of here along the Canadian border."

"When you say pack, you mean *pack*?" Heracles asked.

Even though this was the last place he wanted to start to explain their existence, Nicolae nodded. "Yes. The wolf is our first natural form, and we only transform into our second, the human form, once we reach adulthood around the age of five Lycan-years."

He gave that a moment to sink in, knowing they were all thinking how this would affect Sapphire should she decide she still wanted him once everything was laid out. He glanced back at her, but unlike her family's, her face held a gentle smile. He breathed easier and continued.

"Once we are transformed, we are given the choice of a trade, and from that moment on, we exist within close proximity to each other but lead separate lives for the most part."

"To protect yourselves should anyone be discovered," Zeus added.

Nicolae nodded. "Yes." He hesitated, because this part would be harder for them to hear. "We do gather together once a quarter, deep in the wooded mountains of our home. It is at this time males and females come together to enjoy the freedom of the run, as well as for the unattached males to find a female with which to mate."

The large porch was quiet, and Nicolae knew better than to look the men in the eyes at that moment. No matter the species, males protected their females. He sighed. "The reason we only do this once a quarter is because that is when the females are in estrus and are more receptive to joining with a male."

"So love has nothing to do with it."

Nicolae turned his attention to Sapphire's mother. "Love has everything to do with it. A female will only accept a male she wants. The choice is always hers. But for my kind, the first sign of compatibility is our need to be with the one whose scent draws us. I've never met an unhappy couple. Ever."

Nicolae looked at Garrison White then and was relieved to see no anger, only concern. "When we mate, we mate for life."

Nicolae felt Sapphire's hand slide into his. He looked down at her and smiled.

"So just how old are you?"

Turning to Destiny, he shrugged. "I don't know exactly because my pack was wiped out when I was too young to remember, but the closest I can guess is eight years old in your years, which makes me twenty-seven by human standards.

"So it isn't like dog years?"

Nicolae smiled at Sapphire's sassy sister. "No, Dia. It isn't."

"Well that's good. I was afraid you were going to say you were fifty-six or something gross like that."

"Dia!" several members of the family said together.

Nicolae figured that was a common occurrence and hid a smile.

Since there were no more questions, he continued. "The pack I am now a part of, live several mountains to the north. I don't know for sure how they found me, but I know why they kept me. I was of a different bloodline, and the Alpha at the time raised me with the intention of mating me with his daughter."

Sapphire's sharp intake of breath wasn't the only one. He didn't look at her but squeezed her hand to let her know not to worry. At least not yet.

"The Alpha died a couple of years ago, and his son,

Ion, took his place. Ion was honorable and knew his father's intentions were good, so he took me under his wing and trained me in the responsibilities of an Alpha, should he die before continuing the bloodline. I accepted my fate and was prepared to mate with his sister if he hadn't fathered offspring by the time death took him." He turned his attention to Rayne. "This time it wouldn't be an act of love or desire. It would be my duty. And hers as well."

"He lives then and has his successor," Amen'ra said, as he drew his wife closer to him.

Since Jewell's husband had only arrived as everyone else was finishing their meal, and his attention had been on the news of his impending child, he'd missed most of the day's activities and discussions. Nicolae shook his head. "He's produced no successor, and now he can't. He was bitten by a rabid wolf while in human form and has gone mad since he couldn't seek medical treatment for the rabies virus. I am now the Alpha, and it is my charge to find and destroy him."

Sapphire stepped before him, her eyes haunted. "You are obligated to mate with his sister now?"

"I will not. I cannot. Not now that I have found you. I will leave the pack, and they will have to choose another to take my place. But before I do, I must remove the threat to us all." He pulled her closer and held her within his arms before looking up to those who watched him with a multitude of expressions. "But we must address how to assist Sapphire in her first transition, because, to my knowledge, no human has ever survived."

That brought those sitting to their feet. Nicolae moved Sapphire to his back and held her there, watching each of them warily.

"Relax, son, we aren't going to attack you."

Everyone turned eyes on Tom as he moved forward to

stop in front of Nicolae. "You are of the earth, just as we are."

He glanced back, and though Nicolae couldn't see what the others saw, everyone settled back into their seats or leaning positions against the porch railing. When Tom turned to him once again, there was amusement in his eyes. "We are our own pack, and we welcome you into it, but how will your former pack take this news?"

Tom stepped back to stand behind his wife. Nicolae released Sapphire, and she rejoined him, tucking herself under his arm, making him feel like he had found his right place. He licked his dry lips before speaking. "I don't know. They could simply accept my decision in appreciation for eliminating the threat, they could shun me for being a deserter, or they may try to kill me."

"Which I will not allow to happen."

Nicolae smiled down at Sapphire. "You are brave of heart and more beautiful than my eyes can nearly stand to behold, but you have no power against this pack, at least not yet."

"We could shoot them if they try anything to hurt you. I've been trying to make gold, but silver bullets might be easier."

"Dia!"

Nicolae laughed, knowing for sure now admonishing the perky blonde was a common family occurrence. He smiled at her, yet he tempered it with sadness. "I would ask you to bring no harm to those who took me in and raised me. Our numbers are few, to the extent of near extinction. Just for the record, a silver bullet will only hurt us because it is a bullet, not because it is silver. And even then, only until it is removed and we heal, which happens much more rapidly than humans."

"So we can't kill you?"

"Dia!"

"Well everyone is thinking it, somebody had to say it."

Nicolae laughed. "I would hope you wouldn't try."

She grinned at him. "Just for future reference."

"Dia, that isn't a question you should ask. It makes his kind vulnerable."

Nicolae looked up to Haven, and nodded his thanks for her understanding. But he'd promised them the truth. "If I am to gain your trust, then you must have mine. It is true we do not die easily, but there are ways. One is to be burned to death. Another is to be decapitated. And then there is drowning. All of these require one to get close enough for it to be accomplished without the one trying to kill us losing their own life instead." He looked at all those assembled. "The only time one of us has a right to kill a human is if we are protecting our own life or the lives of our kind."

"That's the same for us. Self-defense is always justifiable," Sapphire added.

He glanced down and she looked up, and he wished they could go back to her place so he could kiss her silly. She grinned at him, making him wonder if she too could read minds, or if he was so hungry for her it showed on his face. He hoped not. Her father was watching.

Nicolae schooled his face before lifting it. He looked to each matriarch in turn. "If there are no more questions, I will ask you ladies, what can we do to safeguard Sapphire's life during her transition?"

All three stood at the same time and moved toward them. Nicolae felt no threat from them and could do nothing but admire the beauty from which his Sapphire had spawned. Rayne took one more step than her sisters, then leaned forward and kissed his cheek. "You keep her safe, and we will seek the answer."

Nicolae nodded. "I promise, unless there is more activity from Ion that I must address for the safety of all, I will not leave her side, until this is done."

Garrison cleared his throat loudly. "Is *that* really necessary?"

Rayne laughed.

Sapphire groaned.

And Nicolae was completely in love with her *and* her family.

****

"It's hard to believe I've only known you since this morning."

Nicolae nodded and adjusted his pillow. "I know. But then today has seemed years long."

Sapphire laughed. "My family will have that effect on you." She snuggled into him, wishing he'd get over his fears of hurting her and get naked.

"I like your family. A lot."

"They like you, too. Even Daddy. He just doesn't want to show it." She slid across him, determined to make him make a move. When he only lifted a brow at her, she groaned. "You're not playing nice."

"I'm trying to respect your father's wishes."

Sapphire sat up and looked down at him with a frown. "What are you talking about? What wishes?"

Nicolae grinned. "He cornered me while you were helping your mom and aunts clean up and asked me to respect you enough to keep my paws off of you."

Horrified, Sapphire couldn't immediately find her voice. When she finally did, she sputtered a curse word, making Nicolae laugh. She didn't think it was funny at all. "Did he actually use the word *paws*?"

"He did, but at least he was smiling when he said it."

"What is *wrong* with him? My dad is never disrespectful!"

"He's being a dad. I don't hold it against him."

Sapphire wasn't feeling quite as generous toward her father at the moment, but she loved him too much to say so out loud. "Well, he should be ashamed." She slid back across Nicolae's chest, and wiggled around, hoping to get a reaction. When his arms captured her and his eyes turned to gold, she knew she had him.

"You are playing with fire," he growled. He took a deep breath and held it until his eyes returned to normal. When he exhaled, he shook his head. "I promised."

Sapphire flung herself off him, bit her bottom lip, and then smiled. "Be right back!" She jumped from the bed and ran down the stairs to dig her extra pairs of handcuffs from the kitchen drawer where she kept them. She tucked each set within her palms and closed her fingers around them. She ran back up the stairs, took a flying leap, landed upon his chest and, to her delight, caught him by surprise.

She knew *that* wouldn't happen often.

She handcuffed one wrist and slapped the other end to one of the wooden slats that made up her headboard, before she stopped and grinned into his stunned eyes. "You may have promised, but I didn't."

He didn't fight her or pull against the restraints as she took his other arm and pulled it above his head. This time she took her time, delighted he was going along with her, and not resisting her idea of a way to play.

"You know I could either break the headboard or turn into my wolf and slide right out of these, right?"

Sapphire frowned since she hadn't *actually* thought of that. She remained straddling his chest and looked down. "Are you going to break my bed?"

Nicolae shook his head. "Nope."

She laughed. "Are you going to turn into your wolf and slip out of my restraints?"

He grinned. "Not yet."

She giggled. "Good, because now that your *paws* can't touch me, I'm going to *touch* you!"

Nicolae's blue eyes began to transform with sunbursts of gold, but she watched him struggle until he was completely in control. "I'm not sure how long I'll last before I have to tell you to stop."

Sapphire leaned forward and kissed him hard. "I'm in charge here. I'll tell *you* when I have to stop."

Nicolae laughed so hard he nearly knocked her off his chest. When he had himself under control, his eyes sobered. "I would give anything to take this to its natural conclusion, but we can't. Not until you transform and are strong enough to handle both man and beast."

She took a great breath and then slid down him. "Tell me, what is the worst you could do to me?"

Nicolae shook his head. "I don't know. That's what scares me."

Sapphire looked deeply into his eyes and nodded. "Okay, you get to decide when we stop. But I'm just letting you know now, I want all of you, for now as a man, but later, when I am fully transformed, as the wolf."

He closed his eyes and threw back his head and his howl went right though her. Everything inside of her quaked with need, and she was certain neither of them would have to wait much longer to fulfill her demand. She studied him as his eyes returned to normal, and wondered if she was being fair.

She kissed him gently and slid from his body to sit at his side. "Transform and slide out of the cuffs. Then lie beside me and let me fall asleep petting you."

Surprise lit his eyes and then understanding. "You are too precious for words."

"And you, my wolf, hold my heart." She shook her head. "And frustrate me to no end."

Nicolae transformed and rolled onto his side without

responding. Sapphire worked the T-shirt from his wolf's body and then pulled the deflated jeans and boxers away from him. She stretched out beside him and ran her fingers through his fine coat, and marveled at its softness. He stretched his massive neck and licked her hand, before settling on his side to stare at her. Knowing she'd teased him enough, she turned away and banked the small lamp on her bedside table. Not that it made any difference.

Sapphire suddenly felt the chill of the room and wiggled around enough to get between her sheets and comforter, knowing he'd need nothing to keep him warm. She leaned over once more and kissed his head, just as she would have kissed Ellie's, then settled onto her side facing away from him.

She felt his body jerk on the bed and her own heart rate increase when the howl of a lone wolf sounded through the walls of her cabin. She turned to him, and he touched her face gently with his hand. He was once again a man. "Don't worry. It isn't Ion. Just go to sleep. I'm here."

Sapphire settled back and watched with her night vision as he moved over her to swipe his lips gently across hers, before he too lay back down. But she couldn't go to sleep without asking, "Is it her?"

Nicolae said nothing for a moment, but finally filled the quiet with one word. "Yes."

"Does she know about us?" Sapphire asked, ashamed she was afraid.

He pulled her to him, still keeping the comforter and sheets between them, and Sapphire remembered he'd now be completely naked. "Get under the covers. It's getting colder."

"I'm fine. My body regulates itself."

"Well, that will be handy."

He chuckled. "Yeah, it is. And I don't think she does. I don't want her near you until you've transformed. And preferably not even then."

"Will she try to kill me?"

Nicolae pulled her even closer. "I will never let that happen. Rest now. Tomorrow is another day with your family." He let that hang and then added, "And we both know how exhausting that can be."

Sapphire grinned. "I think my dad is holding Ellie hostage just to make sure we come back tomorrow."

"He's a smart man."

Sapphire giggled and reached out to cup his face, before leaning forward for a final kiss. "Good night, Nicolae."

"Good night, my brave beauty."

Chapter Twelve

Clouds hung low over the mountain, obliterating vision. The air held a crispness that threatened snow or worse. Sapphire held her coffee cup in both hands as she faced the whiteness from her front porch, realizing, though her vision penetrated the darkness of night, it did nothing for fog. The sound of the door closing at her back made her sigh.

"Is she out there?"

Nicolae slid uncloaked arms around her and pulled her back, against his bare chest. She inhaled the scent of her own shampoo and wondered when her body, too, would stop feeling the cold penetrating her thick jacket. She held the handle of her coffee cup away from them as she turned within his arms.

"No. She is not near."

"How can you be sure?"

Nicolae leaned down enough to bury his nose in her hair and then pulled back to look into her eyes. "There's little ice balls forming on your lashes."

Sapphire sighed again, this time with contentment. Not only was she with the one who held her heart, his warmth was now warming her as well. "You haven't answered my question. Tell me about her."

She felt his minute jerk, and knew she'd hit on a sore subject, but knew too he always told her what she needed to know. "Just who she is as a human. What she does. If she's in love with you."

Nicolae's mirth-filled chuckle was sharp. "Sabia loves

no one but Sabia. She is a diva of the highest rank and spends her days plotting to become the Alpha Female. Her brother always took care of all her needs, as she has never had the disposition to work with others. She has anger-management issues...*to put it mildly.* If Ion had sired a successor, the plan was for Sabia and me to begin a new pack so she'd still retain an Alpha place and title. Eventually, it was expected that we'd merge the two packs again, once we had mature pups."

"You would have been Alpha either way."

Nicolae ignored her statement and loosened his hold enough to take the steaming cup from her hand to place it on the porch railing. "I don't want you to scald yourself."

"Thanks. I guess it wouldn't hurt you?"

He grinned and pulled her back against him. "Only for a minute." He kissed her nose.

"Tell me about Lycanthrope packs. Are they all related? Are they like the average wolf pack in hierarchy and rules?"

Nicolae smiled at her. "Thank you for not saying *normal* wolf packs, and to answer your question...yes *and* no. Unlike the average wolf pack, each adult Lycan member isn't required to be a blood relative. It did start out that way, way back when, to avoid the chance of inbreeding. But our numbers have dwindled so drastically over the last century, our only safety is having many mature males to protect the pack, regardless of their line. Even mature males born within the pack are no longer required to leave, to search for alternate packs with untapped bloodlines for mate-able females." He looked at her with sadness. "There just aren't many left, and none left on this continent, as far as I know. This has further depleted our numbers."

"So if I can live through the change, another new bloodline is available to you and your kind."

"That has nothing to do with my wanting you."

She nuzzled against his bare chest, loving his natural scent, before laying her head against him. "You're deflecting."

He rolled his eyes and shook his head slightly, obviously uncomfortable with the direction the conversation had taken. "Yes. It could make a great difference. But I will not have you thinking it has anything to do with my feelings for you. My *need* for you."

"Tell me about Sabia."

Nicolae shook his head harder this time, as his eyes sharpened in anger. "I don't want to talk about her."

Sapphire reached up and gently slid the back of her fingers against his cheek in a caress. "I am not pushing you out of idle curiosity, I need to know." His sigh was so deep it nearly took her off her feet.

"I know."

"So tell me, and I'll never ask again."

"I never mated with her."

Relief washed through Sapphire, but only until her next thought. "But she wishes to mate with you. And expects it as her right."

"Yes. She has tried to…entice me. On more than one occasion."

"Is she beautiful?"

"Not as beautiful as you, but yes."

"Has she come to you while she was in estrus?"

He hesitated. Then, "Yes."

"How did you resist?"

Nicolae pulled her back a little to look down at her. "Why all *these* questions?"

Sapphire studied the beauty of his face and eyes and knew the magnificence of his form. She understood the she-wolf's reasons to resent not only the loss of high position among their kind, but the loss of the wolf/man as well. *She* couldn't understand any woman or she-wolf putting position above desire for Nicolae.

"Because I need to know how deep her desire for you goes. How her mind works when she feels something has been taken from her. If ever the time comes when I must fight her, I need to know everything about her. Most importantly, to what lengths she will go to get you back."

"That isn't her choice."

"You said it was always the female's choice."

He chuckled. "You are tenacious. *What I said* is it is the female's choice to accept or reject a male. Not that she got to dictate whether he wanted her to begin with."

"So males reject females who want them?"

Nicolae shook his head. "Rarely, but there is me." He grinned at Sapphire. "I may very well be the first."

"What if we go talk to her and explain what is happening."

"There is no talking to Sabia. She talks and expects others to follow along."

"Maybe I could try, woman to woman."

"She would eat you alive. Literally."

"That would make her a murderer. You said that never happens except in self-defense."

"She would consider you a threat to the life she expects to live. She'd justify it. Even if we had to put her down for it, that wouldn't undo what she will have already done to you. We can't risk that possibility."

"You make this all sound impossible. Your pack may fight us. Sabia certainly will. Why would you give up everything you expected your life to be, just for me?"

Nicolae dropped his arms only to grasp her jaw and pull her to him for a kiss that stole her breath and ignited her body. When he pulled back, he continued to hold her so she was forced to look into his golden eyes. "Because you are the life *I want* to have. Because you stood up to your family and staked your claim on me when they would have happily put a bullet into my heart. Because I can't imagine going through another day of life without you by my side. You are everything to me, Sapphire. *Everything!*"

Sapphire shook with the desire his huskily spoken words evoked and pulled his face back to her own. She delved into their kiss with her heart and soul, and the wolf within her grew as a growl in her throat. She didn't fight it, willing to embrace what was meant to be without fright, without hesitation. The sharp pain that hit her in the abdomen was as surprising as it was sudden. She gasped and broke from him to stumble back a few paces.

Nicolae was at her side immediately, but Sapphire couldn't straighten from her doubled-over position. He swooped her up into his arms and carried her into the house.

"Hold on!"

He took her to the couch and placed her on it gently. Sapphire could do nothing but roll into as tight a ball as she could, as tears spilled from her eyes. The pain was agonizing, ripping through her like a double-edged knife. "My mom," was all she could get past her lips, but she knew Nicolae would understand.

"Already called her on your cell, didn't even have to speak. She's on her way, she said her sisters too."

He knelt before her, his eyes filled with a panic she doubted had ever been in them before. She tried to smile but another sharp pain hit her, and she could do nothing but scream.

****

Nicolae's heart raced with panic, his eyes filled with terrified tears. Though he never remembered crying even once in his life, he understood now the agony one faced with the fear of losing a mate. He listened intently for the sounds of a car on gravel, and was startled when sparking mist came down from the ceiling instead, encircling them both. His heart nearly stopped until he realized it must be Sapphire's aunt. Nicolae held his breath as he watched, hoping Destiny's presence did something, *anything*, to alleviate Sapphire's suffering. When she continued to moan and cry in pain, he couldn't hold back any longer.

"Do something!"

The mist stopped moving around them to slide by him, and it felt as if a hand had caressed his cheek. Before he could react, Destiny's essence blanketed Sapphire, and then they were both gone.

Nicolae stared at the empty couch as his mind tried to catch up to what he was seeing. Fury filled him that Sapphire had been taken when she needed him most. He threw up his head as a terrified man, transformed, and howled with anger and loss as the wolf. His scratched the boxers off his much leaner hips and headed to the door. Finding it closed, he turned to the large front window and jumped through it, not caring about the damage to the property or himself. He had neither the time nor the will to transform back into the man. If her family thought to use their magic to take the wolf from her against her will, his Sapphire would be lost.

He ran in the direction he knew her parents lived, and though he could not see very far ahead through the thick fog, his footing was sure, his intent defined, and his fear they would take her from him, for all eternity, mammoth. His heart pounded, his breaths labored, and he pushed his body to its limits. When another wolf jumped in his path, he skidded to a halt, and his furry intensified.

"Get out of my way, Sabia!"

She stood her ground with legs locked, head lowered to shoulder level, ears pinned back, and teeth flashing as she growled, *"Where do you go in such a hurry, Alpha?"*

Nicolae knew he couldn't answer in truth, or pass her and lead her to Sapphire, or her family—no matter their intent. He forced himself to relax slightly and was relieved when she did as well. "I look for Ion, she-wolf! You are interfering!" he spat back, hoping to intimidate her.

Sabia's head danced in denial. "You do no such thing. Ion is out of your reach."

Her words jolted him. Nicolae transformed and protocol demanded she do so as well. Seconds later, as if trying to decide if she would, she did, but the insult was there all the same. The beauty of her face was lost to the evil intent in her eyes, and Nicolae wondered how he'd ever entertained mating with her.

"What are you saying? Have you hidden him?"

Sabia laughed with confidence. "You are such a fool, Alpha. Do you think I would answer that true?"

He advanced on her and took her thin but muscular arm in a tight grip. Instead of fear, her eyes reflected desire, and he released her and stepped back, disgusted with everything she was. "You will answer me true, female. And you will do so now."

She pressed her lips together and then sighed. "I wish no fight with you, Alpha. Give me what I want, and I will give you all you need. Including the whereabouts of my brother. Believe me, this is information you will wish to know."

Nicolae couldn't respond to that. His answers would only anger her, and he knew her well enough to know he'd get nowhere with an angered Sabia. "Why are you not with the pack? You were to follow Jaspon, it was a direct demand from an Alpha."

Her eyes shined with laughter. "You are too easy to read, my Alpha, and we both know I will eventually get what I want. But I will play your game and answer, *only* because we all need you to quit wasting time and do your job. I *allowed* Jaspon to follow *me* back to the pack, and he did so like a good little puppy, but once I was there Heburue thought to take me against my will.

"Because you have failed in your duties, in more than just mating with me, my brother followed us there. He is nearly completely mad now but had a moment of lucidity. It only lasted long enough for him to see I was endangered. He killed Heburue's human, but almost immediately, Heburue awoke and went after other members of the pack. We all scattered, so I have no idea who made it and who didn't. But there are at least two rabid Lycanthropes now. And it is all your fault."

The stunning news nearly took Nicolae's feet from beneath him. As desperate as he was to get to Sapphire, there was no choice but to leave Mystic Mountain and return to whatever was left of the pack. His heart bled, his soul cried out in anguish, and his wolf howled in outrage and mourning. When his head lowered and Sabia was nearly flush against him, he knew it might be a very long time before he saw his Sapphire again.

If ever.

****

"Where's Nicolae?"

Sapphire could hardly speak, but the pain had eased some since Haven pushed the vial of morphine into her veins. She looked around the room, not certain where she was.

"We don't know, honey. He was with you when we aided Destiny in bringing you to us, but we've heard nothing from him since. I'm sure he'll find his way here."

"Where is here?"

Rayne pushed the hair away from Sapphire's forehead before placing a cold wet cloth on her fevered brow. "We are at Tom and Destiny's cabin. We thought it best to bring you here. Many of us need to fit in here to assist you. And, it brings us closer to the ceremonial grounds, should we need to be there to help you through this…situation."

Sapphire swallowed and felt another sharp punch within her stomach, but the drug had dulled the pains considerably. "Please don't take my wolf." The sadness in Rayne's eyes was replaced with assurance, but Sapphire knew her mother well, and the bravado was just that. "Mom, I'm serious. You can't take my wolf."

"I can make no promises, Sapphire-mine. You are my child, and I will fight to save you *no matter* what it takes. You cannot ask me to let you die, so you may be that which you aren't."

"But it *is* what I am. Don't you understand? I cannot be anything else and be happy."

"You're asking too much of us, Sapphire. Especially of your mother."

Sapphire glanced over to see her father standing in the doorway, and her heart sank. She knew her mother was always his highest concern, but she knew the loss of one of his children would devastate him. She shuddered at the thought of giving up her wolf, of never knowing the joy she experienced in her dreams, but mostly, of losing Nicolae. If she could not transform, they could never make a life together. She looked up at her mother, and the tearful understanding in Rayne's eyes took any objections she'd thought to make and turned them to dust. "If you must take my wolf to keep me, then do so, but know I would rather die."

The choking gasp from her father before Garrison turned and left the room only served to compound her guilt, but there was nothing she could do about it. Destiny and Haven entered the room as Rayne settled herself on the bed at Sapphire's side. "I know what it feels like to love so deeply. I could never imagine living without my man." She glanced back at her sisters and then turned back to Sapphire. "We all do."

Sapphire didn't have to look away to know her aunts agreed. She already knew this. "Then how can you ask me to live without mine?"

It took a moment before Rayne could answer; her struggles were obvious to see. Sapphire gave her that time, as another slice of pain came and went. When Rayne seemed to have herself in hand, she lifted and rubbed Sapphire's hair between her forefinger and thumb.

"We will do everything we can to save your wolf. Everything. But if it's a choice, I would rather die myself than let you go."

Haven stepped forward and placed her hand on her sister's shoulder. "I think I've found a way so no one needs," she glanced at Sapphire, "or *wants* to die."

Sapphire knew her mother and Destiny turned to Haven, though her aunt was looking at her instead of them. "How?"

Haven held up a small book and handed it to Rayne. "I called the aunts yesterday, just as they were about to board the plane to Athens, then Gavin, once Aunt Soleli told me about a small box of things Momma had left for us. She said she'd kept it, until she knew we'd need it. Gavin located it in our Los Angeles house and overnighted it so it would arrive first thing this morning. The box arrived only seconds before you called us about Sapphire."

"Those women are something," Destiny said.

Sapphire couldn't figure out if that was a compliment or an insult, but she was more interested to find out what help the little book might be. "What is it?"

Haven smiled. "It's the diary of one of our ancestor aunts, who fell in love with a werewolf."

"You're kidding!"

Haven grinned at Destiny. "I'm not."

"Do they have anything else of Mom's we should know about?"

Rayne looked up then and smiled. "When Mom came to me the day we saved Gavin, she told me things happened when they were supposed to. At least that's what I remember. It's been so long ago now, her exact words have faded with time. I'm sure we weren't supposed to get this until now."

Silence filled the room, and Sapphire knew her mother and aunts were taking a moment to mourn the long ago loss of their mother. She didn't mind giving them time. Losing Rayne Cavanaugh-White would devastate Sapphire and her sisters...and the morphine was making her sleepy.

"Well, onward," Rayne said, breaking the silence. "Let's see what is what."

Sapphire's eyes drooped and she felt herself falling. She jerked and forced them back open to watch as her mother opened the little book. Heavy eyelids caused repeated labored blinking as her mother turned page after page, then, settled in to silently read. As much as Sapphire wanted to ask what her mother had found, she couldn't overcome the need to close her eyes, and finally gave up the fight.

Sapphire dashed as fast as she could, knowing her time was running short. She jumped from one mossy rock to another then skittered across the narrow stream, barely even wetting her paws. The cracking of small branches and snapping twigs warned her the monster was closing in fast. Fear had her heart pumping painfully and she could only wonder why Nicolae had left her unprotected and broken hearted.

As if her thoughts of him had stirred magic within the air, he was suddenly there. Her heart jumped, this time in glee, but she knew the threat was still near, gaining on her, and now Nicolae was in danger as well. She wanted to nuzzle him, wanted to rub up against him from nose to tail, but all she could do was follow his lead as he moved ahead of her and turned in a different direction than the path she'd been taking. When he stopped abruptly and swung around with a growl, she knew the threat had caught up with them. Instead of the monster she'd envisioned, the wolf who'd been chasing her was a female, though the snarling, growling mouth made the she-wolf look as if she might be a deadlier threat.

Her.

Sapphire knew it was she, Sabia, *the Alpha Female-wanna-be, who would challenge Sapphire's right to mate with Nicolae. She felt hackles rise along her back and stepped ahead of him, determined to show the she-wolf she would not give up her wolf without a fight. She met growl for growl and stood her ground when Sabia took a menacing step forward.*

Sabia took another slow step before leaping. Prepared, Sapphire met her mid-air with mouth opened, and murder in her heart.

"Sapphire, *baby*, wake up!"

Chapter Thirteen

Nicolae left his heart behind and ran for nearly a day and a half at full speed, stopping only long enough for an occasional drink from a stream. Sabia stayed with him, periodically grumbling he needed to slow down, or to state she was hungry or tired, or to raise her tail teasingly at him when he stopped for the required hydration. A small storm moved in, then moved back out, soaking them, but Nicolae didn't mind, he appreciated the cool down. The sun was high, but the air cooled as a front moved in by the time he reached the clearing where his pack met for their mate meetings and any other pack business.

He stopped along the tree line and inhaled repeatedly as he turned in each direction. As far as he could tell, he and Sabia were the only wolves in the immediate vicinity, which wasn't surprising. All who could, would have gone back to their daily lives. If there were some who couldn't, the others would know about it, and he needed that information as soon as possible. Nicolae opened the pack's telepath-way to alert the pack he was back and at the clearing, though he was concerned doing so would also alert Ion and Heburue. There was no choice. He needed the pack to assemble, not only see who was left in the area, but also to determine if any more were infected, or dead.

Sabia changed, smiling with pride as she happily displayed her naked body. "Now that I have you alone again, I will give you one more chance. We have time before the others come. You can solidify your place as Alpha, *now*, by mating with me before they come. I am willing to do so in either form. It is your choice."

Nicolae forced himself not to react in any way, refusing to display his human form to her until Jaspon brought him the clothing he'd requested while communicating with the pack. To say *anything* negative to Sabia at this time, whether with his human voice or telepathically, would only cause him more problems. He was *already* concerned the pack would be questioning his role since he hadn't taken care of Ion before this latest disaster. *"I need all my strength, Sabia. There will be time for such as that later."*

"You do not question why I changed my mind and am willing to give you another chance?"

Though he didn't *need* to ask, as he already knew she desired him above all others, he also knew she would tell him anyway. Figuring it would give her confidence—that he was possibly considering a union between them—and keep her busy so she didn't continue to attempt to tantalize him, he settled back against a tree trunk and looked over at her. *"So why did you decide to give me another chance?"*

She pressed her lips together, her annoyance clear. "You insult me, Alpha. Change and let me look upon you as a man."

"Sabia, I told you I am too tired, and I need my strength. This way I am less tempted to deplete my strength further," he lied.

She smiled and settled herself at his side. "I do not mind opening myself to you as I am, with you as you are. It has always been a secret desire of mine."

Nicolae was shocked and more than dismayed. There were only a handful of rules that were steel-clad within their world, but to have human and beast mate was as taboo as it got. He swallowed, relieved another member of the pack responded for him.

"Shame on you, Sabia Ilie!" Halivia Ilie hissed, as she approached her daughter with clothing, so Sabia could cover her body. "Put these on and shame this family no more!"

Sabia had the grace to look contrite, though Nicolae didn't believe she felt any shame at all. Not for a minute. But the elder former Alpha female wasn't done, as she turned angry eyes on Nicolae.

"And shame on you as well, Alpha! Though I don't believe you deserve the title. Your failure to stop my son, as well as your hesitancy to mate with my daughter, tells me you are too weak to take the reins from my family! But we have no other choices now, do we?"

She turned angrily and walked away, and Nicolae wanted to call her back and tell her to choose Jaspon or one of the other remaining males for the position. He'd never wanted the job, had only been willing to do so to please those who had raised and cared for him. He wanted nothing but his woman, who even now he feared was dying without him there to comfort her or try to save her. But Nicolae couldn't walk away until he knew the rabid brothers were dealt with. If nothing else, he owed that much to the pack that had taken him in.

"I told you they'd be angry you haven't mated with me yet. Now even my mother has turned against you. And she always thought your *scat* didn't stink! Guess you fell off that pedestal everyone put you up on!"

She pulled the dress over her head and glared at him before running to catch up with her mother. Now that her father and brother were no longer around to support her, Sabia knew which side of the bread she needed to butter, at least until she could secure a mate who suited her...which meant him. Nicolae sighed, knowing they were all going to turn against him if he didn't get this rabies situation under control...and soon. He thanked Jaspon when jeans and a T-shirt were dropped before him. After transforming, he quickly pulled on the jeans, but once he looked up, he knew all eyes were on him, anyway.

Sabia lifted a brow from across the field and smiled with satisfaction. Her mother's gaze was more speculative and accessing. The other mated as well as unattached females were clearly as interested in checking him out, though they were at least trying to be a little less obvious about it. Nicolae blew out a breath of frustration. He knew their interest had little to do with him, his looks, *or* endowment, but more to do with bringing new blood into the several nonrelated lines within the remaining small pack. Mating with Sabia, first, was expected, to make her his official mate and an Alpha. But he'd also been raised to expect to join with any other female who wished it. Growing up, the obligation was one he'd never given thought to, as the couplings would have meant nothing more than doing his duty. But that had changed. He no longer had a desire to touch another female besides the one he feared he'd never be able to touch again.

Refusing to accept that until he had to, Nicolae glanced at Jaspon. "I guess I need to get this over with. Let's go."

Jaspon followed slightly behind him, proper protocol when with an Alpha, but Nicolae felt it an outdated rule. He slowed his steps, glanced back, and signaled for the next Alpha heir to walk by his side. The slight shake of Jaspon's head was surprising, but then maybe not. With things being so out of control, Nicolae understood and allowed the male to follow as he'd been taught.

The pack members walked forward also, to create their version of a Circle of Trust. Nicolae took a moment to see who all was present. Besides Jaspon, Sabia, and her mother, Halivia, seven female members stood silently, and Nicolae felt the first stirrings of fear. He looked to Jaspon, knowing his action was something of a slight to Halivia, but right now he needed answers, not condemnation. "Where are the others?"

Jaspon shrugged. "Heburue and Ion are lost to us, as I'm sure you know, but still remain a threat. Kaspor, Teagan, and Domeno are on the hunt for them and left me to protect our females. As for Keeleen and the others, I have no idea. They have disappeared and have not been heard from. We are expecting the worse."

Nicolae nodded, swallowed, then looked to the females who now depended entirely on him unless, and until, those whose mates were currently hunting or missing, returned. "I am sorry I have failed you and understand you may wish to replace me as Alpha. I will step down now and hand the title to Jaspon if that is what you wish."

"Are you a coward as well, then, Nicolae Lupei?"

Having expected Sabia's mother to be the only one to respond, he was already facing her before she asked the question. "I am as afraid as you are, but, no. I am not saying I will hand over the responsibility of capturing and killing those who threaten us. I am willing to do my duty without the title."

Surprise and approval settled in the elder woman's eyes. "Then you are still our choice as Alpha. Without the other males here, and with only the two of you before us alive and well, we cannot take any more chances. You or Jaspon must mate with each of the fertile females this day...with me as well. We cannot allow the loss of either of you to end our line if you should fall and fail again, Nicolae. I will take Jaspon first, and Sabia was always yours to mate with. Afterward, the others will take their turn, if their mate has not already impregnated them. We must all be carrying young before you depart again."

Nicolae was rocked by her decree. Everything within him protested with anger and resentment. He struggled with the howl of rage that pressed against his throat. He bled tears within but dared not let them show. As much as he wanted to deny them all, to tell them to go to hell, he couldn't, because she was right. No matter where his heart lay, his body belonged to the pack, and his soul to the continuation of their kind.

Sapphire!
Sapphire!
Sapphire!

Moving like a prisoner being led to his death, Nicolae slowly removed his jeans and then changed into his wolf. One after another, the rest of the pack undressed and did the same, until he was facing she-wolves who seemed no more eager than he. He understood and felt bad for those who were already mated, or were looking forward to a mating. Halivia stepped forward and crossed the large ring. She barked sharply once, making Jaspon jump. He moved forward and met her in the center of the ring. Nicolae turned his head away, not interested in witnessing the mating, then turned back, because he had already insulted them enough.

Halivia circled Jaspon and then stopped. He then circled around her and placed his nose at her tail. She immediately swung around, backed a step, then lowered her head and growled. When she settled, Jaspon approached her slowly, taking his time as he walked around her, periodically glancing back to see if she would turn and nip at him once he'd again gotten to her flank. When she remained still, he turned his body so he was facing her tail. This time she lifted it and allowed it to fall to the side, flagging him that she was receptive.

Privacy while the mating ritual was enacted wasn't something his wolf had ever given thought to before. He'd witnessed them periodically since being taken in by the pack. This time, he found it hard to watch, knowing it wasn't a natural act of selection by his kind, but an act of desperation on the part of the pack to survive.

It felt like prostitution.

He started to turn away, but Halivia's sharp bark indicated they'd broken apart, and that it was Nicolae's turn to do his duty. He inhaled deeply and turned back, watching as the elder she-wolf approached her daughter to nudge her.

Sabia needed no nudging. She pranced to the center of the circle and turned so all could see her beauty before facing Nicolae fully. She lifted her head with pride, awaiting him. Nicolae knew he could walk away, and likely be attacked by her and her mother, and maybe even the others. He didn't fear them. But he knew he'd end up hurting them, or worse, kill them, if a fight ensued. He couldn't do that.

"You hesitate to take me, Alpha? Why do you insult me so?"

Nicolae cringed at Sabia's taunt. He knew he couldn't continue to deny the inevitable, and he'd pay dearly for this slight in the years to come even if he didn't stay with the pack. He moved forward and stood before her. *"I will ask you again to take Jaspon as your mate. He will be honored to join with you and make you his Alpha when I leave this place. I will leave the title to him, without reserve."*

"You will do your duty! Your seed belongs to us! We took you in and raised you. We fed you. I fed you! Besides, if Jaspon mates with us all, the next generation will be forced into a first generation inbreeding, and we are all but doomed!"

Nicolae closed his eyes and nodded. He knew Halivia was right. There *really* was no choice at all. *"I will do this, then, and I will seek those who threaten us all, but once that is done, I will leave this pack and never return."*

Not a sound stirred; even the wind stopped blowing. Nicolae knew he'd shocked them. With so much else to worry over, he hated making his stand now, but his life would never be his own if he stayed. Since no one said a word, Halivia glanced at her daughter and nodded.

The ritual only took seconds to commence since Sabia was more than eager to take center stage. She circled him, pranced in front of him, rubbed against him, then lifted her tail and backed into him. He looked at her engorged vulva and smelled her scent. The wolf in him emerged as his penis extended beyond the fur sheath that protected it. He mounted her and rammed himself forward with more anger than desire. Sabia's yelp indicated his roughness, and his anger turned internal. It wasn't her fault he desired another, and in turn was repulsed by her. No matter what he'd told the others, no matter what he'd told himself, he just couldn't continue with this farce.

Abruptly, before there was time for blood to completely fill his *bulbus glandis*, he pulled out.

Nicolae turned and ran as fast as he could to the closest stream, choking on the vomit climbing up his throat. He knew the other females would be confused by his sudden desertion, and Sabia would be howling in anger at his abrupt departure, but just like the most male part of him, everything within his soul was tainted with the stain of her blood.

He *knew* the matings weren't his choice to make, but that made no difference in his need to run. As a man, he could have gotten away with the lack of desire Sabia failed to inspire in him. He wouldn't have gotten erect and been able to perform. But as the wolf, he'd only had to smell her and see her swollen and dripping vulva, and the rest was nothing more than a chemical reaction within his male wolf brain.

Only it wasn't that simple.

His brain wasn't completely that of an animal, even when he was the wolf. He was also equal parts man. And though he'd penetrated Sabia out of obligation to the pack, he hadn't been able to force himself to push in far enough for his *bulbus glandis* to take hold, swell, and lock them together to complete the copulatory tie.

It made no difference that he hadn't given her his sperm.

At least not to him.

He'd still joined with her. He'd sold his soul to keep his family's future secure and had still failed when it came down to it because he didn't love her, or the others, only his beautiful Sapphire. Though he knew, even as he stepped into the stream to wash the she-wolf's blood from his body, even if Sapphire lived, he could never look her in the face again.

The sound of another wolf approaching rapidly finally penetrated his turmoil, and the sounds of the rushing water. He looked up, fully expected Sabia to launch into an attack, but the sight of Heburue breaching the tree line with red eyes and a foaming mouth nearly stopped his heart.

Chapter Fourteen

"She's still out cold."

Sapphire heard their voices and knew her mother and aunts were in the room. She wanted to open her eyes, to move her body, but she couldn't. She tried to moan, to do anything to let them know she could hear them, but every time she tried frustration resulted.

"How do we do this?"

That was her mother's voice. She sounded so tired.

"We have to find Nicolae. I can't believe he ran off like that. He was terrified when I took her from him."

Nicolae, terrified? That doesn't make sense. He isn't afraid of anything.

"Did you explain to him you were bringing her here, so we could help her, Destiny? Or did you do what you always do and just snatch her and disappear?"

"Well, what would you have done? Maybe you should have created a storm and had the wind blow her this way."

"Sisters, I swear, I'll knock your heads together if you don't stop. My daughter's life is in danger."

If she could have, Sapphire would laugh. Her aunts were always picking at each other. According to her mother, they always had. It was like an earlier generational version of Dia and herself. Though there was love, there was just a little bit of angst too. Although now, she realized what she'd felt toward Dia had less to do with personality conflicts, and more to do with the realization she'd blamed Dia for being a part of her own mistake in killing that boy, all those years ago.

"I think she's waking up! I saw her frown."

Sapphire opened her eyes to find three identical faces staring down at her. She looked from her mother to her aunts, and as they moved back, the array of intravenous drips at the four corners of the bed. She looked toward her mother again. "What's going on?" Rayne smiled down at her with a gentleness that told Sapphire just how sick she was.

"We have kept you in a coma for the past week, in an attempt to keep the changes your body is experiencing from killing you with the shock of excruciating pain."

Sapphire looked over to her aunts as she tried to lift her hands. The realization she was restrained sent her heartbeat into overdrive, which was as evident in the increased beeps of the monitor somehow attached to her as the hard thumping within her chest. She breathed through the horror of being tied down as she tried not to let her family see her panic. She'd expected to go through the change with Nicolae at her side, guiding her, not being treated as a threat to the ones she loved. Needing him more than ever, she sought her mother again. "So I've changed?"

Rayne shook her head. "No, sweetheart. From what we've deduced, it's a process, not an event. At least not yet." She settled against the bed. "I know you can't stand being tied down, and I think it may be safe for us to release you, at least for a while. But I need you to understand that we'll have to tie you back down soon."

"Why?"

Destiny stepped forward, drawing Sapphire's attention. "I will tell you everything we know, if that's okay with you. This is hard on us all, but your mom most of all."

Sapphire nodded. "Okay."

Destiny smiled. "We read the diary our great-aunts, *in their infinite wisdom*, decided we didn't need to see until now. We all had an ancestor who was like you in many ways. She was independent, and brave, and didn't use the magic that was hers."

"I've had my reasons," Sapphire said quietly, knowing her family had always wondered.

Haven stepped forward. "I'm sure she had hers, too."

Tears filled Rayne's eyes. "Can you tell us? It might be important."

Moisture flooded her own eyes as her shame came to the surface, but she nodded. "The only time I ever used it, I killed someone."

Sapphire could tell she'd shocked all three of the women whose purpose had always been to do only good.

After several seconds of silence passed, Rayne shook her head. "That isn't possible. You've never used your magic even though we've all felt the strength of it in you since the day of your ascension."

"Your mom's right, Sapphire. The power within you has always radiated to others. I am energized by it in the same way a storm fills me with power." Haven said, smiling.

Destiny stepped closer. "And my senses are filled to capacity and are more defined even when I'm not trying to use them when you are around. What you have is special, pure. It would not be so if you had killed someone. I would feel the stain on your soul. You must be mistaken."

Sapphire wished that were true. She'd give *anything* for that to be true. Shaking her head, she expelled a breath, knowing she might as well confess all, just in case she didn't survive what was coming. "I did. It isn't a mistake. I killed him with angry magic."

"Tell us exactly what happened."

Sapphire hated having to tell her mother what she'd done, but it had to be said so they would understand why she hated magic so much. "There was a kid who always taunted us in school. Steven Hart was his name. He started kindergarten with us, went all the way to high school in a class with at least one of us or with our cousins. He was equally mean to all, but he made fun of Dia more than any anyone." She paused, swallowed, and then forced the words to continue. "He said he was going to do something really awful to her, and I pointed at him and told him to die. He did. That night."

Relief filled all their faces. Sapphire couldn't believe their reaction, but she could think of nothing more to say.

Rayne took her hand, reminding her she was still restrained. "Honey, I remember when that kid died. You didn't do that. He had a heart condition that was revealed during an autopsy."

Sapphire shook her head. "I did it, though. I stopped his heart."

Haven stepped forward and took her other hand. "No, sweetheart, you didn't. I was with Logan when the kid was brought in. We both examined him, and though I couldn't tell the hospital, I knew he was going to die."

"Couldn't you stop it?"

Haven pressed her lips together. "No. I can only heal when my gift will allow for it. It wouldn't that time. I think it was because, had he lived and grown into adulthood, he may have been a really bad man. I tried really hard because it was a child, and I didn't know then, what I know now—if wickedness is within the heart and mind of the one who needs healing, light magic can't fix the problem. It took me years to figure that out because most people are basically good. But not everyone is, and those people aren't meant to be saved with light magic. If they can be saved at all, it must be done with dark forces, and that only encourages rotting of the soul."

"It's true," Rayne added, and then looked up past her head. She smiled gently and nodded. "Steve is here, honey."

Sapphire shook her head. She hadn't seen her mother

connect with a spirit for years, and she wasn't really up to dealing with her doing so now. "Why? Am I about to die? Has he come to mock me?"

Rayne shook her head, amusement in her eyes. "No, honey. He came to tell you it was never you. He died of natural causes and feels blessed to have done so. His soul has grown and matured on the other side, and he is sorry for all the pain he caused others. Because now he is at peace. And says you must be also."

Sapphire took a deep breath and felt years of guilt fall from her own soul. Tears of relief followed, and she struggled against the restraints. She opened her mouth to tell them to release her, but a knife-slashing pain cut through her abdomen. She buckled up as far as her restraints allowed and then fell back against the bed.

"What is it?" Rayne asked, jumping back while reaching forward. "Is she changing this time? Open the morphine, quick!"

Sapphire shook her head from side to side until the pain eased enough for her to gasp, "It's not me! Save Nicolae!"

****

Sapphire awoke, this time able to open her eyes as soon as she was conscious. Unlike before, the room was empty. She inhaled deeply and scanned the immediate area for the scent of her mother, aunts, or any other members of the family, and then realized what she was doing. She closed her eyes and focused on the sounds throughout the house. There was the resonant tap of a branch against a window she believed was located in the kitchen, and she remembered her father warning Uncle Logan the crape myrtle he'd planted a few years before as a gift to the Whitehawk couple was too close to their house. There was another sound, and she smiled, thinking how horrified Aunt Destiny would be to learn a mouse had taken up residence in her pantry, and if she wasn't mistaken, those were potato chips it was nibbling on. Since Destiny and Tom only ate the healthiest of foods, that probably meant Heracles made regular appearances to visit his parents, and undoubtedly ate them out of house and home. Nobody could snack like her cousin and not gain weight. Except, maybe, the additional mice that were now joining the first.

She listened for more noises, but all she heard was the ticking of the large clock hanging above the rock fireplace and chimney that divided the living room and kitchen from wood plank floor to wood plank ceiling, and the steady beep of the monitor in the room she occupied that displayed her heart rate. She inhaled again and realized the fire was dying down as the aged logs took on a different scent when they were reduced to glowing embers.

That all this information was available to her, without her having to move an inch, was astounding, to say the least. But that wasn't the only change happening. She felt strong and alert, even though the small bag hanging at the end of the bed, infusing into the saline drip, indicated she should still be stoned out of her mind. She pushed her lips together and stared at the clearly labeled narcotic, then realized the writing was tiny and just her focusing on it made it magnified.

"Hellooooo!"

Sapphire waited a second before laughing at herself. "Well, it was worth a try… and I'm talking to myself. *Great.* Now I'm going crazy, too."

She tried to tug at the restraints when gravel crunching under tires caught her attention. The slamming of a car door and the sound of someone running toward the house filled her with relief. It was about time! "Somebody get in here and get me out of these damned things before I break the bed!"

The crashing of the front door was unexpected. The face that appeared in her room with a gun pointed at her, seconds later, even more so. Sapphire stared at the middle-aged stranger with eyes so wide they hurt, but he only glanced down at her, at the screaming monitor, and then the restraints, before turning and leaving the room again. The heart monitor, already screaming, went wilder and the muscles in her arms strained until the restraints broke at her wrists. She sat up and tore the others off her ankles as if the three-inch-wide leather bindings were made of string.

It filled her with confusion that her family had left her unattended, but there was still no way she'd allow a thief to steal from them.

Sapphire swung her feet down and had to catch herself when her body immediately tilted toward the floor. She took several breaths and waited for the room to stop spinning, but time was of the essence and waiting until her head was completely clear wasn't an option. She jerked the IV from the back of her hand, wincing when the tape ripping off her skin hurt more than removing the needle. She pulled the sticky pads from her chest, and the monitor flat-lined, putting out an even tone. Fully naked once the sheet hit the floor, she searched the room desperately for something to throw on.

The dresser revealed sweatshirts and pants, and she had them on in a flash. As they apparently belong to one of her male cousins, she had to push up the sleeves and was thankful for the elastic around her ankles. She tied the string to hold the pants up, and then snuck to the door.

And came face to face with the business end of the gun.

He was as surprised as she was and took a step back. "I won't hurt you."

Sapphire should have reacted like the cop she was, or

at least like the animal she was turning into, but she'd never encountered a thief who looked like he was one step away from madness. His eyes darted around the room, bouncing back to her, before darting again. His hair stood on end, as if it hadn't been brushed in weeks. His hands shook, and the barrel of the gun looked more menacing each time he swung it her way.

"How did you get out of the restraints? I had to make sure no one else was around, before I released you. I've already called 911, and they'll have someone here soon. Are you okay? Your eyes are doing funny things."

Sapphire realized the drugs were still affecting her, but knowing others would soon descend on the Whitehawk home, she knew neither one of them could stay like they were. "Please. I'm fine. You don't understand."

Realization lit his eyes, and he stepped back and held the gun higher, his hands shaking furiously now. "You're one of them, aren't you?"

Before Sapphire could ask him what he was talking about he lunged forward and instinct took over. With one swipe of her fist against his jaw, he hit the floor. She stared down at him, unable to believe she'd done it again. Only this time she hadn't used magic.

"And everyone in your family thinks Dia is the one always making trouble."

Sapphire jerked back only to find Heracles staring down at the unconscious man. She swallowed. And wanted to wipe the smile off his face when he looked up. "He broke in."

Heracles nodded. "I can see that."

"He came here for a reason, but I don't know what it is. Worse, he's called the police."

A rare frown crossed Heracles' lips. "That isn't good."

"What are you doing here anyway? And where is everyone?"

Heracles shrugged. "Don't know where they went, but they left a voicemail for me to get right over here and take care of you."

"So they just left?"

Heracles shrugged. "Don't know for sure but probably not. I was sleeping in. When I woke up and saw the message, it showed it was several hours old." He grinned. "But it looks like you are doing just fine."

Sapphire loved her cousin, she assured herself she really did, but she wanted to deck him too. "No, I'm *not* doing fine. An unconscious man is on the floor, a bed with a morphine drip is hanging at its foot, with shredded restraints that could never be explained to *my coworkers* who might arrive at any moment."

Heracles looked at her with a frown. "Well, you don't have to get testy about it." He grinned. "Besides, you look really cute wearing my sweats."

Knowing there was no use expecting Heracles to be anything but who he was, a good guy with a heart of gold *and* a head as hard as a boulder, Sapphire pointed to the man. "Get him out of here and hold him somewhere until I get rid of the police. Hopefully Aunt Haven can fix him. If I didn't kill him, too."

Heracles started to open his mouth, but the sound of sirens cut off whatever it was he'd planned to question. Without another word he lifted the man, threw him over a shoulder, and headed out of the room. Sapphire bit her lip before running to jerk the morphine bag from its stand. She lifted the sheet from the floor and threw it over the bed, covering restraints and all. Then she hurried to the living room and lay across the couch, and awaited the knock, belatedly realizing the stranger had broken in.

"Police! Put your hands where we can see them."

One after another the officers came in, guns raised, eyes intense, and breathing hard. Sapphire raised her hands, glad the large sweatshirt sleeves had fallen, and were now covering her hands. "It's just me guys," she said weakly.

Guns were slowly lowered as Brad crossed to her and stooped in front of the couch. "What's going on? The door's broken, and we got a call that there was someone here being tortured."

Sapphire shook her head, hoping her look of *that's ridiculous* worked. "No. Just me. I'm still trying to recover from the rabies bite. I should have listened to everyone and stayed down longer."

Brad looked at her with brows drawn together. "You look great."

Sapphire laughed, though she kept it light. "Thanks. I think. You don't have to frown when you say it."

The other officers started moving around, and Sapphire sat up a little straighter. "You guys, really, everything here is fine."

"Then who broke the door?"

Sapphire didn't like the doubt in Brad's voice, but she understood it. She'd have reacted the same way. "My cousins are twenty-three-year-old little boys who like to wrestle with each other. They still end up breaking things when they tussle. It's a burden my aunt and uncle deal with all the time."

Brad grinned then. "My brother and I were the same way. Twins?"

Sapphire didn't like to give out family information, but Apollo worked at the fire station, and they likely had that information. Though there was no reason for Brad to ever see it, she didn't want to take any chances. "Triplets, actually."

"Wow."

Sapphire did laugh naturally then. "You have no idea."

Though she didn't want to delay his departure, Sapphire was curious. "How did you guys get here so quickly?"

Brad grimaced. "We were just a couple of miles up the mountain. Got a call this morning that there was more carnage on the road. Thankfully, this time it was only a couple of deer. Looked like they'd been dead for some time though. Well, what was left of them. Best we can figure, they rolled down from the cliff after the last rain. Don't look like they were killed on the road. Someone would have reported it sooner."

Sapphire tried not to let the news upset her, so she attempted a smile. "Well, thanks for coming."

Brad nodded, as if sensing that was his clue to leave. "Okay then…It's good to see you. Hope you can make it back soon. I miss working with my partner."

Sapphire grinned at him more naturally. "I miss it too." She looked at the other officers and realized they were looking at her and Brad with interest. He was, after all, down on one knee. Determined not to roll her eyes at them, she smiled and flashed a wave. "Take care, you guys. I'm sure I'll see you soon."

The other officers made the appropriate responses then filed out before Brad rose and walked to the door. He turned back and shook his head. "Seriously, for a sick woman, you look amazing." He grinned, turned, and minutes later Sapphire heard the squad cars leaving.

"Burden? Our mother loves it when we wrestle."

Sapphire did allow her eyes to roll then when she looked at Heracles, making him grin. "What did you do with him?"

Still smiling, Heracles headed to the kitchen. "He's tied up in the greenhouse."

She heard him rummaging around before he screamed and then cursed. Sapphire laughed, wondering if he was more upset by the mice or the fact that they'd eaten his snacks. She embraced the moment of normality before a tingling started in her abdomen. Lying back against a decorative couch cushion, she closed her eyes and breathed through the oncoming pain. "Hey, did your mom say when they'd be back?"

****

"You're okay! Nicolae! You're okay!"

Nicolae stared in shock at the three women, wondering how he'd gotten from an oncoming attack while he'd been standing in the stream to the grassy field the four of them now stood in. Each of them on two legs, him on four. He changed and then lowered his hands to cover his genitals. "How'd you get here?"

Rayne waved her hand over the ground. His heart thumped, and he jumped when cool leafy vines coiled and climbed up from the earth to wrap around his legs. They continued upward, weaving through each other, until he wore a natural loincloth. He held his hands out in front of him until he was covered completely and looked from the vines to the woman who made them spring to life. "I hope that isn't poison ivy."

Rayne laughed. "No. Japanese arrowroot."

"Known as kudzu around here," Haven added. "I could have done that, you know," she said, turning to Rayne.

Rayne raised a brow. "I waited, but you seemed more interested in what the vines were covering."

Nicolae noticed there was no denial, nor indication from Haven Cavanaugh-Hansen that she cared one way or the other. They really were a fascinating bunch of women. He turned to Destiny Cavanaugh-Whitehawk. "So I guess you went misty and brought me here?"

"It was a joint effort." She grinned. "Rayne turned you into mist, if you want to call it that. Haven called in a strong breeze, and I dragged you out of danger and into the sky with me."

Completely captivated, he looked from one to the other. "So why don't I remember it?"

Rayne grinned. "I put you to sleep when I changed you. Destiny was afraid you'd freak out and parts of you would end up in the mouth of the rabid wolf."

Nicolae's head jerked up. He inhaled deeply but didn't smell *any* members of his pack.

"He's...neutralized."

He looked at Rayne. "You killed him?"

"No. We need him."

Destiny moved toward him. "We found a spell that will help Sapphire, but it requires the blood of the one who infected her." When he shook his head, she hurried on. "We aren't going to stop her from becoming one of you. She wants that, and it is her destiny."

"And her desire," Haven added, her voice filled with sensual promise.

"No!" Nicolae felt the taint of his actions with Sabia, but when he realized he'd shouted, he gentled his tone. "I'm sorry, but no. If you can stop the change. Then you must."

No one spoke. Destiny's emerald eyes became speculative. Haven's disbelieving. And Rayne's brewed with anger. He inhaled, knowing he'd have to explain, knowing they'd all hate him once he had. "The wolf you snatched me from is not the one who infected Sapphire. But even if he were, I cannot continue to be with her."

Rayne stepped in front of Destiny so he'd have to look her in the eyes. "Why? She's willing to change her entire existence to be with you. She was willing to give up her family if that's what it took!"

Nicolae squared his shoulders, certain he was in more danger now than he'd been with Heburue. "My reasons are personal."

Rayne's hair lifted in the breezeless air. "Not good enough."

"Rayne…" Haven stepped forward and placed her hand on her sister's arm before she faced him. "What have you done?"

Destiny stepped around Rayne and stood on her other side. She looked him over and gasped.

Figuring now was not the time to remind her she'd promised not to read his mind without permission, he swallowed, refusing to let them see he feared their power. "I have a duty to my pack." He shook his head. "Had."

"And?"

He locked gazes with Rayne. "I was expected to mate with the daughter of the royal line. They've always been the Alphas of our pack. Long before her brother, Ion the reigning Alpha, was infected, I was chosen to mate with Sabia Ilie. Once he was infected, I was destined to be the next Alpha male to her Alpha female. I was never taught to expect anything else. It was the destiny chosen for me as a pup, when my own family was wiped out. Until I met Sapphire I never even dreamed there was another…*choice*. Once I met her, everything within me rebelled against my duty. I tried to refuse them, knowing I owed them my life, also knowing to do so now, meant the almost certain extinction of our pack."

"But?"

Nicolae nodded. "Yeah, *but*. I was convinced by Sabia's mother that I had to fulfill my duty, and I knew I did, so I decided I could never be with Sapphire again, even though, in the end, I failed them all."

Rayne's eyes sharpened. "You didn't go through with it?"

Nicolae huffed out a laugh. "I tried. I went so far as to mount her but pulled out immediately. I just couldn't do it.

But that doesn't change anything. I still breached her and am not worthy of your daughter."

Rayne splayed her fingers and her sisters each took a hand. Nicolae waited for lightning to strike him, or the earth to gobble him whole, but when all three smiled at him, he wasn't certain if he was to be spared, or if they were just going to enjoy sending him to his death.

But there was one thing he had to know, no matter how things ended for him. "If the three of you are here, who's taking care of Sapphire?"

"Apollo."

Destiny shook her head, sending Rayne a grimace. "No, he had an emergency call."

Rayne frowned. "Zeus?"

Destiny answered more slowly. "No...he is in Europe."

Rayne's eyes grew large. "Not Heracles!"

When Destiny nodded, Rayne disappeared.

Nicolae felt the breath leave him and warily looked between the two remaining sisters. "So what happens now?"

Destiny shrugged. "Looks like the three of us have to find Ion Ilie and take him home."

Chapter Fifteen

Sapphire was cramping so badly she wasn't sure what to do. Heracles was no help. He flittered from one room to another, then came back to ask her if she was hungry, or thirsty, or needed help going to the bathroom. When she refused everything, he kept walking around in circles, rubbing his hands together, and practically fell all over her mother when she suddenly appeared.

"Thank goodness you're here! I gotta go!"

Sapphire watched him run out the door. She sighed in gratitude that her mother was back and Heracles was gone. "If changing into a Lycan didn't make me crazy, he would have."

Rayne smiled and approached her daughter. "How are you doing?"

Sapphire didn't know where to begin. "Well, not great. I'm hurting again, but not as bad as before. At least not yet. But we've got other problems."

Rayne's brows rose. "As in?"

Sapphire pointed to the front door, explained what happened, and then curled into a ball when the pain increased. "This is getting worse."

Rayne bit her bottom lip and helped Sapphire up and back into the bedroom. She pulled back the sheet and looked at each shredded restraint before sending Sapphire an inquiring lift of her brows.

"I know, but that guy broke in, and I just…did it!"

"Well, lie down and I'm calling your dad. If we need to restrain you, for your safety as well as ours, we need something stronger."

"Have I tried to hurt anyone?"

Rayne shook her head. "It was just a precaution. If you don't want us to do it again, we won't. I just didn't want to have to use magic on you, unless we needed to."

Sapphire frowned. "Why? You could restrain me with a thought."

Rayne smiled. "But you hate magic."

Sapphire looked at the broken leather. "I hate those more."

Chuckling, Rayne hugged her. "Good enough. The only restraints from now on are the ones we create." She took a deep breath. "I guess I'd better go see what's going on with the man in the greenhouse."

Concern had Sapphire taking her mother's arm before she could turn away. "Be careful, Mom. He said I was *one of them* before he tried to attack me. I don't know if he knows I'm changing into a Lycanthrope, or if he knows we hold magic, or if it's something else altogether. But he was really angry."

Rayne nodded. "Don't worry about it, honey. By the time I get done with him, he won't even remember he was here or why."

"Mom, wait." Sapphire inhaled as another sharp pain zinged up her spine. "Can you put the morphine drip back in? I think I'm getting worse."

Worry pulled Rayne's brows together, but she went to the tray that was placed on the nightstand and pulled new tubes and needles from their plastic packaging. She wet the back of Sapphire's hand with an alcohol swab and dried it with a cotton ball. "Haven's better at this than I am."

Sapphire smiled through the pain. "It's okay, Mom. Just do it, please."

Once Rayne had the saline drip with the morphine all set up and working again, Sapphire felt instant relief. "So what are you going to do? Wipe his mind completely?"

Rayne shook her head. "No, just the last couple of days, a week tops. Anything beyond that takes my actions from being *familial*-defense and leans toward cruelty. Hopefully, whatever he's up to will have generated within that timeframe. I can't take away all his memories. He wouldn't know how to function or know who he is." She made a face. "Even criminals have families."

"I don't know if that's going to be good enough, Mom. He seemed almost triumphant that he'd found *one of them*. People who are that angry at someone they don't even know...it has to take more than a week for that kind of rage to develop."

"Sometimes it takes a lifetime of being raised with prejudices," Rayne agreed. "Did you know him?"

Sapphire yawned and settled into her pillow. "No. Never saw him before...ever. Probably about your age. Maybe a little older. Nice looking criminal, though, if you discount the fact that he acted like he was on drugs and probably didn't bathe regularly."

Rayne smiled at that. "Don't worry about this. You're half asleep already. Give in to it and I'll take care of the other."

Sapphire nodded, and closed her eyes. "Mom?"

"Yes?"

"Where's Nicolae?"

****

Nicolae glanced from Destiny to Haven. "So you aren't going to kill me?"

Haven laughed. "We don't kill people *or* Lycanthropes. Not that we actually knew you existed before now." She grinned. "We only do good, not harm, unless someone or something threatens the life of one of ours."

"That's a relief." He looked at Haven since she consistently felt the less threatening of the three sisters. "What about Ion and Heburue?"

"Well, we thought we'd have to kill them, and if it comes to it, we may, but we're hoping we can help them instead."

Nicolae's chest expanded with the relieved breath he then expelled. "How?"

Destiny walked toward him and held out her hand. Nicolae looked at it, then at her, before taking it. He'd expected her to read him again, but the scenes that flashed within his mind were of his pack, happily laughing and playing together, and Ion and Heburue were among them. The scene ended abruptly, and he found himself looking into her eyes. She smiled with a gentleness that mesmerized him.

"We will have to find them first, and get them back home where we will have to cage them. The three of us will join forces to enchant them into a docile state, until we can find a way to eradicate the rabies from their blood." Her brows pulled together, and her eyes filled with sadness. "But there are risks."

Since he'd already decided the three older Cavanaugh women could do just about anything, he didn't question the enchantment, but he needed to know the risks and said so. Destiny looked from him to her sister, and Haven nodded.

"They did not receive immediate attention to kill the rabies strain, so conventional medicine will not help. If we had gotten to them as early as we did Sapphire, they would already be well. Since we will have to be aggressive with what we will create to cure them, we risk it will also kill them *or* make them...*different*."

"Different how?"

Haven swallowed. "Bigger, meaner, and stronger maybe. We don't actually know."

The thought of something more threatening than what they were now facing was horrifying. "But, if you do nothing, they will continue to kill and infect others. So there is no choice."

Destiny nodded. "Yes. That is true."

"So how do you know what to create, if you never knew we existed before?"

Destiny opened her hand and a little book suddenly appeared in her palm. "We are of a long line of mystics, who experienced many things over thousands of years. Our ancestors have chronicled their lives since the time of the Egyptian dynasties, and those tomes are in our possession. We just learned there was an ancestor who fell in love with a Lycanthrope. She found a way to make him completely human by creating a potion using his blood."

Nicolae shook his head. "But you aren't trying to change them, are you? I thought you wanted to save them, as they were meant to be."

Haven nodded. "That's where the danger comes into play. We can't use her potion, but we are trying to use her notes to figure out a way to alter it to make it work for us. We're still working on that."

"Ion can't be in very good shape. I can hardly believe he's still alive. Heburue, and possibly others, will have been infected more recently. Do you think there is hope for them all?"

The sisters sighed at the same time, and Nicolae was afraid he knew their answer.

Destiny shrugged and frowned. "If not, then we will have no choice but to take their lives."

Nicolae felt the first stirrings of hope and wanted to hug them both. "I need to tell the pack. They need this hope. And I need to apologize for failing them." His excitement dwindled. "But I still don't know how I will ever look Sapphire in the eyes."

"She will be angry," Haven agreed, before pressing her lips together.

"And she may forget she hates magic and turn you into a cockroach," Destiny added, before they both laughed. When he just sent them a look that expressed his opinion about their amusement, Destiny continued, "Listen, we understand family, and the protection and continuation of our kind comes before all else. Sapphire will be hurt and angry, but she also has a just heart. I believe she will find her way through this."

Nicolae hoped so; otherwise nothing else would matter.

"Well, let's get this party started," Haven said, and held out her hand to both Nicolae and Destiny. Once their hands were joined, the sky turned dark, the wind picked up, and lightning crackled continuously. Clouds swirled, tornadoes dipped teasingly, and then one stretched out to encircle them. His heart raced, his body trembled, and his feet lifted off the ground. Nicolae nearly jerked his hands free, but Haven held on tight. She smiled at him, and he took a shaky breath before nodding to her. Once he forced himself to relax, they took flight.

Nothing could have prepared Nicolae for the exhilaration of flying. He'd always wanted a chance to parachute from an airplane, but this had to be better. He wasn't simply falling, he was moving with the sisters across the sky in the eye of a storm. Although he could only see swirling clouds and flashes of lightning between him and the small area of the greenish-brown earth far below, he was filled with an exuberance he'd never before known. Sadly it was over too soon, and they were slowly descending until Nicolae was once again standing on solid ground next to the stream.

He laughed at Haven's smile of satisfaction. "That was incredible!"

Destiny rolled her eyes. "Show-off."

"Like you weren't when you made him essence and transported him to us?"

"That was necessary."

Haven raised a brow. "So was this. Now we're back where he started." She turned to Nicolae. "Where do we find them?"

He tried to settle from the excitement he'd just experienced, knowing his welcome by the pack would be less than thrilling. "If they are still gathered, they'll be about a half-mile from here. Come on."

"You could have at least dropped us there."

"Don't be lazy. A half-mile is nothing. Besides, we would have given them a heart attack."

Nicolae lead the way, smiling at the whispered exchanges going on behind him. He liked Sapphire's family; *no*, he adored them. He just hoped she'd be able to find a way to forgive him and let him be a part of their craziness.

Since Haven's storm had drenched the area pretty well, he maneuvered though the path in an attempt to keep them from getting any muddier than necessary. Twenty minutes later he stopped at the tree line to tell them they'd arrived, but when he looked back both women were not only dry from head to toe, they looked as if they'd just stepped from a salon. He grinned, knowing his actions to protect them were unnecessary. "We're here. They are too, but they sense us and are staying hidden."

Destiny placed her hand on his shoulder. "Can you communicate to them that we mean no harm?"

"I'll try. Right now, I'm probably the last Lycanthrope on earth they want to see. Unless it's to kill me."

"Try," Haven said, before the palms of her hands started to glow.

Nicolae looked from her hands to the clearing. "I know you are out there. We are here to help. Not hurt."

"How dare you come back here, Alpha? My daughter is shamed!" Halivia hissed, telepathically.

"I come with those who are willing to restore our brothers. It is the only chance this pack has to survive. Speak out loud, and show yourselves."

Nicolae stepped from his position and Haven and Destiny followed. One by one the members of the pack emerged, though they stayed in their natural form. Sabia stood close to her mother; her gaze speared him with defiance. He ignored her and addressed them all. "I came back to give us all hope for a future. These ladies are my friends and have special powers. They are trying to find a way to restore Ion, Heburue, and any others who may have become infected to health."

Halivia changed to her human form and the pack followed suit, except Sabia. She growled and snapped her teeth. Her mother turned to her and smacked her muzzle. "Enough! If this is true, Ion will once again reign! Change, as is our custom when an Alpha demands it."

After a slight hesitation, Sabia transformed. She stood there with anger radiating from her nude body, looking from him to the women. Nicolae knew she was furious with him, rightly so, but he was as sure her anger increased greatly with jealousy of the two beauties at his side. The Cavanaugh women were a sight to behold at any age. Which was something he looked forward to, if Sapphire allowed him in her life again.

"Tell us how this is possible!" Halivia demanded.

Destiny stepped forward and clapped her hands. Just as Rayne had done for Nicolae, vines stretched and swirled at the Lycanthropes' feet. The women and Jaspon yelped, fearful, but remained frozen in place as their bodies were covered. Nicolae didn't know if fright had kept them from running or if one of the sisters had forced them to remain still. Either way, by the time they were cloaked, everyone was looking at each other with wonder, and there were even a few smiles.

"You and Rayne are invading my space." Haven glared at Destiny. "I'm supposed to handle things like that!"

Nicolae had to keep from smiling. "I think you are all amazing."

Both sisters smiled at him, and then the three of them advanced on the pack. Halivia moved forward to meet him, and he shook his head, now fully understanding Sabia's assessment of the only other male present. Jaspon would never make Alpha. No male Lycanthrope worth his salt would allow a female to take the lead in a situation where there was the threat of the unknown. Halivia met them in the center of the field, and Nicolae had to push away memories of his failed attempt to mate with Sabia. It shamed him, both that he had mounted her, and that he hadn't fulfilled his duty.

"We see these women have magic. But what can they do to restore our males?"

Nicolae turned to Destiny. "This is Destiny Cavanaugh-Whitehawk. Destiny, the she-wolf who raised me, Halivia Ilie." The two women nodded at each other, Destiny with a smile, and Halivia with reserve. He smiled, turning to Haven. "This is Haven Cavanaugh-Hansen. Haven, Halivia Ilie." Again a smile...and caution.

"My apologies. I forget my manners. Introductions should have come first. Welcome to our home. Please, what can you do for those who have become infected? We need our men." She looked pointedly at Nicolae.

He said nothing, knowing he deserved that. But she needed to know up front he would not be returning to them, no matter the outcome. "I am not your Alpha, Halivia. Your son is still alive, and if everything works out the way we hope, he will continue to lead you all. The others must be found, but not engaged in confrontation.

We don't want anyone else infected."

Nicolae looked up to the rest of the pack and addressed them with authority. "Those who have mates, call to them through the private channels of the mated. Once they respond that they are on the way, or you sense they are, get back down the mountain and hide. The remainder, go back to your daily lives. We will keep you informed, but you must all be out of harm's way. It is my hope no more are infected, but I believe we would have heard from them by now were that the case."

He turned back to the sisters. "Will you be able to contain many at once?"

Haven shared a look with Destiny before turning back with a nod. "We may need Rayne and Destiny's husband to join with us, but I believe we can."

Nicolae took a deep breath and turned back to Halivia. "Sabia needs to be contained. Her anger at me will make her reckless."

Sabia advanced on the group quickly, stopping only feet before Nicolae. She glared at him, the irises of her eyes spinning with the need to change. "Do not think I cannot hear you, Alpha! How dare you treat me like a child? I am more worthy than you to bear the title Alpha! I am Sabia Ilie, daughter of kings! I will tear your throat out!"

She changed and leaped, only to dangle in the air before him. A collective gasp filled the air, and all eyes turned to the two sisters. Each held up a hand, their eyes focused on Sabia with purpose. She yelped and wiggled, but her struggles did nothing but cause her mother to laugh. Uproariously. The remainder of the pack joined in, and Nicolae had to bite his lip to keep from joining them as well.

Halivia finally settled, her eyes still filled with mirth as she smiled at the sisters. "I've wanted to be able to do that since she was a brat of a pup. Please release my daughter. I will control her."

Instantly Sabia hit the ground, and then slowly rose to her feet. She looked from the Cavanaugh women, to Nicolae, and then turned and ran across the field and into the trees. They all watched her go, and Nicolae could only hope it was the last he'd ever see of her.

Halivia turned to the pack. "Do as Nicolae instructed, I will see you all back in town." She glanced back at the sisters. "I hope your magic is our salvation." Then to Nicolae, "Let me know if there is some way I can help." She nodded to each and then changed, before following the path of her angry child.

****

Nicolae didn't even jump when Rayne Cavanaugh-White and Tom Whitehawk suddenly appeared and stood before him. If he wasn't so burdened with what life had thrown at those he loved, he'd laugh at his complete acceptance of the impossible.

"Is Sapphire doing okay?"

Rayne smiled and nodded to Nicolae. "She is holding her own. We are keeping her on a morphine drip to ease the pain and to allow her to sleep, but I'm afraid if we keep doing this, she will become addicted to the drug. How long before this all ends?"

Nicolae was relieved, but understood Rayne's concern. "I believe it will happen on the night of the Hunter's Moon. This year is particularly important because it will also be the thirty-third moon since the last time a second moon appeared within the same month."

Haven smiled. "*Yes!* That makes sense. We know and understand the value of Luna's cycles. Magic increases on nights such as those. People call it a Blue Moon, but we know it as the Mystic Moon." She looked at him with satisfaction. "And this time, it falls on All Hallows Eve."

Nicolae felt her excitement, but his was tempered with reality. "That's great. But Sapphire will be in grave danger when the physical transformation happens. Her bones will break and reform, her heart rate will increase dramatically. Her body will go into shock. Lycanthropes are born with the ability for our form to change from wolf to human and back, she was not." He looked at her mother, his heart heavy. "No human has ever survived that I know of."

Rayne inhaled then closed her eyes. When she opened them, she nodded. "I know. Sapphire told me you explained that to her, but she's willing to chance her life for this, for *you*."

"Did you tell her?"

Rayne didn't question his question. Her smile was sad. "No. That is yours to tell."

Relieved, yet still filled with sadness, Nicolae nodded. "She should know *before*. If you have the ability to stop her transformation, I need to let her have the choice to change her mind before the night of the Mystic Moon."

"I agree."

"Send me to her. Give me about an hour and then bring me back. No matter her choice, I have to save my brothers."

Rayne nodded and waved her hand. Instantly Nicolae was standing in a room filled with beeps and the scent of morphine. But the only thing he noticed was the dark-haired beauty asleep on the bed.

Chapter Sixteen

"Sapphire!"

As if she heard his silent exclamation, Sapphire's eyes fluttered and opened. She looked to where he stood at the foot of her bed and her eyes lit with recognition and relief. She held out her hand as her lips lifted in a welcoming smile.

"I thought you had left me."

It pained his heart to know she would wish he had, once she heard what he had to say. He moved to her side and took her hand. Everything within him shook with the emotion of touching her again. "How are you feeling?"

Sapphire grinned. "Better now. I've missed you so much."

"I've missed you too." He leaned down and kissed her forehead gently.

"That isn't the welcome I was hoping for."

Nicolae nodded and blew out a breath. He couldn't find the words to begin his confession, so he looked around the room, aware her eyes were still on him. "It's good they are giving you something for the pain."

"Nicolae? What's wrong?"

He returned his attention to her. "I have come here to ask your forgiveness."

She laughed in relief and attempted to sit up, but she gasped and lay back down. "Oh, good grief, I'm dizzy from lying here so much." Her smiling eyes looked him over. "You are forgiven for being gone, now that you're back. What have you been up to?"

Nicolae stalled, not sure if he should walk into it slowly, or back into it like a coward. He shook his head, feeling more cowardly than wolf. "There's no easy way to tell you that."

Concern pulled at Sapphire's brows. "Tell me *what*?"

"Okay…I was coming to find you after your aunt *misted* you out of your cabin."

"Good so far."

After a slight hesitation, he continued. "Sabia intercepted me."

The heart monitor she was hooked up to increased slightly as Sapphire's gaze sharpened. "And you've been with her ever since?"

Nicolae nodded and then shook his head. "Yes and no. She told me another member of the pack was infected, and I had to go back."

The monitor settled a little. "So you weren't with her, you were with them all."

Though this time she made it a statement, Nicolae gave the same response. "Yes…and no."

Sapphire attempted to rise again, this time she succeeded, and slid back against the pillows and headboard. "Tell me the entire story. Now."

Swallowing, he informed her of the threat to his Lycanthrope family, the possibility of more infestations, and closed his mouth when he was at the part where he and Jaspon were made responsible for the continuation of the pack. He swallowed again, and then hurried through the mating of Halivia, and then, finally, told her the worst.

The pictures on the walls shook, the bags of saline and morphine swung, and she jumped forward to slap him hard on the cheek. Tears streamed from her face, growls of pain and anger tore from her throat as she turned to the bedside and lifted the lamp to throw at him. Nicolae didn't flinch but stood there embracing her anger. Once she calmed and curled so her face was buried in her knees, he gave her a moment more, knowing to touch her now, or to continue with the story, wouldn't be well received.

"What's going on in here?"

Nicolae turned. Tom Whitehawk stood in the doorway without expression. He looked at the room, at Nicolae, and finally at Sapphire, before moving forward. He stepped to the opposite side of the bed and checked the monitor, then touched Sapphire on the shoulder.

"Be at peace, child."

Sapphire's whimpers eased as she looked up at her uncle, and Nicolae's heart crumbled at seeing her so broken. When she turned her teary gaze on him, she shook her head.

"You should go."

"No, sweetheart, he shouldn't. You need to hear him out."

Sapphire looked back at her uncle in disbelief. "You don't know what he's done!"

Tom smiled gently. "Neither do you."

Nicolae held up his hand. "She's right. It doesn't matter. But thank you, anyway, Mr. Whitehawk. I'll go now." He looked back at Sapphire, knowing it would be the last time he would ever see her beautiful face. "I'm really sorry. For *everything*."

He turned and walked out of the room, ran down the hall shedding his leafy clothing, and flew out through a broken front door. Nicolae transformed as he leapt off the porch and ran, hell bent, for the trees. He kept running for miles as his wolf, over rocks and streams, through brush and briars, knowing, if he stopped to catch his breath, he'd want to curl up and die.

Once his legs ached and he felt his heart was about to burst, he had no choice but to stop at a stream. He threw up his head and howled in hurt, in sorrow, in loss. When his voice was so hoarse he couldn't continue, he lowered his head and drank his fill, then lay down and closed his eyes. He knew the sisters would zap him back soon...he just hoped what was to come would be over with quickly, and then he could disappear from all their lives, for good.

****

Tom Whitehawk stood silently where he'd been for the past thirty minutes, while Sapphire waited for him to leave her to her misery. It had taken everything in her not to tell him to get out, but she'd not only been raised better than that, she loved everything about her uncle...except *now*, that he had endless patience. "Say what you have to say, Uncle Tom," she finally said, resigned.

Tom smiled and moved to the foot of the bed where he could face her. "Do you love him?"

Sapphire closed her eyes for a few seconds. "He *mated* with another!"

Tom raised his brows. "Do you love him?"

"No!"

Tom smiled. "Do you love him?"

Tears threatened and spilled. "I hate his guts right now!"

"I know you do. But do you *love* him?"

Sapphire took a deep breath. "Yes." She looked down at her hands, then her feet, and her breath caught.

"Do you want to live the rest of your life without him?"

"Huh? Uh...I can't think about that right now."

"He's gone, Sapphire. Forever, likely. Unless you let him know you can forgive him."

As much as that was unthinkable, Nicolae was the least of her problems right now. "It will have to wait. I'm not sure what's going on, but I think my fingernails have grown half an inch since I fell asleep earlier."

Tom frowned and looked down at her hands, then back up. "At least they aren't claws."

Sapphire almost found that funny enough to laugh, but laughter wasn't in her at the moment. "Cute. So, where are Mom and the aunts? I can't believe they left me again."

"Well, my guess would be that they are calling Nicolae to them right now."

Sapphire frowned. "Why?"

"Your mom, Haven, and my Destiny are helping him. They are trying to save the pack."

"What are you talking about?"

"What has Nicolae told you about the pack?"

Sapphire took a moment to play everything he'd told her through her mind, while trying to ignore the pain settling in her lower back. "That they are a small group. That he is their Alpha. And his responsibility. One he never thought of giving up, before he met me." She grimaced. "Apparently, he's changed his mind...."

"Mmm!" Sapphire jerked with the pain that was shifting within her. She leaned forward, trying to ease the ache threading through her like a snake in the marrow of her bones.

"You're hurting. I'll increase the morphine."

Sapphire shook her head. "No. It will make me loopy. I need to think right now. Tell me what's going on."

Tom nodded. "Nicolae didn't get a chance to finish telling you his situation. The female he was...to mate with is the last member of a long line of royals. It was up to her to carry on the royal line, and Nicolae was chosen as her mate when their family first fostered him, when he was still too young to remember."

"I know all this! That doesn't change anything."

Tom smiled with his normal gentleness. "Let me finish."

Sapphire couldn't believe her family was taking Nicolae's side. She shrugged. "Finish it then. So I can." Tom held his grin by pressing his lips together, but Sapphire saw it in his eyes. Her anger was nearly as strong as the pain now radiating throughout her body.

"The other males in the pack, with the exception of one, went after the other two known infected Lycanthropes. They haven't come back and the pack expects the worst has happened, and that they, too, are infected. The...let's call her *queen*, or former Alpha Female, Sabia's mother, insisted he had to save them all, and by save them, I mean continue the line with half. Leaving the other half to the other remaining male." At the horror in Sapphire's eyes, he nodded. "The queen mother took on the other male herself first, then demanded Nicolae service Sabia."

"He would have been sick at the thought! Not only because he can't stand her, but because their kind mate for life! Exclusively."

Sapphire felt sick. And she hurt like hell. She wished she could call Nicolae back and tell him she understood. The continuation of her own family was something she would have done anything to preserve. How could she ask less of him?

"I need to go to him and tell him I understand. I need to apologize for being a jealous brat. I need, *agh!*" She doubled over, and Tom grabbed her to keep her from rolling off the bed.

"You aren't going anywhere, sweetheart. Lie down. I'm increasing your morphine and calling your mother."

Sapphire had no choice but to accept her uncle's help and follow his instructions. But she couldn't have him disrupt whatever her mother was doing. She owed Nicolae that much. "Don't call to her. Just drug me more. I'll hold."

At least Sapphire hoped she'd hold. She didn't want to

go through the change without her mother and aunts present, but mostly she didn't want to do so without telling Nicolae she was sorry.

Just in case she didn't survive.

Sapphire didn't fight the sleepiness overtaking her. She embraced it but couldn't give in until she said one last thing. "Uncle Tom?"

"Yes?"

"Tell them... all... I love them. Tell... Nicolae...."

The wind was in her face. Trees flew by with breathtaking speed. Animals small and large skittered out of her way, even the large black bear that she sensed would usually be willing to engage in a confrontation with her young so close. Sapphire reveled in the freedom, trusting her instincts to guide, her muscles to support, and her heart to lead. He was everywhere and nowhere; his shape in the twists and turns of a gnarled branch, his voice in the howl of the wind racing through the trees, and in his scent, which was as pure as the land she tread upon, called to her, as nothing else could.

She finally saw him *at a small clearing close to the edge of a cliff and slowed to a stop. Everything inside of her wanted to jump on him playfully, lovingly, but he held his ground and stared at her with caution. She approached him gradually, inching her way, lowering her head in submission, yet keeping him within her sight.*

"I love you."

Her voice was her own, yet her mouth didn't open. He continued to stare at her, until he shook his head. "You don't."

Sapphire took a tentative step forward, needing him to know she spoke the truth. "I do. I love you!"

"You hate me."

It was her turn to deny, but she chose instead to take another step. Even his low growl didn't stop her, though she felt a moment's fear. "I love you, Nicolae! From the first moment you walked into my life. I've loved you."

"He's mine!" a she-wolf hissed, suddenly appearing by his side.

Sabia! Sapphire growled low in her throat. "He was never

yours!"

The she-wolf laughed mockingly. "Has he mated with you? No? I didn't think so. Be gone, bitch! Nicolae is mine!"

Sapphire and Sabia leaped at the same time, meeting in midair. A sharp pain tore into her neck; she yelped as they hit the ground together. Sabia was quicker to roll to her feet, and Sapphire felt another deep bite as she attempted to stand. But the more seasoned Lycanthrope knew just where to hit and bite into her leg. Before long Sapphire was forced to remain still as teeth hovered on the fur just over her jugular.

"Enough! Sabia, get over here, now!"

Sabia hesitated long enough to let Sapphire know the she-wolf only had to snap her strong jaws together, and her life would end. She waited, panting, refusing to cry out at the pains radiating throughout her wolf's body. Sabia stepped back, growled deeply, and backed away until she was once again by Nicolae's side. Sapphire looked at the pair and didn't even flinch when Nicolae simply stared back as Sabia licked his jaw.

"Go home, Sapphire. You don't belong in our world." With that he turned and took his time walking away. Sabia turned as well and then looked back, once, in triumph, before they both took off and were soon out of sight.

Sapphire pulled herself up, her heart as broken as her body. She limped her way to the edge of the cliff and, with a cry of anguish, threw herself over.

"Sapphire! Wake up!"

Sapphire shook her head as she awakened, angry her wolf's body never made it to the rocks at the bottom of the cliff. She slid a glance to her uncle, knowing she must have been crying out in her sleep for him to look so distraught. She smiled a sleepy smile she wasn't feeling and lifted a heavy arm to point at the morphine drip. "Turn it up. And don't stop."

Tom shook his head. "No. No more. I'm calling your mother and her sisters home, and we are putting a stop to this now."

Sapphire shook her head. "You can't. They would have just called Nicolae to them, they have to help him."

Tom tilted his head and looked at her with his brows pulled together. Understanding entered his eyes and his features relaxed. "Sapphire, honey, you've slept through the last week. They've been searching and rounding up the infected pack the entire time and have just about captured all but one."

She stared at him in disbelief. It felt as if she'd just closed her eyes long enough to have that terrible dream. "What is today's date?" she asked, but before he could answer her body seized, cracked, crunched, and she screamed.

Chapter Seventeen

Sapphire!

Nicolae nearly missed dodging Domeno's punch, as his mind wasn't squarely on his mission but on the unexpected telepathic scream he'd heard from the woman he loved. He threw one of his own, relieved Rayne had placed a holding spell on all Lycanthropes within the hundreds of miles her magic could reach. Now none of them, including himself, could transform into their wolves. But that didn't mean they'd lost any strength. If anything, the rabies infection was making them even stronger than before.

He wanted to glance back and see if any of the women had returned to the clearing, but he didn't dare take his eyes from the foam-mouthed brother who was doing everything in his considerable power to bite. Though Domeno was in man-form, the possibility that his saliva was still diseased wasn't something Nicolae was willing to risk.

When his adversary suddenly froze mid-strike, Nicolae stepped back and swung around to see the three sisters had all returned together and had the others in the same frozen state. He breathed heavily, knowing his exhaustion wasn't something to give into yet. "Thank you!"

Rayne, Haven, and Destiny held their hands out, each controlling the invisible magic that kept their adversaries in thrall. None looked his way, but all kept their concentration on the men, whose varying stages of decay possibly indicated the order in which they were infected, or at least, the advancement of their illness. Nicolae couldn't believe the Cavanaugh women were still capable of such strength after the last two days without sleep or food, followed by however many days they'd searched together before splitting up. He felt shaky and about to drop.

"We have to get these guys home. Sapphire's in trouble. I think she's finally changing."

Nicolae nodded, relieved Sapphire's mother knew what he believed was happening too. As he attempted to catch his breath, he took a second to try to figure out which day it was, as the sun was already heading over the mountain.

All Hallows Eve. *Halloween.*

Certain Rayne was right, he forced out one last shaky breath. "How do we do that?" Two more harsh breaths. "And what do we do with them once we get them there?"

Domeno was suddenly dragged toward the others, his toes barely touching the round. When he, Kaspor, Teagan, and Keeleen were with their backs together, they each leaned forward as if a rope had been tied at their collective waists, bundling them. Rayne looked over at him then, while the other two kept their hands up, facing the men.

"We are going to work together to transport them as one into a cage Garrison and Logan built, and Tom enchanted. It should hold them until we can whip up the inoculation we believe will cure them." She frowned. "We're still missing one."

Nicolae nodded, still relieved to have learned other males who hadn't been infected were now in the town with the she-wolves. "Ion. I think Sabia knows where he is. I just don't know how she's kept him from infecting her too." He grimaced. "*If* she has."

Rayne nodded. "Give us time to get these home and caged. Then I'll come back for you."

Nicolae wanted to protest. He needed to see Sapphire. Needed to do whatever he could to ease her suffering. But he knew she never wanted to see him again. And he had to finish this. "I'll keep the telepathic lines open," he said, looking at Destiny. "I'll let you know if and when I find them."

She nodded, as Rayne walked forward, taking him into a hug. He hugged her back, appreciating her compassion and understanding. When she stepped back, she took his hand and led him to Haven.

"He needs strength, sister."

As Rayne lifted her hands toward the Lycanthropes, Haven's hands fell, and she turned to face him. She held her palms inches from each other and they began to glow. Nicolae stood motionless, knowing she wouldn't harm him.

When she placed her heated hands upon his chest, he inhaled sharply at the infusion of energy filling his body. She smiled up at him with a twinkle in her emerald eyes.

"Be well, Nicolae, be well."

Haven lowered her hands and stepped back before she turned to lift them once again toward his brothers.

And just like that, they were gone.

Nicolae inhaled a deep breath, and smiled. His hunger had disappeared. His thirst was sated. And his energy level was extraordinary. He felt as if he'd feasted and rested for days. He thought of his wolf and was relieved when he was able to transform, and then amazed when he looked down at one huge paw, then the other. He laughed inside his head, realizing he was no longer the size of an average male wolf, but much larger than he'd ever been before.

He crossed the field and lowered his head at the spot he'd last seen Sabia before she'd entered the tree line all those days before. Nicolae sniffed around until he caught her scent and then sniffed some more to make sure it was the strongest leading into the trees. With the rise of the moon only hours away, he knew he had to find and catch his prey, and quickly, or the vicious cycle of murders and infestations would continue. But mostly, he wanted to be there, even if he wasn't wanted, when Sapphire embraced her wolf for the first time....

If she hasn't changed her mind.

Having no time to dwell on the *should-have-beens*, Nicolae increased his speed until he was in an all-out run, to only have to double back occasionally when Sabia's scent weakened. Then he would start the hunt all over again.

Though much of the landscape was identical to Mystic Mountain, the differences were astounding. The air wasn't as sweet, the earth wasn't as rich, the tree branches merely swung, not danced in the cooling breeze. In what he figured was a couple of hours, he stopped at a stream and partook of refreshment, but even the water wasn't infused with the same clean taste, silky texture, and mystical energy he'd come to expect.

"So you've come for me after all."

Nicolae jerked his head up and swung around, ready to engage, but Sabia was in human form, and doing nothing more than eyeing him with confusion.

"How the hell did you get so big?"

Nicolae considered staying as he was, but after lifting his nose to assure himself they were alone, he changed, and stood before her. "Where is Ion?"

She looked him up and down, and smiled. "I see those witches didn't increase the size of your package." She laughed. "Not that there was a need."

Nicolae ignored her comment. "Where is Ion?"

"I told you once before, you give me what I want, and I'll give you what you want to know."

"I don't have time for this, Sabia. He's dangerous. How have you stayed unaffected?"

She shrugged. "It would seem he can't bite me. Which is very sweet, when you think about it. Every time he's gotten close, smelled my scent, he recognizes me as family."

Filing that away for future use, Nicolae nodded.

"That's great. But you are endangering everyone else by hiding him. Those women may be able to cure him!"

Sabia shook her head. "I don't want him cured."

Stunned by her selfishness, though he had no idea why it stunned him, Nicolae advanced and grabbed her by the arm. "You little bitch! He's your brother!"

Completely unfazed, she looked from the fingers biting into her flesh, back to his face. "And if he's cured, I am no longer in control. He will become Alpha once again, and you, or whomever I'm forced to mate with, will not be able to give me the life I deserve."

Nicolae released her and stepped back as fury engulfed him. "I am done playing your games. You will tell me where Ion is now, or I will use you for bait, after spraying your entire body with my scent."

Sabia's eyes widened. "You would not!"

Nicolae's lips lifted in what he hoped was a devious smile. "I will. You have two seconds, then all bets are off."

Anger distorted her otherwise lovely features. "All right! You are such a disappointment! If my father had known this was how you'd turn out, he never would have killed your family to get you for me!"

Nicolae stumbled back as his mind reeled. Sabia's eyes widened as she slapped her hand over her mouth. She shook her head. "I didn't mean it! I'm lying! I was just angry!"

Anger like none he'd ever known had him changing without conscious thought. He advanced on her then waited, but she refused to change as well.

"Change, damn you! I cannot fight you like that!"

Sabia's eyes filled with tears. "I can't! I'm trying, but I can't! Please don't hurt me. *Please*, don't kill me!"

In what was the first honest emotion Nicolae believed she'd ever displayed, Sabia fell apart, crying so hard she slid to the ground and curled into a ball, her distress soaking her face and the hands she kept wiping on her cheeks. He changed back, realizing the sisters had left him with an advantage—only allowing him to transform, not any other Lycanthrope in the area.

He loved that family more by the minute and allowed their acceptance of him to temper his anger. He stared at the pitiful foolish female, knowing he couldn't let her see he was no longer out of control, or she'd use it to her advantage.

"Where is Ion? This is your last chance," he said, barely moving his mouth.

Sabia uncurled and sat up, reluctant acceptance in her eyes. "He's about ten miles from here, in a cave. He's dying. He can barely even sit up now. He isn't a danger to anyone."

Relief washed through Nicolae as he advanced to pull her up. Once she was standing he glared at her. "Lead the way. Looks like we're going to have to make this trip on two feet. But you'd better run your ass off, because I'm out of patience."

"What I said before, about your family. I had nothing to do with that. I was just a whelp. I didn't know about that until years later when I overheard my father telling Ion why you were treated like a son. My brother has always been jealous of you, you know. He never even liked you."

Nicolae shook his head at the deceptions, trying to ignore the pain her words caused. "*You* should have told me when you learned the truth. Instead you went along with their plans for me. *You* made sure I was always aware of your presence and position, and the packs expectations for us. *You* teased and tantalized me, and I almost bought into it all.

"My entire life with this pack was a lie. But we don't have time to deal with that now. I need to get your brother help before his time runs out."

Sabia looked at him with disbelief. "Why would you help us now? Why do you even care?"

Nicolae's laugh was flat. "I don't. But I'm not letting the likes of you and yours endanger others any more. Once this is done, your family will leave this side of the country and never return. I don't care where you go, but I had better never see any of you again."

Sabia shrugged. "As you wish, *Alpha*. But does it occur to you, that you will be the end of *your* line?"

Nicolae hoped not, but yes, he knew it was a real possibility. "You stall any longer, and yours will end today as well."

Sabia's gaze spit fire, but she wisely kept her mouth closed. She turned and started jogging and, once she knew he was behind her, set out at an inhuman run.

It took nearly three hours and darkness had fully set in when they stopped at the opening of the cave. Nicolae pushed Sabia in before him, testing her words that Ion was incapable of attack. When they entered his eyes adjusted to the complete darkness, and he spotted Ion immediately. For once her words were true. Her brother was flat on his back, and his human chest barely moved. Nicolae opened his mind to Destiny and she responded immediately. Within minutes a glittering mist entered the cave lighting it, before she cloaked Ion's form and they disappeared.

Sabia watched it all with her mouth hanging open and then turned to him. "What was that?"

Nicolae smiled. "That is my real family."

I hope.

As his own body began to tingle and lighten, and he was certain he too was turning to mist, he heard Sabia's scream of fear and anger, and then he was standing beside Rayne.

Nicolae took a deep breath and inhaled the sweet scent of Mystic Mountain. Whether Sapphire accepted him or not, he knew he'd come home.

****

"Sapphire, hold on!"

Sapphire clinched her teeth together to keep from screaming, again, but it was getting harder with each wracking pain. She held tightly to Aunt Haven's hand and doubled over. "I can't do this. Where's Mom? Where's Aunt Dee? Oh my, ahhhh! Where the hell is Nicolae?"

"I'm here!"

Sapphire looked up as he stalled and then stopped. It was obvious he'd been running by the harsh breaths and rapid rise and fall of his chest above his completely exposed male parts. She looked from them to his face. "Where...have you...been?"

Nicolae looked from her to Haven. "Rayne and Destiny need you outside. They're ready to start the spell. I've got this."

Haven looked him over and grinned. "Yes. I can see that you do." She hurriedly kissed Sapphire's forehead, whispered in her ear, and winked at him as she left the room."

Sapphire grunted through another pain. "I'm dying here and my aunt is checking out your package."

Nicolae grinned. "That one is something, for sure. But what about you? Do you want me to call your uncles or dad in? They're out there watching your mom cook up what she called a *brew*, of all things."

Sapphire whimpered, bit her lip, and swore before responding. "Yeah, I know. Kettle. Fire. *Hokus pokus*, and all that. It's what they do. But no. I don't want the men or them. I need *you* to distract me. All I can think about right now is the pain, and what Aunt Haven said would help me through it."

Nicolae nodded. "I understand. Help, but get lost afterward."

Sapphire wanted to throw something at him, and would, if she wasn't dying with each crack of her bones. "*No*, you idiot. I want your lips on mine. I want your naked body on mine. I want you to fill my body and mind with *you*, not *this*!"

Nicolae's brows shot up. "But I thought…."

Sapphire growled deep in her throat. "Stop thinking, dammit, and get over here."

Nicolae approached the bed and stood at the side. "I don't understand."

"Oh for Pete's sakes! Sex! I want sex, and I want it now!"

The look of shock on his kisser would have made her laugh under any other circumstance.

"But you hate me."

Sapphire really *was* going to kill him. She didn't have time for conversation. But she knew to make it right, she had to say the words. "I don't hate you. I love you. Now will you shut up and get on top of me, *please*!"

Nicolae said nothing more, but it could have been because his lips were on hers instantly. Sapphire didn't know if her aunt knew what she was talking about because she could barely focus on Nicolae's deepening kiss with so much agony screaming throughout her body. But gradually, the pain eased and was replaced with pockets of pleasure when his hands massaged and soothed, and as his kisses eased to tease and tantalize. His hard body braced hers until she relaxed. Then he began to move, foraging around her face with delicate kisses before lowering his body slightly as he nibbled and licked the raging pulse at her neck. He lifted a hand to his mouth, licked his finger and thumb before he angled his body to tease a hard nipple. She actually *felt* the flood of endorphins entering her brain, tricking her pain sensors into focusing on the pleasures of new stimulation, the anticipation of what was to come. She moaned, as his mouth replaced his fingers, and again when he teased the other with his free hand.

Long, laborious licks of his magical tongue continued down her body, and Sapphire held her breath with hope and a tinge of trepidation. She'd lain in the bed for so long, and though she'd been sponged thoroughly only the hour before, she stopped him. "I haven't bathed properly."

Nicolae looked up at her, his eyes lit with the fire of his passion, and the threat of his wolf emerging. "Your scent is pure, and calls to me, female!"

Sapphire felt her inner-wolf answer, as something alive and robust stirred within her. Unlike before, where that something broke and tore at her insides, this *something* knew his scent was the counter to her own and craved it desperately. As her mind accepted, her body relaxed, and she embraced the pleasure of his hands lifting and spreading her legs apart, so he could look at her fully. He growled deeply, and she did so in response, wanting to dance around him, and prance until she could lift her tail and tease him until he lost control. Yet she was still she, and there was no tail.

As her mind accepted the coming change, the threat of another wave of pain approached rapidly. Sapphire stiffened, bracing for it, but it never fully manifested, much less peaked. Nicolae's mouth was on her, stopping all other thought, eradicating all pain, as his tongue delved and laved at her most hidden treasure. She threw back her head, allowing this new wave that threatened to overtake, to build without fear, without resistance. Nicolae continued his sweet assault, making her limbs shake, making her heart race, taking her breath completely. She wanted to reach for him. Wanted him to share in the wondrous agony of anticipation of what she was becoming and to partake in the destruction of a lifetime filled with denial of who she really was. She felt her magic stir, magnify, before erupting and shattering all the barriers she'd spent so many years building. Sapphire embraced every nuance of the experience before pulling herself from beneath him to turn over and rise to her knees, giving him free access to all he desired. He was on her immediately, sliding into her, breaching her barrier, and rode her until she shattered, and howled....

And changed.

Sapphire howled again, this time Nicolae responded, his wolf transforming in tandem with hers. He continued to ride her until he too was replete, and his *bulbus glandis* drained of the blood that kept them locked together. He backed away slowly and then made his way up to lie at her side to lick her face, and snuggle in the softness of her fur. They stared into each other's eyes, and she felt his joy. It matched her own.

"Tell me all that has happened, since last I saw you."

Nicolae snuggled, licked, and pawed at her as he relayed the events, ending with the deception the pack had played on him all his life. She nuzzled him with affection and encouragement when he relayed Sabia's assertion his family had been murdered because the Ilie pack wanted him. When he was done, Sapphire curled up around him as much as her wolf's body would allow. She nipped his ear playfully then, hoping to lighten his mood, and bring back the joy of their union.

"Well, isn't this cozy."

Nicolae jumped and hunched his back where the hairs stood on end. Sapphire rose more slowly and looked at the strange woman standing in the doorway. She turned to Nicolae, not needing to ask who the woman was, but wondering how she'd gotten in her aunt's house. And wondering what her presence meant for them.

Nicolae slid Sapphire a wolf smile of encouragement and then changed. He pulled the sheet with him as he climbed from the bed, to face their adversary. Sapphire concentrated, and was finally able to change as well, keeping her eyes on the woman.

"I should have known! You would have never given me up unless you found another!"

Sapphire slid to the side of the bed where Nicolae stood and he handed the sheet to her. She wrapped herself quickly, realizing there was no more pain, but that of a woman in love, having another woman look upon her naked male with as much lust as anger. She stepped forward. Nicolae reached out quickly and grasped her arm protectively. She smiled back at him. *"I've got this."*

She faced Sabia, not in the least threatened by the woman's physical beauty knowing how rotted was her soul. "How are you here? My mother and aunts would not have allowed it."

Sabia smiled, her eyes reflecting her humor at catching them unawares. "I grabbed Nicolae's fairy-dust foot before that witch pulled him away. Apparently that stupid bitch wasn't the only one who never knew I was there." She laughed, looking Nicolae over with disdain.

"Actually, the stupid bitch did, but had more important things to handle at the time."

Sapphire had to keep from yelping as her aunts and mother filed into the room, with Jewell and Dia following. She ignored them all and dropped the sheet, while allowing her magic to engulf her. She smiled at Sabia, before lifting her hand. The vindictive female gasped as she rose into the air.

Her family looked on with a mixture of reactions: Rayne smiling with delight, Destiny biting down on a grin, Haven winking and glancing over at Nicolae, Jewell looking anywhere but at the naked couple, and Dia frowning.

"I knew it! I knew you had the power I wanted all along!"

"Dia!" nearly everyone in the room said together, but that didn't discourage her at all.

"Well, don't think I'm giving up, because I'm not." She sent Nicolae a bold up and down look then turned her attention back to Sapphire. "But you do get points for *that*."

"Dia!"

"Everybody out!" Sapphire said firmly, and her family immediately vacated the room. With her attention fully back on Sabia, she spoke slowly and precisely, so the Lycanthrope would know she meant ever word. "I am giving you a second chance at life. I hope you make better use of the next one."

With that, she envisioned a whelp, and seconds later a barely toddling Sabia was peeing on the hard wood floor.

The laughter from behind her had Sapphire turning, and she went straight into Nicolae's open arms. They sighed deeply together, and Sapphire knew her life had not just changed, it had only just begun.

Epilogue

Sapphire stood beside her Alpha, smiling at all those assembled. Four weeks had passed since the night of the Hunter's Moon, and the entire pack, their health and stature renewed, stood in the ceremonial clearing her family had always used for rites of passage and family celebrations. Tonight's celebration not only included the Lycanthropes from the Virginian Mountains, but the Cavanaugh-Whites, Cavanaugh-Hansens, and Cavanaugh-Whitehawks as well. Side by side, the werewolf clan stood together in a large circle with her family to witness mankind's version of a wedding. Though with humans, mystics displaying their magic, and Lycanthropes in their natural form, present, there was little about the gathering that was common.

Thomas Whitehawk, the spiritual leader of his Native American family and her dear uncle, stood at the ancient stone slab altar and raised a chalice filled with the waters that flowed from the top of Mystic Mountain down to the vast pool long known as Mystic Lake. He whispered to his ancestors in his native tongue, and then increased his voice in volume so all gathered could hear the blessings he petitioned for Nicolae and Sapphire, as he joined them in marital union. His softly spoken words brought tears to Sapphire's eyes, as she stood on the opposite side of the altar, facing Nicolae. He smiled at her with love filling the blue of his eyes, and her heart felt filled to bursting.

When it was time for them to speak, she nearly choked on her tears, but proudly said the words, "Forever and for always, yours I will be."

When Nicolae repeated the words, his voice broke, but he inhaled sharply and added, "I will protect you with my life, I will cherish you with honor, and I will strive to please you every day of our lives."

With a smile he threw back his head and howled. Sapphire did the same, as they dropped the white robes and changed, together, into that which they were meant to be. They nuzzled and danced around each other and then ran through the gathering, as the remaining Lycanthropes howled until the mountain was filled with the music of their celebration.

Clapping from her family pulled her attention away from Nicolae, reminding her it wasn't time yet to claim her mate. She ran back to the robes, Nicolae at her side. When they transformed once again into their human bodies and donned the covering, the clapping increased, as each Lycanthrope had changed as well, and joined in.

The celebration flowed, from the rise of the moon until its setting over the mountain. Happily tired family members offered congratulations and eventually headed home, either alone, or in groups, until all that remained were those who Nicolae had known all his life.

He had made peace with his past in the weeks leading to the wedding and had mourned with the rest of them when Ion passed away, his illness too advanced to stop. As she stood at her husband's side, Sapphire knew his heart was heavy now that his family would soon depart as well.

"Thank you all for travelling this great distance to be with us. And I am so happy our brothers are renewed and can now return home. No matter how I came to be a part of your family, I am your family, and I pray we will meet again."

Halivia stepped forward, her eyes filled with tears. "You have been my son all these years, and you are still the son of my heart. I am so sorry for what we have done to you, and I thank you for your forgiveness."

Nicolae smiled, and pulled her into a hug. "I am afraid we have burdened you with raising Sabia all over again."

Halivia laughed. "Hopefully I will do a better job this time."

The light slowly left her eyes as she studied his. "I have no right to ask this of you, and I will understand if you cannot, but please reconsider. Stay our Alpha. We need you and the protection you and your mate can provide. Our numbers are too few, and one disaster could wipe us out. One almost did. Please, Nicolae, consider this."

Nicolae shook his head. "I will not take Sapphire from her family. Now mine, as well."

Sapphire placed her hand on his arm and smiled at him when he looked down into her eyes. "My family *is* your family, but that means your family is also mine. They are welcome to make Mystic Waters their home. And we can all protect each other."

Nicolae pulled her into his arms and took her mouth for a deep and endless kiss. When she was finally allowed to resurface, she had to laugh at all the howling going on, though this time it was done with the pack's human voices.

Halivia laughed too, and moved forward to give Sapphire a hug. "We are proud to call you our Alpha Female, and we will take you up on your kind offer and make this magical land our home."

Sapphire's smile was replaced with her jaw dropping open when a loud pop caused her to look past Halivia at a full-grown Sabia. Before anyone could react she changed and ran into the forest.

Nicolae looked at Sapphire, and she back, warily. "How did that happen?"

Kaspor moved forward quickly, his hands fisted. He looked from Sapphire to Nicolae, panic filling his eyes. "I think I did that!"

Sapphire's brows rose as her heart thudded in her chest. "What do you mean?"

Kaspor pointed downward. "I was pointing to Sabia like this, and I said, 'I hope you grow up.' But I hadn't finished talking, I was going to add, 'a better person.' But before I could say the last part, she was there, all grown up!

"But that's not all…When I was getting better, and the rabies virus was leaving my system like the mystic sisters said it would, I kept getting these…I don't know how to explain it, except to say sparks of energy that heated up my paws, or hands, depending on my form at the time."

Nicolae's brows drew together as he glanced at the others. "Does anyone else feel anything unusual?"

Teagan, Domeno, and Keeleen stepped forward, one at a time, and nodded slowly.

Sapphire looked from the men to her new husband. "Oh dear. They were all cured with magic. I think maybe they wield it now." She grimaced. "My mother and the aunts have some explaining to do."

Nicolae's concerned features turned into amusement. "I think this falls under the category of *all magic has a price*, as your mother told me the day they cooked up the cure."

He looked back at the men, with a raised brow. "As your Alpha, I command you to learn how to use it from those who know how and never to use it unless absolutely necessary once your education is complete."

The men looked relieved, as they nodded quickly and then bowed to Nicolae.

He grinned at the rest of those gathered. "Now, if that's settled, I have a honeymoon to get on with." He dropped his robe and changed. Sapphire laughed as she too changed and followed him in the direction of her cabin…*their* home. She knew there would be consequences of having mystical werewolves running around Mystic Mountain, but that was a problem for another day. Today, she was deliriously happy to simply be the Alpha's mate.

THE END

Take a sneak-peek into the sixth book in the *Cavanaugh Family Series!*

DIAMOND IN THE ROUGH

A Mystic Waters Book

JC Wardon

Prologue

There was nothing better than having your hard work pay off, and for it to come to completion on his twenty-fifth birthday was just the cherry on the whipped cream.

Ryan Steward pushed his glasses up his nose as he knocked on his mother's apartment door. Barely suppressed anticipation filled him with what felt like super-human energy, knowing she would be thrilled for him once she'd heard the news. He was a little early for the birthday dinner she'd planned on his behalf, but he hoped she wouldn't mind *too much*, even though her need for complete order and scheduling bordered on the manic side. His excitement kicked up a notch as he heard the multiple locks being released, so he was smiling like a conquering hero, which he *felt* like, when she opened the door.

Shock, horror, and denial flittered through her eyes, coinciding with the dropping of her lower jaw. Never expecting such a reaction from her, his brows pulled together, and his glasses slid back down, again. "Mom?"

Instead of answering, she moved quickly to the couch and snatched something up to shove into the pocket of her housecoat. Annoyed with his glasses, he took them off and tucked them into his shirt-pocket, and followed her into the room. He didn't know which was more bizarre, her behavior, or the fact that she was already dressed for bed...or *still* dressed for bed. She gathered a pile of used tissues as well, and headed to the wastebasket in her little kitchen.

Which was spotlessly clean, as there was *nothing*

cooking.

Confusion turned to concern. He closed the door behind him, and joined her at the bar that separated the kitchenette from the living room. "Hey, Mom, what's wrong?"

Ellen Steward looked at him as if just realizing he was there. His concern turned to fear.

"Are you sick?"

When she nodded, frowned, and then shook her head, he became more concern by the minute. "Whatever it is, we can beat it. I'll take you to a doctor right now. Give me the name of your physician. You put some clothes on while I make the call."

Ellen didn't move, just looked at him as her eyes welled with tears. She reached into the pocket of her gown reluctantly, and pulled out an envelope, handing it to him. "That's yours."

Frowning, Ryan took the crumpled envelope and looked it over and then put his glasses back on. It was addressed to him at his mother's address, which was weird, since he'd lived on his own since starting college years before. The return address said Mystic Waters Municipal Court, Mystic Waters, West Virginia. Baffled, he turned it over, surprised to see it was unsealed. Looking up, he frowned.

"What is this, Mom? I don't know anyone in Mystic Waters. I've never even heard of it." He said nothing about her opening his mail, since she was already acting so strange.

Ellen's features underwent several emotions before she shook her head. "I never wanted you to know it existed."

Since that made no sense, he pushed the irritating glasses up again, wishing he'd remembered his optometrist appointment. But he'd been so close to finishing his project, and mega-excited the three-dimensional video gaming system was going to outshine the competition at the electronics fair next month, he'd completely forgotten to go.

Ryan put thoughts of his future away as he opened the envelope's flap before pulling out the folded sheet of paper. It was clearly a summons, but while reading one sentence after another, his confusion only increased.

"I don't understand. It says here I need to appear in court to take over my father's power of attorney and his care."

Ellen nodded. "Yeah, I know."

He stared at her, taking in her disheveled appearance, her hunched shoulders, and her watery eyes. "I *thought* my father dead," he said evenly, while watching her every reaction.

"I know. I wanted you to. He's been dead to me for a long time."

Determined not to let rising anger take hold, Ryan tilted his head, indicating they needed to go to the couch. Ellen nodded and shuffled her way there. He waited until she was seated and sat himself. "I need an explanation as to why I've spent my entire life thinking I had no father."

Ellen nodded and bit her bottom lip. She released it on a sigh. "It's complicated. I don't know how to begin."

Ryan stared at her, exasperated. "*Try.*"

She nodded again and chewed on her lip for a minute more as her features played out her fear. Ryan almost told her to forget it, that he'd look into it himself, but the words wouldn't pass his lips. He'd spent a lifetime allowing her off the hook when she didn't want to discuss something with him, but this was too important.

"Mom!"

She sighed. "Okay, already. This isn't a story I ever wanted to tell you, but I guess I have no choice." She focused on her hands, which she rubbed together as if she'd just moisturized them.

"I met your father my first year of college at a frat party. He was dark and mysterious, and I was free from my strict parents for the first time in my life. He had some...*pot* and we got stoned—a first for me." She glanced up at him, but when he didn't react, looked down again.

"He made me laugh with these stories of witches and magic that resulted in murder in this place called Mystic Waters. I thought it all so funny, and that he was making it up to amuse me, or impress me...I don't know which.

"Anyway, *at the time*, I thought it was so cool to be with him. Everything we were doing that night flew in the face of my very religious upbringing." Her gaze flittered Ryan's way briefly before her face filled with color.

"So we hooked up. You know, *had sex*. Another first for me."

Ryan placed his hand on the two of hers that were now tightly clenched together. He figured he knew where this was leading, but he wanted her to say the words "Okay, so you were a normal teenage kid. Go on."

She almost smiled, as if relieved.

"The next morning, I went back to school only to find out he didn't even attend, but was the friend of a friend of a friend, and no one really knew much about him." She paused and then swallowed hard. "You were conceived that night."

Ryan nodded. It was just as he had figured. "So, that's the last you ever heard of him."

Ellen shook her head. "I wish that were true. But...not exactly. Once I found out I was pregnant, my parents had a fit. My father forced me to tell them the whole story, and he had an investigator locate a Clayton Davis. He was from Mystic Waters, West Virginia."

"So you *did* see him again."

Ellen shook her head. "No. He was in a facility for

people with psychological problems. His stepfather was a policeman at the time, and a really nice man. When my father took me there to see them, Mr. Grammar, his stepdad, told us Clayton's emotional problems started when he was a little kid, and since his mother had died years before, Mr. Grammar was raising him on his own." She cleared her throat. "He said Clayton was diagnosed as schizophrenic, and would never be able to help out, but Mr. Grammar would set it up so that I got a check each month from him to cover some of the expenses of having and raising the child...*you*. Of course my father got the money every month, and I never saw a penny." She shook her head. "But that's a story for another day."

Ryan nodded, understanding now why he'd never met his grandparents either. "Tell me more about my father."

"According to Mr. Grammar, Clayton believed there were witches performing magic in Mystic Waters. He also believed one died in his stepfather's house when he was little. The police chief said it caused him all kinds of problems, because he had to be investigated, but of course, nothing came of it. Still, after all that, Clayton insisted he was telling the truth, and no one could convince him otherwise. Not even after years of medication, and therapy. Because they couldn't help him see reality, he started cutting himself, and fighting with people who didn't believe him. He even broke a man's nose and nearly busted open another man's skull for calling him crazy. In other words, he became a danger to himself and others."

"Oh...."

Ellen nodded. "Yeah. Do you really want to hear more?"

Ryan nodded, though he felt a little ill that this man had sired him. "Yes. I need to know everything."

She cleared her throat. "Okay. At that point my father was done pursuing a solution to what he considered *my* problem. We went back home long enough to pack up all my belongings. I was sent to Memphis, Tennessee, to live with Aunt Grace until I had you. The only way I got to continue to live with her once you were born was to agree to never tell you or anyone about Clayton Davis. The family was afraid if you knew, you'd try to contact him once you were old enough. And they wanted nothing to do with a nut case.

"With the exception of speaking with my father once, I never spoke to my family again after Aunt Grace died a year after I moved in with her. She was a mean woman, and she kept my father informed of my every move. Once she was gone, and *surprisingly* left me her house, I sold it and moved to the house you remember growing up in. But I saw the wisdom in keeping information about a mad man away from you. I was afraid you'd be concerned with the hereditary issues."

Ryan didn't know what to say, or how to react. Until she'd said it, he hadn't thought about the possibility of inheriting the condition. It was something he'd have to look into. But first, he needed to meet his father and see what was what, for himself. "I guess I'm leaving tomorrow for Mystic Waters, then. I only have four weeks to get my life in order before I show the world what video games are supposed to look and act like." He laughed, though he was not amused. "How weird is it that my games are all full of witches and dark magic?"

For the first time since he'd arrived, Ellen almost smiled at him. "You finished it then?"

Ryan nodded, all his earlier joy gone. What if he'd inherited his father's craziness? What if what he'd thought brilliant fantasy for a nerd all these years was nothing more than hereditary memory? The thought nauseated him. "Yeah, I finished it."

Whoop-de-do, and Happy Birthday to me!

Chapter One

"I'm sorry, Mr. Steward, but your father had to be sedated again this morning, so he'll be groggy, if he even wakes up. This isn't an uncommon thing with him, though I'd hoped the therapy and medication we've been giving him for the past six months eventually might make a difference. Unfortunately, with many of our patients, it never does for long."

"He's been in here for six months?"

The doctor nodded. "This time. We can only keep him until his insurance stops paying. Hospital policy." He grimaced. "Your father needs to be put somewhere permanently, for his own safety. But that isn't my call."

"So where does he go when he's released?"

The doctor flipped through a manila file and looked back up. "He used to go to his stepfather's house. But the retired police chief has gotten too old and feeble to handle Clayton. I believe the last time he was released he was homeless for about a week or so, then he was found lying in the street, smelling of liquor. When the police questioned him, he went right back to claiming witches had put him to sleep again, only this time, when he awoke, he could only remember that he'd found them, and had planned when he was going after them. He said he knew one was a cop and that he'd been watching her for months. It wasn't until he was brought here, and asked and learned the date, he claimed they'd wiped his memory as well.

"It wasn't the first time he'd told this story, or some variation of it. He's been telling the same since he was a kid."

"Did anyone check into his story?"

The doctor frowned at Ryan. "There is no reason to. Clayton has a lifelong history of mental illness. And no one in their right mind would believe the stories he tells."

A chill rolled down Ryan's spine. "Of course."

"Look, I know this is all new to you, but I've spent a career with these cases. The sad truth is your father should be able to live a normal life with medication and therapy. His condition hasn't improved over the years, and except for the way he acts out at times, it hasn't gotten any worse, either. That's actually pretty remarkable."

Ryan absorbed the information. "How does he act out, other than telling wild stories?"

"He cuts his skin. Since he's been here, he's found several opportunities to do so. No matter what we try to do to stop him. If we take away one thing, he finds something else. But there is usually a long lull between episodes, and since he's so close to being released, again, I'm trying to give him every opportunity to leave his room and socialize with the general population at meal times."

"You said he cuts numbers into his arm. What numbers? Are they significant?"

The doctor shook his head. "He keeps repeating elevens. At first we thought it was just straight line cuts, but a couple of months ago, when he came back out of his latest manic episode, he kept repeating the number eleven. When I asked him what eleven meant, he said he didn't remember, that the witches took his memory, but he remembered eleven, and he had to keep saying it so he wouldn't completely forget what they'd done to him."

"So he still doesn't know what it means, even now?"

Again the doctor shook his head. "I'm sorry, but it probably doesn't mean anything. More likely, this number is something his brain has devised to torment him."

Ryan nodded, pushed up his glasses when they slid forward, and hoped his horror didn't show. He thanked the doctor, before following an orderly down the long beige hallway of the hospital's psychiatric ward. They stopped at the thirteenth door on the right, which he thought appropriate somehow, as he waited until the door was unlocked. The orderly nodded and stepped back, but before he could make himself enter the room, he looked through the small wire enforced window to see his father lying on the bed.

He took a deep breath and moved forward. The door clicking closed behind him once he was inside, sent another shiver down his spine. The entire facility gave him the creeps, but this room was even worse. It smelled like pine cleaner, rubbing alcohol, and bleach, a mixture that instantly made his head ache. He tried to ignore the smells and focused on the middle-aged man strapped to the bed. As if sensing his presence, Clayton opened his eyes, glared, and spit at Ryan, causing him to jump back to keep from being hit.

"Get the hell out of my room!"

Ryan stayed where he was, any hope of a good first meeting gone. "I can't do that. I need some answers."

"What the hell! I don't need other psychiatrist picking my brain!"

"I'm not a psychiatrist. I'm your—" Ryan nearly choked. "*Son.*"

That seemed to startle Clayton, which was good. It took the scowl off his face...at least temporarily. He squinted his eyes and looked Ryan up and down as much as he could.

"I don't have a son."

That question answered, Ryan moved closer. "You do. I'm Ellen Steward's son."

Clayton laughed, a rough gurgled sound that ended in

him coughing until spittle ran down his jaw. Ryan took a hesitant step, then another before he reached for a tissue from the box on the nightstand beside the bed, and held it up. "Can I help?"

Eying Ryan warily, Clayton nodded, and remained still while his son wiped his face. When Ryan resumed his distance, Clayton blew out a long breath. "How is she?"

Taken aback that his father could recall her so quickly, he had to ask, "So you remember her?"

Clayton laughed, "I would think so. She's the only girl who every listened to me for more than ten minutes back then." He scowled. "And pretty much since." His smile returned, but was distant. "So that night produced you. That beats all. Why didn't she ever tell me?"

Not wanting to go into that, Ryan shrugged. "It's a long story. We'll talk about it next time. I need to know something right now though."

Clayton studied him and then nodded. "You want to know if you'll end up in a place like this, with people constantly drugging you."

Surprised by his perception, given that he probably *stayed* medicated, Ryan nodded.

"Let me tell you something, *son*, I am not crazy, at least I wasn't until they did all this to me. I told the truth from the beginning. I know it's hard to believe. But I did. I was a little kid, and I told people what really happened. Maybe if I'd been older, I would have known better than to argue with them when they didn't believe me. But I was accused of lying over and over, and I wasn't. And then this last time, I was still too drunk to think straight and hold my tongue, and damned if I didn't end up in here again!"

Ryan tried not to react to the foolishness his father spouted, since it was obvious Clayton believed what he was saying. "So you say that there are witches here, and they do things to you?"

Shaking his head, Clayton frowned. "No, not here. In the house I used to live in with my stepfather. And they didn't do *things* to me, only one thing that first time. I was knocked out cold for a couple of days right after I witnessed that woman doing things with my stepfather. And, last time? They did it again right before I was put back in this hellhole. Only this time they wiped my memory for weeks."

"Tell me about the first time. What *kinds* of things were done to a woman? And who was she?"

Clayton eyes grew wary. "Why? So you can laugh at me too?"

Ryan shook his head. "No. I don't find any of this funny. I'm just trying to understand."

"Well, I'm telling you!" He took a deep breath when Ryan jumped. "Sorry. Just give me a minute, okay? I'm not as eager to tell it as I once was." He looked around the room and then back at Ryan. "For obvious reasons."

Clayton closed his eyes momentarily and then opened them, determination sharping his gaze. "I witnessed them... uh, damn, doing unnatural things, with my own eyes, and then I fell asleep. When I woke up, it was two days later. But no one else knew that. Somehow the witch was gone, and my stepdad was going about his life as if nothing had happened and life was normal. Only it wasn't. He didn't even remember her, or...*well*, any of it."

Ryan took a deep breath. His father was completely delusional. But he was talking, and that was something. "Why did you think it was two days later?"

Clayton stared up at Ryan, his eyes filled with anger. "I don't *think*, I *know*. But in all the years I've told my story, no one ever asked me about that. They never got past me calling that woman a witch. They never believed she existed."

He took a moment to breathe in deeply and out slowly

and then sniffed. "Okay, I'll tell you how, but you have to keep an open mind."

Ryan nodded slowly. "I'll try."

Clayton nodded, his lips twisted. "That will be a first. But what the hell.

"I was in elementary school. A good student. A good kid, actually. I never lied to my stepfather or caused him any trouble. He was a good guy, and all I had, because my mom had died, and he kept me. He didn't have to, but he did. I was grateful. And he was kind. So when all this happened and he didn't believe me, it really hurt my feelings, and I was already scared shitless. That said, I'm going to tell you every detail I remember. Hell, you may as well know what has haunted me my entire life.

"The day I came home from school was a half-day, so I let myself in and went to my stepfather's room to tell him he forgot to be at the school bus stop to get me. But his door was locked so I figured he was there, but asleep or something. So I peeked through the skeleton keyhole." He grimaced. "That was my first mistake, but I was just a little kid and didn't know any better."

Ryan nodded, and held his tongue. After all, what could he say?

"What I saw caused me to scream. I think." He frowned. "I *think* I screamed…It's so long ago now; I'm not sure about that anymore. But anyway, something alerted the witch that I was there, and all the doors in the house slammed shut. I jumped, startled, but other than blinking, I never stopped looking through the keyhole. My stepfather threw her away from him, and her head hit the nightstand before she landed on the floor. He screamed, and hit the bed as hard.

"Then he was crying and screaming hysterically. Because he knew what had happened wasn't normal. And I think he realized the witch was dead, that he'd killed her.

I'm sure he never meant to, but he did."

Ryan scratched his head, trying to decipher all he was being told. "What caused you to scream? Or do whatever you did to get the woman's attention?"

Clayton stared at him for a full minute, his face expressionless. When he finally spoke, he did so slowly. "They were making love, although that didn't come to me until years later, but they were floating at least four feet above the bed while they were doing it. *That* was what made me scream."

Ryan backed up a step, his mind rejecting his father's words. "You know that isn't possible. Right?"

Clayton closed his eyes. "You may as well leave now. I knew you wouldn't believe me either. But I'm telling you, knowing I'm about to die, that it is not only possible. It happened.

"Just like them witches blanking out my memory again right before I came here this time. That really happened too."

He turned to Ryan and opened his eyes. They were filled with defiance. "And when they are forced to release me this time, I'm going to prove it."

****

Calling himself all kinds of a fool, Ryan drove the continuously curving mountain road, wondering why he hadn't just gotten a hotel room in the valley below, or better yet, tell the court he wasn't about to take on a mad man when his life was just getting where he'd worked so hard for it to be.

Still, since he wasn't one to drop any responsibility thrown into his lap, it would have made more sense to be closer to the hospital, and the restaurants, but there hadn't been much to choose from. From the look of things, the town hadn't changed much in the past century. The only accommodations he'd found were on the extreme eastern side of the town. He'd made the effort to find more but there was only one motel, a single story building that looked like it was built sometime before 1940. His only other option, according to those at the Main Street diner, was to go a couple of doors down the continuous line of stores and talk to a Frank Whitehawk, as he rented out cabins on Mystic Mountain to the tourists who frequented the area from spring to fall. Fortunately or, now that he realized how far he'd have to drive to get back to town, *unfortunately*, there had been a cabin available close to the top of the mountain.

Sighing, he reached into the passenger seat and lifted the directions and address of the cabin he'd rented from the very elderly Native American, wishing he could just enjoy the view as he made his way to ever-higher elevations. But there was too much churning in his mind, for that.

It wasn't that he believed his father was right or even sane, but there was something about his acceptance that he would never be believed that weighed heavily on Ryan's shoulders. Maybe it wouldn't bother him as much if it weren't the man who had sired him. Or maybe he could dismiss it all if the story were something Clayton made up as an adult. Regardless, Ryan knew he'd have to get some questions answered for his own peace of mind before he left Mystic Waters for good.

The clock was ticking.

Hoping it wouldn't take the full three and a half weeks he had before having to prepare to showcase his new game, Ryan trudged on, then jerked his wheel when an explosion sounded, and the road beneath him shook the car. He grabbed the steering wheel tighter, hoping he hadn't rented something close to a coalmine that would turn out to be a constant irritation. If that was the case, he'd go right back down the mountain and give that old man a piece of his mind and demand the rental fee back.

A few minutes later a reflective number stick, indicating he'd arrived, stood beside the gravel driveway he was to take. Ryan turned, surprised he couldn't see anything but thick trees. He proceeded slowly, glad the driveway was relatively smooth, but the more he drove the creepier it all felt, and he wondered if he'd been set up somehow.

Visions of horror movie plots he'd loved as a kid came back to haunt him now, and he kept glancing around him, waiting for something half-human with spiked teeth to jump out and attack the car. His shoulders bunched, his neck grew stiff, and he held onto the steering wheel tightly, ready to floor the gas pedal to run down anything that came his way. By the time the trees thinned and he arrived in the small clearing where a little cabin sat welcomingly, overwhelming desperation to escape, and leave all his concerns behind, had taken over.

He barked out a shaky laugh as he came to a stop before the little house, wondering if his father's stories had messed with his mind and questioning when he'd become such a dork. Pragmatic, staid, by the book Ryan Steward did not believe in things like monsters, witches, or any such nonsense, except where it came to creating interactive games. That his mind had even gone there embarrassed him, and he was thankful no one was around to see what a fool he was being. Especially the woman who had fussed at him all those years ago when he'd gotten caught watching the horror movies he'd regularly snuck into the house and watched while she was at work.

Still, he gave himself a moment to look around before unlocking the car's doors, and stepping from the vehicle.

He'd been told the cabin was in a remote area, he just hadn't expected *this*. He looked around, but with the exception of the small clearing, which might park six vehicles the size of his Volkswagen, there was nothing to see but trees. Ryan shook his head, wondering if he should just get back in the car now and head straight to the motel.

He sighed, discounting that option immediately. The day had been endlessly long, and given the darkness that was falling ridiculously fast, there was no way he would consider it. At least not until morning.

Ryan reached into the back and lifted the two bags of groceries he'd purchased before leaving town. He grimaced, wondering what he'd do with the meat and dairy supplies if he headed back to more acceptable lodgings, but he hadn't expected any of this, so he'd figure that out in the morning as well.

He glanced at the single suitcase he'd borrowed from his mother, before shifting the bags into one arm, to grab it as well. With his hands full, he looked longingly at his laptop in the passenger seat, and decided he'd get settled first, before coming back for it.

Until he'd spoken with his father, he hadn't planned on being in town more than a few days, a week tops. He was now afraid he'd underestimated the situation. Figuring out what to do with his father once he was released would likely take time.

The short walk and the three steps leading to the front porch took no effort, but digging for the cabin's key within the deep pockets of his jeans, while juggling his load, took a little more. He sat the suitcase down while looking at the homey set-up. Hand carved chairs sat facing the railing with a small table between them on one side, while a porch swing took up the other. He rolled his eyes, wondering who in their right mind would vacation somewhere where the only view while sitting on the porch was trees. Not him.

He located the key and unlocked and pushed open the door, retrieved his bag and stepped inside. The darkness engulfed him immediately, so he lowered the luggage again and felt around for a light switch.

There wasn't one.

"You have *got* to be kidding me."

Though not prone to curse, a string of foul words fled his mouth as he sat the bags down and returned to the car. He opened the glove compartment, relieved to find the flashlight had batteries that still worked, grabbed his laptop, and returned to the cabin. He stepped over the groceries as he shined the light around the small room, and his fear was confirmed when he saw the gas-chimney lamps and a large box of matches lying next to them on a nearby library table.

"You have got to be kidding me!"

Fury replaced disappointment as he lit one lamp after another. There was no way in hell he'd stay for more than one night. The groceries would no doubt go bad, and the drinks would be hot by morning anyway, so he didn't have to worry about what to do with them once he returned to town. If mice didn't dwell within the cabin, he'd at least have chips and drinks tonight, and then take the rest to munch on as snacks in the motel room once he got back to town. But the worst thing about what he now knew was a camping trip was he couldn't play his game, and check it and recheck it, to make sure there were no bugs left in the new system or in the new game. Not if there was no damned electricity!

"Mr. Whitehawk, you had better plan to give me my money back!"

Ryan closed the front door and was relieved to see it actually had a lock. He stood in the glow of the little cabin and cursed. When he ran out of words, he carried one lamp, as well as the bags, to the small island that separated the lounging area from the kitchen. To his surprise the light showed a small upright chest that had a sticky note attached to its front door, indicating it was a refrigerator.

Intrigued, he opened the small door and cold air hit

him immediately. Curious now, he held the lamp up and moved it as far as he could around the box. There were no wires, but there was a hose attached to the back of it, and as he chased the line, he found it ran into the cabinet and then attached to the pipe leading to the pipes of the sink's spigot. He could only surmise it ran cold water between the wooden exterior, and the metal open-faced box that would hold his supplied.

"Okay. Now that's pretty cool. But still not enough to keep me here."

The hard knock on the front door startled Ryan, and he yelped before pushing his glasses back up. Knowing he'd have to get a grip, and get it soon, he crossed to the door and moved a sheer curtain aside to look out the window. Fortunately, the face on the other side not only held a flashlight up so he could see it wasn't a polite monster, but a beautiful blonde, instead. Pleasantly surprised, he unlocked the door and swung it open.

"Hi! I'm the Welcome Wagon."

She held up a basket filled with things, but Ryan couldn't take his eyes off her lovely face long enough to look down.

"Actually, I'm the niece of the guy who owns the cabin. My aunt Destiny texted me, because cellphone service sucks around here, and said I should check on you. She wasn't sure Great-uncle Frank told you about the plumbing and things. So how are you? I know it can be crazy scary out here when people come for the first time." She stepped forward, and he stepped back. She went straight to the kitchen then turned with a smile. "I see you've lit the lamps. That's good. Did you see how to use the icebox? Well, it isn't really an icebox anymore, since my dad made it into a water-cooled box. But same difference. You can't leave the door open like that, though, or it won't stay quite as cold. And you should probably close the front door. The temperature is dropping fast. It always does up here."

Ryan nodded and closed the front door once she took a breath and moved to shut the cooler. But before he could answer any of her questions, she started up again.

"This is a nice cabin. Not nearly as far back as mine. I wonder why they didn't send me here." She frowned, looked at an oil lamp and then nodded. "Of course. The lack of electricity. I don't mind being out in the boondocks, at all, but a girl has to use a hair straightener every once in a while." She grinned at him. "You don't talk much, do you?"

He slowly shook his head, a little overwhelmed.

She nodded, and continued. "Most men don't as far as I can tell. My dad is really quiet, and so is Uncle Tom. He's the owner of the cabin, by the way. My uncle Logan talks more than those two, but I think it's because he's a doctor and has to talk to people all day, so he's more social. My dad mostly talks to his wood, and to my mom, but he can get going sometimes when it's just family around."

She pointed upwards to the loft. "That's your bedroom if you haven't already figured that out. I brought clean sheets and put them on earlier. My great-uncle would have done it, but I volunteered. He's nearly as old as these hills but would have a fit, if he *had* fits, which he doesn't, for me having said so.

"You do have a bathroom over there," she said pointing again. "But only cold water. Unless you kicked on the generator out back?"

Ryan shook his head.

"Figured not. You don't look like you rough it. Anyway, no city water, thank goodness. Only well water out here. Runs from the spring. Great for drinking, but cold as an Alaskan's snot to shower in which is why it works so well to keep cold food cold." She grinned.

"Toilet's good though. Has a concrete box in the

ground. Can't remember what it's called, but it does the trick. For you know, catching things. But anyway, I'll show you how to work the generator tomorrow, unless you want to shower tonight." She grimaced. "I'm just afraid it may have spiders since nobody has used the cabin for some time. I hate spiders. Don't you?"

Ryan nodded.

"Thank goodness. I was afraid you'd want to deal with that thing tonight. It isn't hard or anything. Just really dark out there. Oh! I nearly forgot!" She pointed to the fireplace. "I've laid you a fire, all you have to do is light it. The matchsticks you used to light the lanterns will do the trick nicely, just put flame to the paper stuffed below the wood. Do you have any questions?"

His mind whirling, Ryan simply stared at her. By the time he could think to ask her name, she was reaching toward his face.

"You have an eyelash on your cheek." She lifted it from his face and dusted her hands together. "Nice glasses by the way. Makes you look very scholarly. Are you a professor? Oh sorry, I'm being nosy."

Ryan so was jolted by her brief touch, he couldn't tell her the lash had floated onto her jacket, rather than the floor. Once he found his wits and was about to tell her, she turned and hurried toward the door. She opened it and turned to smile at him.

"Sorry, I've got to go. In a bit of a hurry. But you have a good night. I'll see you in the morning. But not too early, unless you need me here early. A girl's got to get her beauty rest, you know?" She smiled again, and pulled the door closed behind her.

Ryan just stood there staring at the door until he heard the sound of a motor starting. That propelled him forward, but by the time he could reopen the door, all he could see were two tiny red lights entering the tree line, and he realized the whirlwind was riding a four-wheeler through the woods to go back to wherever it was she'd come from.

Amazed he hadn't heard her arrival, he closed the door and exhaled, wondering just how much stranger his life could possibly get.

****

Dia hurried back through the trail leading to her cabin, hoping she hadn't been rude. She didn't particularly like being out after dark, even though she'd grown up on this mountain and knew it like the back of her hand. But the darkness wasn't her reason for hurrying. She'd left a new potion brewing on her stove, and she was afraid after the small explosion earlier that she still may not have lowered the ingredients quite enough to prevent it from happening again.

Her dad would have a fit if she destroyed a third stove. As would her uncle if she burned down his ancestral home. But it was finally spring, and the weather was already showing signs of warmth. Soon she'd be able to move her experiments back outside, and into the cauldron her mother gave her as a housewarming gift when she'd moved in. Thank goodness, Great-uncle Frank said the cutie had only rented the place next door for a month; otherwise, she'd have to be more careful. The last thing she needed was someone around to hear her noisy failures, and to get nosy.

She grinned as she sailed over a boulder that suddenly appeared in the path she was taking. They often made up the launching pads she loved to fly over. For those brief seconds she was airborne, and the feeling of freedom was as exhilarating as it was brief. One day, and she hoped it was soon, she'd find a spell that allowed her to fly for real.

She couldn't wait.

Dia pressed her lips together, trying to not let

annoyance set in that Sapphire was the one who'd inherited the celestial gifts. Her oldest sister by only a few minutes didn't appreciate her own power, had denied it for years, and even now barely acknowledged it, as far as Dia knew. Not that she'd seen much of Sapphire since October last. *She* was too busy with her new husband and their pack of Lycanthrope to devote time to Cavanaugh family matters, which was just fine. That meant Dia could work toward creating magic without her sister's constant judgment and condemnation.

Darkness aside, Dia loved the smoothness of the trails she always found while riding the four-wheeler. Since moving into Uncle Tom's one room cabin all those months ago, she'd gotten to ride often while out looking for the wild growing plants she tested once mixed together, with the hope of finding just the right things to cast spells, or alter and create things. It always surprised her that such rough terrain allowed for such smooth travel given the thickness of the pines, and the rockiness of the acreage covering the mountainside.

She spotted the glow from the windows of her cabin and slowed as she came to the little shed her father and Uncle Tom built for her experiments, and parked in the little carport they'd added at its side to keep her generator and transportation out of the elements. Thankfully, the generator was only necessary for the shed's cook-stove and the lighting within. Like she'd told her delicious new neighbor, a girl needed real electricity in her dwelling.

Dia hurried into the shed and breathed a sigh of relief. Her potion was still simmering, the aroma light and pure. She shivered, as the room had grown cool in her absence, and then gasped as an eyelash floated down, landing in the pot of potion she'd so painstakingly concocted. Dia lifted the sterling silver ladle and tried to capture the lash, but it disappeared into the gently bubbling brew, and no amount of stirring brought it back to the surface. Disappointment flooded her, but she knew she'd have to hope no more of her lashes dislodged, and that the one that had didn't make any difference.

Biting her bottom lip, afraid she'd now ruined the day-long experiment, she none the less stirred the rosebud, honey, and wine brew she'd mixed with a peppering of the other lesser but still important herbs, and then grasped a small vial with her tongs. She poured the brew into the test tube and swirled it gently. Smoke rose in a twirling rope-cloud, puffed, and eventually formed a shimmering valentine heart. Excitement caused her to shake so hard she nearly spilled the vile, so she poured what little remained back into the pot.

Have I done it? Did I really create a love potion?

Nerves skittered across her body, sending goose bumps over her skin. What if she had? What could she do with it? She couldn't tell anyone, if indeed she'd been successful, at least not until she tested it. But how? And on who?

Her mother would tell her to destroy the potion immediately and try something else. To mess with someone's will was taboo. Though not exactly dark magic, it bordered there as far as her family was concerned. Which meant she'd have to keep this a secret. Or destroy it. But how could she do that if she'd finally found success after so many failures?

Torn, but unwilling to throw out what might be her first real step into becoming the white witch she wanted to be, Dia set the potion off the burner to allow it to cool. Once it had, then she'd decide what to do. Of course, there was nothing the mixture could do without something that belonged to the one the spell was meant for, and the incantation her ancestor created and recorded in her diary centuries before. Dia picked up Camellia Cavanaugh's diary and read the words aloud, just because she loved to recite the spell:

> *"Three hearts of the precious wild growing rose*
> *Beneath the sun and starry sky, grows;*
> *Three silver drops of honey so gold*
> *Awaken the mysteries of bold, and old;*
> *Three silver spoons of blood red wine*
> *And thee shall be mine;*
> *Thee shall be mine;*
> *Until by will, I set thee free*
> *This is my will, so shall it be."*

Though no longer on the heated coil, the brew went crazy, bubbling and boiling over the sides, sending smoke throughout the room. Startled, Dia ran to the doors and threw them both open, and stood outside coughing until her lungs cleared. Trepidation skittered down her spine as she watched the smoke spiral through the trees in the direction of the rented cabin, its form nearly that of a snake on the hunt.

"Damn, damn, and double damn!"

She wiped at her irritated eyes as she made her way back inside, hoping the guy had gone to bed and wasn't calling the fire department instead. Disappointment flooded her, as it did every time she thought she'd made a breakthrough only to realize nothing had changed. She stared down at the pot. Her potion was now nothing more than glimmering crystalized rosebuds. As pretty as they were, she lifted the pot and threw it across the room, shattering the three little buds on the far wall. Dia watched them float down as red glitter to cover the pot that had hit the dirt packed floor.

Fury overtook her with a vengeance she'd never before experienced, and though her mind rejected the emotion, her mouth took on a life of its own.

"You win!" she screamed, as tears formed and fell from her eyes. "I'm done! I'm never going to be a witch, okay?" She ran outside and shook her first at the star filled sky. "Did you hear me? I get it! I'm done! You win! I'll never again try to cast a spell! Ever!"

Once she caught her breath, and could make herself reenter the shed, Dia walked over to pick up the pot. She extinguished the electricity feeding the stovetop since she'd forgotten to in her earlier excitement, and placed the strangely clean pot on the same cold coil as before. She looked at the glitter left behind from the boil-over but didn't have the heart to deal with it yet. She surveyed the little room, and wanted to cry, knowing all she'd done to make it her own special place, had been a waste of too much time and effort.

Overwhelming sorrow weighed on her as she returned the small bottles of herbs to their rightful places on the shelves her family had helped her build, gather, and stock. Everyone had pitched in from her mother, to her aunts, to her cousins, and even her uncle Tom.

Everyone, that was, except Sapphire.

Dia groaned, knowing her oldest sister would be the only one who wouldn't mourn with her over the loss of her dream. Of course, Sapphire wouldn't see it as a loss. She'd told Dia more than once, "You can't lose something that was never yours to begin with." And now, finally, Dia had to accept her words as truth. But that didn't mean she didn't want to sock her sister in the jaw just once. The only thing stopping her was that Sapphire could now transform into her wolf, and she'd probably been waiting for a reason to bite Dia for years.

Having no idea what is was that had always caused such friction between them, Dia lifted the diary she'd spent the last few years filling with each exciting experiment, and detailed subsequent failure. This time there was no need to write down her concoction, nor its results. She was closing this chapter in her life, and she wouldn't look at the little book ever again.

Reluctantly, she locked up the shop for the last time and went out to turn off the generator before heading to her cabin to get what she needed to prepare for bed. *Tomorrow*, she promised herself. Tomorrow she'd search for the gift that was her birthright, and she'd accept whatever fate had thrown her way.

After all, what other choice did she have?

Since she now reeked of smoke, Dia gathered clean towels and took the path that led to the shower house her uncle had built long before her birth. The freestanding facility was one she treasured, as the toilet had plumbing, but better still, it contained a large shower room that could hold a party of people if one were so inclined. The multiple showerheads allowed her to feel as if she were standing in a steady rain, and could be turned up to torrential, or down to a mist, depending on how much pressure she wanted. The tiles were beautifully designed and the knobs were realistically carved eagle heads, which had been created by her uncle's own talented hands. But tonight, the pleasure of the shower house was lost in the folds of her heavy heart.

The only good thing that had come of this failure was that she was being forced to look forward, rather than back, and now she wouldn't have to worry about the delicious new neighbor discovering her secret. But what in the world would she do with her days? She'd done nothing since returning home after her post-college European trip, but try to perfect a craft that was not hers to begin with.

Burdened by defeat, she made her way back to the one room cabin she called home and locked herself in for the night. Not caring that her hair and body were still damp, she fell upon the bed and prayed for sleep.

Mystic Waters Books
By JC Wardon

The Cavanaugh Series Books Now Available!
(The Cavanaugh Sisters Trilogy)
#1 **Mystic Thunder**
#2 **Touch of Lightning**
#3 **Tempest's Embrace**

(The Cavanaugh Series continues!)
#4 **Jewel of the Nile**
#5 **Sapphire Blues**
#6 **Diamond in the Rough**
#7 **Luna's Landing**
#8 **Celestial Liaison**
#9 **Zeus:** *Unbound!*
#10 **Apollo:** *Unleashed!*

The Cavanaugh Series Books to come!
Heracles: Undone
Soleli's Secret
Gavin's Ghosts

Blood Moon Chronicles
Blood Moon Rising

Visit my website: **www.jcwardon.com**
Facebook pages: **www.facebook.com/jc.wardon** and
www.facebook.com/JCWardonNovelist
tweet me: @jc_wardon

Thanks for sharing my world. I'd love to hear from you!

JC Wardon

ACKNOWLEDGEMENTS

I would like to send out a special Thank You to all who have embraced the Cavanaugh women. May your lives be as enchanted!

I'd also like to thank all those who chatted and commented with and to me at: **ilovewerewolves.com** Embrace your wolf!

Thank you all so much!

JCW

ABOUT JC WARDON

JC Wardon loves writing fantasy and spends her days weaving stories for those who love it as well. Though she has great appreciation for romances, a juicy and complicated plot is what she holds most dear. Danger, mystery, and magic are the life's blood for her Mystic Waters Books. She hopes you are captivated and stimulated, and your hearts become engaged.

If you enjoyed *Sapphire Blues*, please consider telling others and writing a review.

Diamond in the Rough, available now!

www.jcwardon.com

www.ingramcontent.com/pod-product-compliance
Lightning Source LLC
Chambersburg PA
CBHW020600180626
46810CB00007B/2588